"I'm your lawyer—we can't have secrets between us."

"No secrets?" Billy touched a length of her hair that had fallen over her shoulder, his fingers precariously close to the swell of her breast. "Then I guess I should tell you right now I intend to have you again, except this time in a bed, not on a plank wood floor."

Shelby's head swam with a sudden vision of him in bed, his bronzed body erotically bared against pristine sheets. Making love with Billy the boy had been a remarkable experience, but she knew making love with Billy the man would be devastating.

She stepped back from him, leveling on him a look of cool control. "Too bad for you we don't always get what we want in this life."

He smiled. "Too bad for you, I always do."

Dear Reader,

The verdict is in: legal thrillers are a hit! And in response to this popular demand, we give you another of Harlequin Intrigue's ongoing "Legal Thrillers." Stories of secret scandals and crimes of passion. Of legal eagles who battle the system... and undeniable desire.

We're delighted to welcome Carla Cassidy to Harlequin Intrigue. Though *Passion in the First Degree* is her first Intrigue, Carla needs no introduction to readers of romance. She is a multi-published, award-winning author with a keen eye for mystery and a warm heart for passionate relationships. We know you'll love her debut Intrigue.

Look for the "Legal Thriller" flash for the best in suspense!

Regards,

Debra Matteucci
Senior Editor & Editorial Coordinator
Harlequin Books
300 East 42nd Street
New York, NY 10017

Passion in the First Degree
Carla Cassidy

Harlequin Books

TORONTO • NEW YORK • LONDON
AMSTERDAM • PARIS • SYDNEY • HAMBURG
STOCKHOLM • ATHENS • TOKYO • MILAN
MADRID • WARSAW • BUDAPEST • AUCKLAND

ISBN 0-373-22379-X

PASSION IN THE FIRST DEGREE

Copyright © 1996 by Carla Bracale

This edition published by arrangement with Harlequin Books S.A.

® and TM are trademarks of the publisher. Trademarks indicated with ® are registered in the United States Patent and Trademark Office, the Canadian Trade Marks Office and in other countries.

Printed in U.S.A.

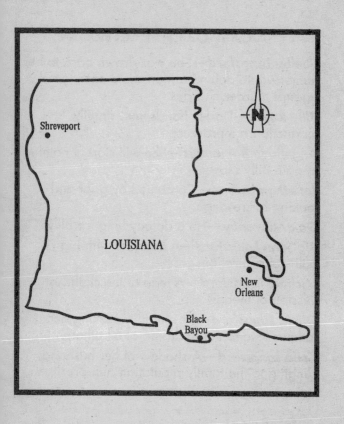

CAST OF CHARACTERS

Shelby Longsford—She was drawn back to her hometown to defend a man she'd once loved against murder charges.

Billy Royce—Darkly handsome, sinfully magnetic...a murderer?

Angelique Boujoulais—She will stop at nothing to gain Billy's love.

Jonathon LaJune—Consumed by grief and looking for revenge.

Gator Revenau—He'd do anything for Billy.

Big John Longsford—A big man with big political aspirations.

Michael Longsford—A man of the cloth...a mission of mercy?

Olivia Longsford—Desperately seeking her father's love to the exclusion of all others.

Celia Longsford—A shadow of her husband, clinging to the family reputation and prestige.

Prologue

Shelby Longsford ran frantically through the swamp, the humid, junglelike air clinging to her like a second skin. Nightmare images whirled in her mind. It couldn't be true. She had to tell somebody what she had seen.

She ducked beneath the Spanish moss that hung like shrouds from the cypress trees, her breath coming fast and furiously. Since she'd lived all of her eighteen years near the swamp, her feet instinctively knew exactly where to step, when to jump to avoid the alligator-infested waters of the bayou.

She focused only on one thing... the tiny flicker of light in the distance.

Her mother had dismissed her, unwilling to listen. "Go away," she had bellowed when Shelby had run to her, confused, frightened by what she'd seen deep in the swamp. "I don't want to hear anything." The biting odor of gin wafted from her mother's breath. "And don't go running down to that old woman. She's dead, died this evening."

Shelby fought her way through the thicket, a new fear riding her back as she ran. It couldn't be true. Mama Royce couldn't be dead. Her heart was too big, too strong to just give up and quit beating.

Tears blurred her vision as she raced ahead. She needed Mama Royce, needed to tell her about the horrible things she'd seen, things she didn't understand. Shelby's mother's drunken rage combined with the haunted images that twisted and unfurled in her mind. The memory of what she'd seen only minutes before brought bitter bile to the back of her throat. She needed to tell. She needed to tell Mama Royce. She'd know what to do.

The moon overhead was full, shimmering its image on the water. Insects buzzed and animals scurried through the thick underbrush. There was never silence in the swamp.

Shelby's footsteps clattered on the wooden bridge that led to the tiny shanty on the water's edge. She threw open the door, gasping as she saw that the rocking chair where Mama Royce had sat for as long as Shelby could remember was empty.

"No." The word slipped out of her mouth as if the mere force of the denial could change what she knew in her heart was true.

"She's gone, Shelby."

She whirled around to see Billy Royce standing in the doorway that led to one of the two bedrooms. His face, always harsh with lean angles and planes, was now stark with grief. At the moment he looked far older than his twenty-one years.

"No," she repeated, tears spilling from her eyes as her heart constricted in pain. Mama couldn't be gone. Shelby needed her. She needed to tell her something . . . something important. She rubbed her forehead, confused, disoriented as too many emotions deluged her, dizzied her.

Billy moved into the room, seeming to fill the small space with his overwhelming presence. "They already took her away. Go home, Shelby. There's nothing you can do here. Go back to your ivory tower."

She didn't listen to him. Instead, anguish usurped her terror. Confused, still frightened, she did something she normally wouldn't do. She moved into his arms, needing his warmth, his strength.

And in his grief he did something he normally wouldn't do. He accepted her.

Shelby began to cry in earnest, her pain so intense she thought she'd go mad. She raised her face to look at him, needing to share the despair, the terror that ripped through her. The moonlight shining into the undergrowth... two figures moving... She shoved the memories away. She couldn't think about them now. Mama Royce couldn't help her, couldn't tell her what to do. A nightmare, that's all it had been.

She clung tighter to Billy, needing to lose herself in him. He was alone now...as was she. In his face she saw her pain magnified tenfold and with a moan of empathy she reached up around his neck and pulled his head down so her lips could gently touch his.

She didn't expect his hunger. The intensity of his response stole the breath from her. With a groan of her name he crushed her against him. She welcomed the strange new sensations that transcended her grief, further banished any lingering fear.

His mouth plundered hers, as if seeking the secrets to her soul. She returned the kiss, tasting the salt of tears but unsure whether they were his or her own.

Together they sank down to the plank floor, the kerosene lantern on the table illuminating the torment in Billy's dark eyes.

"Yes," she whispered as his fingers hesitated on the buttons of her blouse. She wanted to lose herself in his passion, his intensity. He was so big and strong. She could hide in him forever.

Her single acquiescence created a sudden frenzy, an explosion of want and need from him that couldn't be denied.

Their clothes were disposed of, leaving them naked and gleaming in the muted light. His touch was heat and fire, and Shelby fell into the flames, grief displaced by the stronger emotion of passion, fear exiled to the darker recesses of her soul.

There was pain—brief and sharp—followed by a pleasure so intense it once again brought tears to her eyes.

When it was over they lay side by side, the only sound the lapping of the water at the side of the shanty. "Billy," Shelby whispered his name as he stood and grabbed his jeans and pulled them on. "Billy. I never...I didn't..." She frowned, the whisper of something dark and forbidding niggling in her head. Whatever it was, it frightened her. She shoved it away and focused instead on Billy and what they had shared.

He turned and looked at her, his face expressionless. "That...was a mistake." He picked up her clothes and threw them at her.

She stood and dressed, her gaze not wavering from Billy. Where only moments before he had been heat and fire, he was now stone and ice. She approached him hesitantly, still overwhelmed by the intimacy they'd just shared.

"Billy...I love you." The words had been trapped inside her for a lifetime but as they fell from her lips, she knew they were true. She had loved Billy Royce for as long as she could remember. Surely he felt the same for her, especially after what they had just done, what they had just shared.

"Billy?" She approached him and placed a hand on his arm.

He shrugged off her touch, his face twisted with an anger she didn't understand. "Go home, Shelby. Forget what just happened. It was a terrible mistake."

"No... no, it wasn't a mistake."

He grabbed her by the shoulders, his eyes blazing into hers. "Don't be a little fool, Shelby. Go back home to your fancy mansion, back to your society boyfriends. You have no place here."

Shelby tore out of his grasp, a sob catching in her throat. It was too much. It was all too much. "Billy... please." She rubbed her forehead, confused. There was something... something she had to tell.... Why had her mother been angry with her? She no longer remembered. "Billy?"

"Get out of here, Shelby. I don't want you here. I don't need you." His words, coupled with the coldness of his eyes, fired a rage inside her.

She stumbled out of the cabin and across the bridge. She paused at the edge of the dank water, shaking with a myriad of emotions too difficult to distinguish. "Someday you'll come begging to me, Billy Royce," she yelled. "Someday you'll be sorry. You'll need me. You'll need me, Billy Royce," she screamed.

"Yeah, right," he returned just as passionately. "I'll need you when hell freezes over."

Chapter One

"Shelby, there's a call for you on line one."

Shelby Longsford frowned, closed the manila folder of material she'd been reading and punched the button on the intercom. "Who is it, Marge?"

"It's long distance, a Billy Royce." There was a hesitation, then Marge continued, "He said to tell you that hell has frozen over."

Shelby's breath caught in her throat as a loud roar resounded in her ears, the roar of the past reaching out to clutch at her. She pulled off her glasses and pinched the bridge of her nose, fighting against the dark memories that assailed her.

She considered not taking the call. What could he want? She should just tell Marge to hang up on him. She knew he wouldn't call again. Billy Royce didn't give himself or others a second chance.

What could he possibly want? After so many years what could he want from her? Finally it was the nagging curiosity that prompted her to punch the button on the phone and pick up the receiver.

"Shelby Longsford." Her voice held just the right touch of cool professionalism.

"Shelby, I'm in trouble."

His voice, as deep and dark as the swamps that had spawned him, caused an unexpected heat to uncoil in her stomach. Memories swept through her, heated memories of a single night in a flame-lit cabin. She straightened in her chair, angered by his power over her despite the lifetime that had passed since she'd last seen him. "What's the problem, Billy?" she asked briskly.

"I believe I'm about to be charged in a double homicide."

She sucked in her breath and rocked back in her chair. She reached for her glasses, as if putting them on would aid her in assimilating his shocking statement. "Where are you?"

"Here, in Black Bayou."

"What do you want from me?" She pinched the bridge of her nose once again.

"I need a defense lawyer. I understand you're one of the best in the state."

She tapped the end of a pencil on the top of her desk, unmoved by his obvious line of flattery. He'd always been good with slinging blarney. "There are others considerably more experienced. Why me?"

There was a long pause. "You know me, Shelby. I may be many things, but I'm not a cold-blooded murderer."

Yes, Billy Royce was many things. He was a coldhearted bastard, a man raised in wildness, nurtured by hate. He was a thief of hearts, defiance instead of blood pulsing in his veins. He walked the dark side, but he wasn't a murderer.

She shook her head, reminding herself that she hadn't seen him, had heard nothing about him for almost twelve years. Then, he'd been nothing but an angry, rebellious boy. Now he was a man. What kind of a man had he become? Could he have committed murder?

"Shelby?"

She stopped tapping the pencil and allowed it to roll off the desk and onto the floor. "Yes, I'm here." There were a million and one reasons that she shouldn't get involved. And yet at the moment none of them seemed as compelling as the fact that it was time to go back home. All she'd been waiting for was a good reason. "I'll be there first thing tomorrow morning."

"You'll defend me?"

"I can't make any promises. We'll talk tomorrow." She closed her eyes and rubbed her forehead. "Is Martha's Café still on Main Street?"

"It's still there."

"I'll meet you there tomorrow at eleven." Shelby wasted no time murmuring a goodbye and hanging up.

What have I done? She stared at the phone in horror. She hadn't asked him any questions. She didn't even know who he was suspected of killing. She'd shut off her lawyer mode the moment she'd heard his familiar voice.

Home. Back to Black Bayou. Standing, she left her desk and walked over to the large picture window that encompassed an entire wall of her office. Below her the streets of Shreveport bustled with summer tourists.

Black Bayou was no longer her home. She'd turned her back on the town and her family's life-style twelve years before. She'd made a life for herself here, was happy with the slow but steady growth of her law practice. She'd left home at eighteen, a lonely, confused teenager. Now at thirty she was a totally different person.

Maybe it was time to go back, make some peace with her memories, mend some fences with her family. And see what kind of a man Billy Royce had become.

The intercom crackled, then erupted once again. She moved back to her desk and sat down. "Shelby, Juanita Gonzales is on line one."

"Thank you, Marge." She immediately picked up the receiver. "Mrs. Gonzales, how are you doing?"

She settled into the chair and gave the woman her full attention. Nearly a year before, Juanita's fifteen-year-old son, Carlos, had been picked up at two o'clock in the morning in a car he'd hot-wired. He also had in his possession a stolen stereo and a bad attitude.

The prosecutor had wanted to throw the boy away, put him in a juvenile facility then transfer him into an adult prison for as long as possible. Carlos had a list of priors that deemed him an incorrigible.

However, Shelby knew the true culprits in Carlos's case were poverty, an absentee father and a hopelessness that in a fifteen-year-old was both frightening and appalling.

Shelby had argued vehemently, finally getting the prosecutor to agree to two years in a juvenile detention camp in North Carolina. In doing so, she had gained a staunch supporter and friend in Juanita.

"How's Carlos doing?" Shelby asked. "Is he still writing you regularly?"

"*Sí*, once a week. I got a letter from him yesterday. He wanted me to call you to tell you he's decided he's going to be a lawyer like you."

Shelby's heart lifted and she smiled into the receiver. She was glad she had taken the time to write Carlos, encourage him in the idea that education was the way out for him. "You tell him if he keeps his grades up, when the time comes I'll see that he gets into a good law school."

"*Gracias.*" Emotion thickened the simple reply. She cleared her throat. "You got my last check?"

"Yes, Juanita. Two more and the debt is paid in full." Shelby had intended to work for Carlos pro bono, but she hadn't counted on Juanita's fierce pride and scorn of charity. The two women had agreed on a fee and Juanita had been sending Shelby a check every week for the past forty weeks.

"This is a debt no money can ever repay," Juanita returned, her accent thickening as emotion returned. "You saved my Carlos's life, his soul. I am in your debt for all of eternity."

Shelby smiled. She, better than anyone, knew how short eternity could be. After all, she'd once thought she'd love Billy Royce through eternity.

SHELBY AWOKE SUDDENLY, gasping for breath and fighting away the images from her nightmare. Blackness surrounding her... moonlight shining on the murky waters of the bayou. Panic clogged her throat as she ran blindly.

She sat up, aware of the icy perspiration clinging to her skin. Drawing in a deep, shuddery breath, she flung her legs over the side of the bed and stood. She shivered as the air met the nightmare-induced sweat. Wrapping her arms around herself, she turned on the bedroom light, instantly feeling better. Like a child who believes evil can live only in the darkness and shadows, she focused on the familiarity of her bedroom in the bright overhead light.

Almost three o'clock. It was silly to go back to sleep when her alarm was set to go off at five. She had a seven-o'clock flight to New Orleans, then an hour-and-a-half drive on to the little coastal town of Black Bayou.

She went into the kitchen and made a pot of coffee. Sitting down at the table, she waited impatiently for the chicory-laced brew to fill the glass carafe.

In eight hours she would be home. It must have been the anticipation of returning to Black Bayou that had prompted the recurrence of the old nightmare. She'd suffered them nearly every night for months after first leaving home. Nightmare images of moon slivers on swamp waters, fragmented visions of macabre creatures dancing in the distorted moonlight. None of it made sense, and she'd long ago given up trying to find logic or reality in the dark dreams.

Getting up from the table, she poured herself a cup of coffee. But even her hands wrapped around the warmth of the cup couldn't stop the shiver of apprehension that raced up her spine as she thought of returning to Black Bayou...and Billy.

SOMEBODY HAD ONCE SAID you can't go home again, but as Shelby drove down Main Street she had a sense of time displaced. Nothing had changed. It was as if she'd been away from the little town of Black Bayou for only a single day, an hour, the momentary flicker of an eye blink.

Yet, there were subtle changes...changes that reflected her own growth rather than the town's. She'd always thought the Longsford Tower business building was one of the biggest in the world. She now realized the ten-story structure was merely the biggest building in Black Bayou, and was small by most standards. Main Street seemed smaller, more narrow than she remembered, and it was disconcerting to fit reality into her childhood perceptions.

She drove down Main Street twice, although it was already a few minutes past eleven. She needed a little more time to prepare for her meeting with Billy.

Billy. She'd thought of him often in the passing years. Always those thoughts brought a combination of anger and pain, and the overwhelming feeling that she'd lost something to him...something special that she could never regain.

She consciously shoved these thoughts aside, not wanting to remember that single night when passions had flared and emotions had tangled, resulting in lost innocence and the end of girlhood.

She didn't know if she could defend him or not, didn't know if she could get past all the emotions he stirred in her. She'd consciously driven into town with no time to buy a newspaper, hear the local gossip or listen to any information that might taint her ability to make a decision to defend him or not. She needed to hear it all from him before she could make a decision.

Pulling into an empty parking space before Martha's Café, she turned off the engine but didn't move to leave the car. Martha's Café had been a favorite place for Shelby and her junior high school friends to hang out. The main attraction had been that Billy Royce worked there as a busboy. As the darkly handsome, older Billy had cleared tables, Shelby and her friends would watch, and giggle in adolescent fascination.

Billy was forbidden fruit. Swamp trash. It was rumored that he was wild, that his father had killed his mother, then hung himself from one of the trees deep in the swamp. But despite the rumors, Shelby knew that each and every young girl of Black Bayou had at one time or another entertained thoughts of making love with Billy. She'd had the reality of that particular fantasy, and once had been quite enough.

She picked up her briefcase from the seat next to her, realizing it was time to put the past behind her. Time to move ahead and see what had happened to Billy Royce in the passing years.

Getting out of her car, she was instantly hit with the sultry heat of the town. She'd forgotten how oppressive, how thick the air was here. Underlying the scent of hot concrete, the fragrance of blooming flowers, the aroma of Cajun cooking, was the pervasive odor of the nearby swamp waters . . . the smell of something mysterious and rotten.

Stepping into the cool, dim interior of the café, she waited a moment for her eyes to adjust from the glare of the sunshine. Here the scent of Cajun spices and frying fish filled the air and caused Shelby's stomach to rumble in hunger. There was nothing better than Martha's spicy gumbo.

"Shelby?"

She turned and immediately found herself enfolded in a fierce hug. Being embraced by Martha was like sinking into a warm foam mattress. "It's about time you got your skinny butt back here where you belong," Martha said as she finally released her. "Let me have a look at you." She stepped back and looked at Shelby, her dark eyes holding the wisdom of more than one lifetime. She looked long and hard into Shelby's eyes, then nodded, as if pleased with what she saw there. "You home to stay?"

Shelby shook her head and smiled affectionately at the big black woman. "I'm surprised to see this place still here. I figured you'd be retired by now."

"Huh, what am I going to do? Sit on a porch and rock till the good Lord takes me home? Bah, why make it easy for him?" Her dark eyes sparkled. "He's gonna have to catch me to take me through them pearly gates."

Shelby laughed, then sobered as her gaze darted around the room. Half a dozen of the tables were occupied, but at none of them was the man she had come to see. "Is Billy here?"

Martha nodded and pulled Shelby closer. "He's in the back. Since the murder he's not too popular 'round town. He thought it'd be best if you meet him there. Go on. He's waiting for you."

The back room in Martha's Café had entertained a colorful past. According to local rumors, at one time or another it had served as a meeting place for bootleggers, the rendezvous point for an affluent businessman and his mistress, and the hottest spot on Friday and Saturday nights to find a high-stakes card game.

And now it was where a prospective defense lawyer would talk to a man who was on the verge of being charged with a double homicide, Shelby thought.

She saw him the moment she walked through the doorway that led into the small room. He sat at a table for two, the chair tipped on its hind legs as he leaned back against the wall. As she walked toward him, the only things that moved were his eyes. Dark and hooded, they followed her progress like a wild animal eyeing prey.

He was just as she remembered him. Darkly handsome with an intensity that was both compelling and off-putting. The years had done nothing to diminish the animalistic quality that radiated from him. If anything, age had chiseled his features, ridding him of any minute vestige of boyhood or innocence that he might once have possessed.

"Hello, Billy." She stopped just in front of his table, fighting to control her pulse rate, which had picked up in the moment she'd seen him.

His chair fell forward, the front legs landing with a dull thud against the tiled floor. One eyebrow lifted and a corner of his mouth curled sardonically. "Well, well. Shelby Longsford, all grown up."

She pulled out the chair across from him and sat, placing the briefcase on the table between them. "People tend to grow up in the course of twelve years," she replied briskly. She snapped open the case and withdrew a notepad and pen, intent on keeping this meeting as professional as possible. Reaching into her purse, she pulled out her glasses and slipped them on, then looked at him expectantly.

When he didn't say anything she cleared her throat, self-consciously aware of his dark gaze studying each and every one of her features. She finally sighed impatiently. "Billy, I've come a long way to be here. If you want my help, then you're going to have to tell me what this is all about. Why do you think you're about to be charged with a double homicide, and who was murdered?"

He leaned back in his chair, for a moment his eyes reflecting the look of both the hunted and the haunted. It was there only a moment, then quickly gone as he rubbed a hand across his lower jaw. "You remember Fayrene Whitney? Two days ago she and Tyler LaJune were found dead in Tyler's apartment. They'd been stabbed to death."

"Oh, Billy," Shelby gasped, knowing how close Tyler and Billy had been when growing up. Despite the differences in their backgrounds and physical appearance, as boys they had been like bookends, always together. She fought the impulse to reach out and take his hand, knowing instinctively that Billy would grieve as he'd always done everything else . . . alone.

"They were viciously stabbed in what the police are now characterizing as a crime of passion." His voice was dispassionate, as was his face. "There were no signs of a break-in. Nothing was stolen. No clues, no leads."

Shelby frowned. "Then why do you think you're a suspect in this case?"

He smiled, a bloodless, caustic smile. "Because Fayrene Whitney was my wife."

Chapter Two

Shelby stared at him for a moment, searching for something to say. In all the years, in all her fantasies, she'd never once considered that Billy might have married.

Fayrene Whitney. Shelby had a vague memory of a sullen blonde in tight jeans with a cigarette dangling from her mouth. Fayrene had come from the wrong side of the swamp and had had a reputation for being promiscuous. However, the penalty for teenage abandon wasn't murder.

"We'd been separated for a couple of months," Billy said, filling in the silence that hung heavily between them.

Shelby pulled off her glasses and rubbed her forehead. "And am I right in guessing that it was not an amicable separation?"

"That would be a fair assumption," he agreed, a mocking smile curving his lips. He tipped his chair back once again. "At least I don't have to worry now about a nasty divorce," he added.

She drew in a sharp breath. She'd forgotten about his wicked irreverence, the taunting chip-on-the-shoulder attitude he'd always worn like a shield.

Shelby threw her notebook back into her briefcase. "I can't defend you if you aren't going to take all this seriously." She slammed the briefcase shut and was about to lock the clasps but gasped as his hand tightly encircled her wrist.

"Don't walk out on me, Shelby." Gone was the mocking smile. His chair crashed to the floor with a resounding bang. His grip on her wrist was painfully tight. His eyes once again reflected the look of the hunted. "Everyone in this town has already judged me guilty. For once in my life, I need somebody on my side."

She tore her wrist out of his grasp, rubbed it unconsciously as she noted that once again his eyes were as black, as enigmatic as the darkest swamp water. The momentary flash of vulnerability was gone, making her wonder if she'd only imagined it.

Averting her gaze from his, finding it difficult to think, she focused on the top of the table, scarred with cigarette burns and knife cuts.

"If you won't do it for me, Shelby, then do it for Mama Royce."

Jerking her gaze back to him, she glared, resenting his overt manipulation of her emotions. "Damn you," she said through clenched teeth. "You play dirty."

"I play to win."

Once again she put her glasses on, as if the lenses could protect her from old memories, past pains and a burning bitterness that ached inside her. "Billy, I just don't think it wise that I represent you."

"You have to. I can pay, Shelby. Whatever your price I can meet it. I've been lucky with some investments."

She didn't ask him about his finances, didn't want to know how he'd supported himself through the years. Whatever it was, she had a feeling it would fall into a gray area of the law. "Billy, I'm not going to give you an answer now. I just got into town. I need to check with the police, find out more about what's happened." She locked her briefcase and stood. "Why don't we meet back here tomorrow morning about nine?"

"And what happens if I'm arrested tonight?"

"Call me."

He stood and walked with her to the front of the café. She frowned, aware that he walked too close, invading her space with his flagrant masculinity. They stopped at the café door. "You'll be at the mansion?" Again she was aware of his proximity, the evocative heat of his body.

She nodded curtly and took a step back from him.

His gaze bored into hers, then pointedly traveled down the length of her throat, lingering a moment on the thrust of her breasts, then swept the remainder of her body. "You've grown up mighty fine, Shelby." His voice was softly insinuating, brazenly sexual.

"I'll see you tomorrow." Without waiting for his reply, she turned and stepped out the door into afternoon sunshine.

She gulped in the stifling air and realized that she hadn't drawn a normal breath the whole time she'd been in his presence.

Getting into her car, she decided that before she investigated more deeply into the crime she needed to go to the mansion and get settled in.

The mansion. Funny how she'd never referred to it as her house, although it was where she had been raised. Everyone in town thought of the Longsford place as "the mansion." Built by Shelby's grandfather as a young man, it rose at the edge of the swamp, an arrogant affront to the primal wildness at its back door.

It had been twelve years since she'd been home, but as she pulled up in front of the huge antebellum house she noticed once again that it was as if time had not found Black Bayou. The mansion looked exactly the way it had looked the last time she'd seen it, as an eighteen-year-old going to live with her aunt in New Orleans. At that time, all she had wanted was to get away from this place and the people in it.

Her parents had agreed, obviously wanting to get her away from the swamp and its influences. Shelby had a feeling her father feared she'd embarrass him, become a hindrance to his political aspirations. Shelby's mother had intimated as much when she'd agreed to Shelby going to stay at her aunt's.

Now, as she sat in the car and stared at the pristine white house with the wide wrapping veranda and the fat columns that supported a balcony, she felt a curious pang of homesickness. Huge urns of vivid flowers dotted the veranda, and she knew their sweet, cloying scent would enter the house with each opening and closing of the front door.

She should never have allowed that single night with Billy to drive her from her home so many years before. Although she'd maintained contact with phone calls and letters, the contact had been casual, like that of an acquaintance rather than a family member. As she looked at the house where she had been raised, she realized she'd missed her family.

She got out of the car, wondering how she'd be greeted. She wondered if her father still controlled the family like a dictator, if her mother still had a tendency to drink too much. She pushed these thoughts away, wanting to make a fresh start with no preconceived ideas, no festering, bitter seeds of the past tainting her homecoming. Funny, it was as if for the past twelve years she had allowed herself to feel nothing, and now that she was back, her mind and heart were flooded with emotions too intense to sort out.

The humid air, as thick as syrup and scented with fragrant flowers and the underlying odor of the nearby marsh, wrapped around her as she walked toward the massive front door.

Although most of the family members and friends used the back door, Shelby felt that after twelve years' absence, the formality of the front door was more appropriate.

She raised her hand to knock, but before she could, the door swung open and Shelby found herself engulfed in a bear hug that squeezed the breath out of her. "I thought I heard a car and when I looked out, I couldn't believe my eyes."

"I should have called." Shelby moved out of the embrace and stepped back, eyeing her brother with genuine affection. She reached up and touched the clerical collar at his thick neck. "Father Michael." She smiled and shook her head. "Mother wrote and told me you'd become a priest, but I found it difficult to believe."

He grinned. "Believe it, little sister. It's one of the few things in my life that makes sense."

Shelby studied her brother. At thirty-four, Michael Joseph Longsford had the brilliant blue eyes, the sensual full lips and the widow's peak that were maternal gifts and St. Clair characteristics.

Out of all of her siblings, Shelby had always felt closest to Michael, who, despite his towering height and bulging muscularity, had always been gentle and sensitive.

"Ah, Shelby, it's about time you came home where you belong." He wrapped her up in another bear hug, then led her from the foyer into the living room.

As Michael walked to the wet bar, Shelby hesitated in the doorway, surprised by the changes that had taken place in the room. "Wow. When did this happen?" She skirted the edge of the large, overstuffed sofa. Decorated in navy blue and burgundy, with oversize furniture, the room had a distinctively masculine feel.

"Big John finally got his way." Michael held up a bottle of brandy. Shelby shook her head and he poured himself a splash in the bottom of a snifter. "He carted all of Mama's things up to her suite, said, 'A man can't plant his rear on them spindly-legged chairs.'"

Shelby laughed at his perfect parody of their father's smoky, blustering voice. "So, where is everyone else?" she asked, sitting on one of the bar stools.

Michael shrugged, then sipped his brandy. "Mother is napping, who knows where Olivia and Roger might be, and Big John and Junior are in New Orleans on the campaign trail. They should be back by suppertime."

"How's the campaign going? Does it look like Junior is going to be able to fill Big John's shoes?"

"Hmm, too early to tell. Personally, I don't think Big John will be satisfied with Junior just filling a seat in Congress. He won't be happy until Junior is seated in the White House and everyone sings 'Hail to the Chief' each time he passes by."

Shelby smiled ruefully. "At least nobody can accuse Big John of not having grandiose dreams for his children."

"And other than Junior, I think I can safely say we have all been giant disappointments." He raised his glass once again, as if to hide the slightly bitter twist of his lips. He set the snifter down, once again a warm smile lighting his features. "Now, not that I'm one to look a gift horse in the mouth, but what brings you back here?"

"As I live and breathe," a feminine voice said from behind them. "Baby sister has finally returned."

Shelby swiveled on the bar stool and smiled at her sister. "Hello, Olivia."

Olivia Longsford moved across the floor with the sensuous grace of a panther. With her sleek, dark hair shorn in a boyish cut that flattered her features and wearing a black jumpsuit that emphasized her exquisite shape, she glided across the room and sat next to Shelby. "How about a gin and tonic, Father?"

"Sure." Michael fixed the drink as Olivia studied Shelby.

Shelby had always been ambivalent in her feelings toward Olivia. Three years older than Shelby, Olivia had been a childhood torment while they were growing up. They had never developed any kind of sisterly closeness and Shelby had learned early to be wary of Olivia's spiteful temper and vicious tongue.

"Well, baby sister, as Michael asked before I so rudely interrupted, what brings you home?" She nodded her thanks as Michael set her drink before her.

"I got a phone call yesterday from Billy Royce," Shelby explained.

Olivia poked an ice cube with one bloodred fingernail as a dark brow lifted elegantly. "Surely you aren't going to defend that madman. Everyone in town knows he's guilty as hell."

"I don't." Shelby flushed beneath her sister's scrutiny.

Olivia stared at her another long minute, then laughed. "Oh, God, this is rich. You always did have a crush on that swamp rat. And I never did understand why you spent so much time in that shanty with the old woman."

"Mama Royce was a wonderful, wise person. I...I loved her."

Olivia smiled knowingly. "I wonder if you'd have loved her as much if she didn't have a grandson as sinfully attractive as Billy?"

"Billy had nothing to do with my relationship with Mama Royce," Shelby protested. Olivia merely smiled smugly.

"Ladies, ladies." Michael held up his hands like a football referee signaling time out. "Shelby, I suggest you think carefully before taking on Billy as a client. From what I hear, it's a losing case."

"He's as guilty as the swamp is bug infested," Olivia stated flatly. "Everyone knows it."

"I haven't made a decision yet," Shelby observed.

"Big John will pop a gasket if you defend Billy Royce," Olivia predicted.

"I'm not making any decisions until I talk to the sheriff and the prosecuting attorney. Besides, I quit making my decisions based on what Big John approves or disapproves of a long time ago."

"Good for you," Michael declared, covering Shelby's hand warmly with his.

"And now I think I'll unload my bags, then head back into town to see what I can find out about this mess." Shelby slid off the stool.

"What you're going to find out is that Billy Royce stabbed Fayrene and Tyler in a fit of jealousy. Fayrene and Billy's fights were legendary. Everyone knows those swamp people are barely civilized." Olivia stabbed at an ice cube once again. "From what I've heard, Billy and Fayrene's whole marriage was volatile."

Shelby frowned. "I still can't believe Billy would kill Tyler. They were best friends."

Olivia smiled thinly. "Best friends shouldn't mess around with best friends' wives."

"Why don't you see if Mother will embroider that profound statement on one of her little decorative pillows," Michael said dryly.

Home, sweet home. Shelby sighed.

TWENTY MINUTES LATER Shelby parked in front of the Black Bayou sheriff's office, wondering who was now in charge of law and order in the town. When she had left, it had been Raymond Clausin, a fat, lazy man who preferred to do all his police work from the comfort of his desk.

Walking into the station, she was surprised to see one of her old classmates wearing the sheriff badge. "Bob? Bob Macklinburg?"

"Shelby. Shelby Longsford." Bob stood, walked around the desk and greeted her with an outstretched hand. "Last I heard you were up in Shreveport defending the underdogs of the world."

"That's right, and that's what brings me back here."

"Billy Royce?" As she nodded, Bob whistled beneath his breath. He motioned her to a chair in front of the desk, then resumed his seat behind it. "The crime was ugly, Shelby. Real ugly."

"Murder usually is," she replied dryly.

Bob shook his head. "Not this ugly. I've been the sheriff here for the past three years and have studied the files from the last ten years. I've never seen such a vicious killing."

She leaned forward in the chair. "So, tell me what you have. Billy seems to think he's a suspect."

Bob frowned and raked a hand through his wheat-colored hair. "He's our only suspect."

"What kind of evidence?"

"Circumstantial," Bob admitted reluctantly. "It was one of the bloodiest crime scenes I've ever seen ... and one of the cleanest as far as evidence. We found a knife, one that

Billy owned, but it wasn't the murder weapon. Still, it's only been forty-eight hours. We're still putting together the case against Billy."

"Could I get copies of all the reports as soon as possible?"

"Sure. I'll have Linda send somebody over with what we've got first thing in the morning." He leaned back in the chair, his gaze warm. "Damn, Shelby, it's so good to see you again. You planning on being in town a while?"

"I'm not sure what my plans are right now." She smiled at the attractive sheriff.

Bob had finally grown into the slightly protruding ears that had kept him from being a heartthrob in high school. Maturity had thinned his face to a fine-honed elegance. However, his brown eyes hadn't changed. They radiated a lively intelligence and curiosity. Quietly handsome. Safely attractive.

"I'd better get moving." She stood and headed for the door. Bob immediately jumped out of his chair and followed her.

"Shelby, why don't you have dinner with me this evening?" Bob walked with her toward her car. "There's a new little place on the outskirts of town that's supposed to have terrific food."

Shelby hesitated, unsure if dinner with Bob would be wise. After all, he was the sheriff and it was possible that she might be defending his number-one murder suspect.

Still, Shelby was savvy enough to know that it happened all the time—prosecuting attorneys drank with the defense team, judges golfed with both sides. An incest of sorts, where outcomes of cases were often decided at a cocktail party or over the eighth hole.

"Shelby?"

She looked back at the appealing law officer. "I'd love to, Bob." What the hell, she could be ethical and just enjoy a pleasant dinner without any ulterior motives. Besides, she'd always liked Bob, had fond memories of him, big ears and all.

"Great." He opened her car door, then closed it once she was settled in. "I'll pick you up about six."

She nodded. She started the engine, then waved to Bob as she pulled away from the curb. She made only one stop on the way back home. Running into the offices of the *Black Bayou Daily News,* she bought papers for the past three days, knowing details of the murders would be splashed on the pages.

Driving back home, she thought about her date that evening. Dating had never been an integral part of her life. Before leaving Black Bayou, even though she'd been eighteen, according to Big John she'd been too young to officially date. Over the years her energy and focus had been on her work, with little time left over for relationships.

Her head exploded with memories of a single night in Mama Royce's shanty. She'd been too young to date, but that hadn't stopped Billy from sweeping her from the innocence of childhood into the passionate world of adulthood.

Leaning over, she flipped the air conditioner fan a notch higher, heat sweeping over her, through her as the memories of that night tumbled unbidden to her mind.

She'd loved Billy with the pureness of innocence. The memory of their explosive physical union had the power to stir her blood, dry her mouth. However, remembering that night also evoked in her an odd feeling of horror, of ugliness, of something in her peripheral vision, something she couldn't quite see.

She tightened her grip on the steering wheel, wondering again if she should...if she could defend Billy. At this time she wasn't sure if he was guilty of the murders of Fayrene and Tyler. But he was guilty of another murder. Twelve years before, he'd murdered her ability to love. What she had to figure out was whether she had been drawn back here by the desire to help him or the overwhelming need to pay him back.

Chapter Three

Evening shadows fell dark and long on the ground beneath Billy's feet. He leaned against a tree trunk, his eyes narrowed as he watched the back of the mansion from his vantage point at the edge of the swamp.

He didn't wonder what had drawn him here, had never felt the need to analyze what pull the big house had maintained on him over the years.

"You covet it," Fayrene had often said. "You want all that they have—the money, the house, the respectability. They belong...and no matter how much you try to change, no matter how much money you make, you'll always just be a swamp rat."

God, Fayrene had been difficult. She'd been so unhappy, and wanted everyone around her to be equally unhappy. She'd known each and every button of his to push. One thing was certain, he didn't covet the house, nor did he long for the respectability the Longsford family enjoyed.

In truth, the family fascinated him, had fascinated him ever since the time that Shelby was small and had escaped this beautiful home to spend all her spare time in his grandmother's shanty.

Shelby. His muscles tightened in response to thoughts of her. Over the years he'd occasionally thought of her, wondered about her and tried to suppress the memory of their single night together. They'd been kids, and in his mind Shelby was all twisted up with his own grief over his grandmother's death.

But she wasn't an innocent young girl any longer. Shelby had grown up. Seeing her that morning, despite the gravity of circumstances surrounding the meeting, he'd responded to her on a physical level that had surprised him.

At the sound of tires crunching gravel, Billy instinctively took a step backward, melting into the lush, slightly cooler embrace of the brush. His eyes narrowed once again as he recognized the car that pulled around the back of the house. Bob Macklinburg. What was he doing here?

He watched as the sheriff got out of his car and knocked on the back door. He wasn't in uniform, so Billy assumed it wasn't a business call. Besides, had it been business, he would have pulled up front instead of driving around to this informal driveway. The door was opened and Bob disappeared inside. Minutes later he walked out, with Shelby at his side.

In a flame-colored dress, she was a vivid splash of color against the pristine backdrop of the house. Her hair was caught at the nape of her neck with a matching ribbon, much as it had been worn earlier in the day. Billy's fingers had itched to remove the clasp that had held the dark hair so neatly, wanting her hair wild and abandoned around her face as it was in his memory.

As the couple got in the car and drove back down the driveway, rounding the side of the house and disappearing from view, Billy turned and began the short walk to the shanty.

Maneuvering easily through the forest that had been his real home and family for as long as he could remember, Billy thought of the trouble he was in.

He'd never been a stranger to trouble. Mama Royce had often told him that trouble was like a mosquito, always buzzing around his head and looking for a place to bite. "You must have sweet skin," she'd say, "'cause trouble always bites you no matter how you try to hide."

It had been a hell of a bite this time, he thought with a frown, one he couldn't heal by himself. He couldn't go to prison, not in this lifetime. And he'd always had an instinctive distrust of lawyers, defense or otherwise. It would be too easy to sell him out, plea-bargain him down the river...one less swamp rat to sully the town of Black Bayou.

He'd do anything to stay out of prison. Whatever it took. He only hoped it wouldn't become necessary to destroy Shelby Longsford in the process.

"HOW ABOUT SOME DESSERT?" Bob urged as the waitress returned to their table. He grinned as Shelby groaned.

"I couldn't," she protested. "But I wouldn't turn down a cup of coffee."

"Two coffees," he told the waitress. As she moved away he pulled a pack of cigarettes from his pocket. "Do you mind?"

Shelby shook her head, then settled back in the chair with a sigh of contentment. The food had been delicious and the conversation pleasant. As they had eaten, Bob had caught her up on many of their classmates' lives—who had married whom, who'd had children, who had moved away. As he'd talked, Shelby had fought a swift wave of nostalgia, of time lost. She'd left Black Bayou just before the end of her senior year, missing the parties and the actual ceremony of graduation.

At the time she hadn't cared about graduation or her classmates. She'd wanted to get away, needed to get away from Billy. She couldn't even remember now whose idea it was for her to go live with her aunt.

She now found herself wondering how different her life would have been, how different she would have been if she'd stayed here.

"You're suddenly very quiet," Bob observed.

Shelby smiled. "Just thinking." She tilted her head and gazed at him curiously. "Why hasn't some girl snapped you up and given you a dozen babies?"

He smiled, an endearing crooked one that only accentuated his clean-cut good looks. "I guess all the hometown honeys got tired of me obsessing over my career." Stubbing out his cigarette, he looked at her proudly. "But the obsessing all paid off. I'm the youngest sheriff in the entire state."

"Quite an accomplishment."

He nodded, then released a deep sigh. "Little did I know that when I gained the public trust, I'd also gain a file full of unsolved swamp murders and now the latest, a grisly double homicide."

"Unsolved swamp murders?"

"The swamp serpent."

Shelby frowned. "What's the swamp serpent?"

The waitress reappeared with their coffee. When she'd left, Shelby looked at Bob expectantly. He stirred creamer into his coffee, then sighed once again. "The swamp serpent is the popular name for Black Bayou's very own serial killer."

"Serial murderer?"

Bob nodded. "The murders began years ago, about the same time you moved away from Black Bayou. All the victims have been from the swamp, and that's where the murders occur and the bodies are found." He shook out another cigarette and lit it. "The first victim was a middle-aged man. He'd been stabbed twice and left to bleed to death. Altogether there's been fifteen victims, all of them stabbed the same way as the first."

"My God," Shelby gasped. "I'm surprised the men of this town aren't out with their shotguns to catch whoever is responsible."

"Ah, but there's the rub. These aren't . . . weren't town people." Bob blew a stream of smoke to the ceiling, then looked at Shelby once again. "They were swamp folks, and my predecessor didn't exactly bust his butt to investigate the crimes."

Shelby frowned thoughtfully. "I guess some things never change." She could remember Mama Royce telling her there were two kinds of law—town justice and swamp injustice.

Bob leaned across the table. "I intend to make some changes," he said earnestly. "I want these crimes stopped, the perpetrator caught. I'm in the process of reopening the investigation, but so far it's like spitting in the wind." He sighed in frustration.

"Any clues? Leads?"

Bob shook his head. "Nothing. No clues, no discernible pattern that I can detect. And the frustrating thing is that I can't get any of the people in the bog to cooperate with me. Hell, I don't even know how many families live in that swamp. I sure as hell can't get anyone to talk to me about the murders."

"When was the last one?"

"A little over a year ago. A couple of months before I became sheriff." He raked a hand through his close-cropped hair, then put out his cigarette. "I've tried to do some follow-up, but it's a near impossible task. Anyway, I'm going to have to put it on the back burner for now. I've got a more pressing matter to attend to."

"Fayrene's and Tyler's murders."

Bob nodded. He sipped his coffee, then looked at her curiously. "You going to defend Billy?"

With two fingers she rubbed her forehead thoughtfully. "Yes. Yes, I think I am."

"You've got one hell of a battle ahead of you."

Shelby flashed him a smile. "I always did like challenges." She stared at Bob for a long moment. "Do you think he did it?"

Bob shrugged. "I truly don't know what to think. Nobody was surprised when Billy and Fayrene separated a couple months ago. Their fights kept the gossipmongers happy for years."

"So it was a violent marriage?" Shelby asked, feeling like a kind of voyeur, yet needing to understand the dynamics at work. She couldn't imagine Billy abusing any woman. Mama Royce would spin in her grave at the very idea.

"Depends on who you talk to. When Fayrene and Billy moved into the apartment here in town, she was always calling us, telling us Billy was being mean to her. I went out to the apartment several times to talk to Billy. He always insisted he never hit her, only restrained her from hitting him. Truth told, I never saw a mark on Fayrene." Bob laughed. "To be perfectly honest, I think we all knew Fayrene was crying wolf to get attention."

"Whose idea was the separation?"

"Again, depends on who you ask. Fayrene told everyone it was her idea, that she wanted out." Bob stared down at his coffee. "She called me a week ago, said Billy was stalking her. Hell, it was never easy separating Fayrene's stories from the truth. I didn't pay it much mind at the time." He looked back at Shelby. "The way I figure it, Billy didn't want that divorce. The night of the murder, he must have followed Tyler and Fayrene home from the bar where they'd been drinking together. He saw them go into Tyler's apartment and he just lost it. Tyler was his best friend and Fayrene was his wife. He went crazy and killed them both."

Shelby frowned, trying to fit this picture to Billy. "I don't know. I just can't see Billy as an out-of-control stalker."

"Shelby, I don't want to believe Billy is responsible for this crime. Hell, I'd prefer nobody I know be guilty of such viciousness, but the fact remains that the crime did happen, and Billy is the only one I know who had both motive and opportunity." He grinned. "And now you know why I'm not married. Every time I get a gorgeous woman to go out with me, I bore her with stories of criminals and crimes."

Shelby returned his smile. "You aren't boring me. But—" she looked at her wristwatch "—I should be getting back to the mansion. I imagine by now my father and brother will be home."

He nodded and signaled the waitress for their check. "Did you see the new community center over on Magnolia Drive?" Bob asked minutes later as they drove back toward the Longsford house.

"No. What I noticed when I came through town earlier was that it didn't look like anything had changed in all the years I've been gone."

"There's been changes, they've just been slow in coming. We've got several people on the town council now who have made a commitment to helping those families living in the swamp. That's what the community center is all about, providing a safe place for the kids to hang out."

"The town built the community center?" Shelby asked in surprise.

Bob shook his head. "Actually, an out-of-town company put up the money for the building and furnishings. The city staffs and maintains it along with a bevy of volunteers. Your family is one of our best volunteer sources."

"Who's the prosecutor now?" Shelby asked, her mind scooting back to Billy's case.

"Abner Witherspoon."

She looked at him in surprise. "I thought he was dead. He worked as a campaign manager for my father about a hundred years ago."

Bob laughed. "There are some who wish he'd retire and get out of town. He's the leader of a small group of the old guard still left, men who don't want to see any change."

Abner Witherspoon. Uncle Abe, as she had called him in her early childhood. If Shelby agreed to defend Billy, she would face Abner in a courtroom. It was a daunting thought. Abner had a reputation for being shrewd, manipulative and a master at legal maneuvering. He would be a lethal adversary.

"Shelby, I really enjoyed this evening," Bob said as he pulled the car around to the back of the house.

"I did, too." She was surprised to discover she meant it. She had enjoyed his company, found him pleasant . . . safe. Frowning, she wondered what had made her think of that particular adjective.

Bob walked her to the door, his hand at her elbow in courtly fashion. Shelby could smell his after-shave, a pleasant light spicy scent. They paused at the door.

"Will you have dinner with me again?"

She smiled. "You promise to talk about your work again?"

His eyes lit with pleasure and he reached out a hand and swept a strand of her hair away from her shoulder. "I think we could come up with some sort of a compromise." He leaned closer to her, his fingers softly caressing the side of her face. "We'll talk about my job over dinner, and we'll talk about yours over dessert." He smiled and stepped away. "Good night Shelby... and welcome home."

She stood on the veranda and watched until his car lights disappeared from sight. Still she lingered, reluctant to go inside. The night air wrapped her in a humid, sweetly perfumed embrace and the moon overhead hung low, a crescent moon like a sliver of ripened fruit.

Shelby had always loved the night. Countless nights in her youth she had sneaked out her bedroom window, climbed down the column and run to the warmth and love of Mama Royce's cabin. The swamp had never frightened her, despite the inherent dangers. Mama Royce had taught her to love the marshy bogs, the roots and flowers that grew in dank, shady places, the untamed wildness filled with mystery and beauty.

On impulse, she kicked off her shoes and stepped off the veranda. The grass licked her feet with cool dampness. The night spoke to her in buzzes and clicks and throaty croaks. It was a nighttime lullaby, a childhood melody she'd missed.

The slice of moonlight silhouetted the trees at the outer edge of the swamp but couldn't illuminate the heart, which remained dark and mysterious.

As Shelby stared at the moon-dappled trees, her throat closed up with fear. A memory tapped on her brain... figures dancing in the dark, the moon a silver orb hanging low, a scream trapped deep inside her. Fear, rich and full, shivered through her and she took a stumbling step backward, back toward the safety of the veranda.

Something in the swamp. Something ugly... something horrid. The scream that clogged her throat cut off her breath. She couldn't breathe. The need to scream clawed at her insides. Turning in panic, she released the scream as strong hands grabbed her shoulders from behind.

"Shelby."

She whirled around and stared at Billy. Without thought, acting only from need, she threw herself against him and wrapped her arms around his neck. His arms instantly responded in kind, enveloping her against his hard strength. "I don't know what the good sheriff fed you for dinner, but he ought to do it more often." Billy's deep voice vibrated inside Shelby, and as quickly as the inexplicable fear had appeared, it vanished.

She jerked out of his grasp. "What in the hell are you doing sneaking around out here in the dark?" she demanded, anger safer than fear. The moonlight stroked his dark hair, causing it to glimmer as if shot through with shards of silver.

"I must hand it to you, Shelby. First day back in town and you snag a date with the town's most eligible bachelor. How is the good sheriff?"

"Have you been watching me?" It was an unnerving thought, that he'd hidden in the wall of brush, beneath the cypress trees, and watched her leave with Bob.

"Are you going to defend me?" He took a step toward her, bringing with him the smell of the swamp, a dark, mysterious scent that stirred her senses as Bob's pleasant spice smell never would.

"I told you we'd talk about it tomorrow."

"He didn't kiss you good-night. He's either an upstanding gentleman, or incredibly foolish." His teeth flashed white in a smile. "I would guess that he's a fool." He stood so close to her she could feel the heat from his body, see the moonlight reflected in the depths of his eyes.

She had never forgotten the feel of his callused hands against her bare breasts, the taste of his mouth so hungry against hers. No matter how she had tried to forget that single night with Billy, she couldn't. And she hated him for it. She hated him for branding her with his touch, his possession, causing an indelible mark no amount of time had erased.

Gazing at him coolly, she wondered if he could hear the fierce pounding of her heart. "What are you doing here, Billy? I thought we'd agreed to meet in the morning."

"I decided not to wait until morning." He bent and picked up her shoes, then motioned for her to sit in one of the wicker chairs on the veranda. "I've always done my best negotiations after dark."

"I'm sure," Shelby answered thinly as she sank onto the chair.

He went down on his haunches and lifted up one of her feet. Sliding on her sandal, he let his fingers linger on the delicate skin of her ankle, making the act far too sensual for Shelby's comfort. She snatched the other shoe from his hand and maneuvered it onto her foot.

He stood and crossed his arms, a lazy grin of amusement curling one side of his mouth.

She stood back up, her face flushed with heat. "I don't like you spying on me." She hesitated a moment, then continued, "I heard today that you were stalking Fayrene before her death."

His eyes narrowed slightly. "You've been listening to rumors and innuendo." He leaned a hip against the veranda railing. "So, are you going to represent me?"

"Why was a knife belonging to you found at the murder scene?"

He grimaced. "I gave Tyler that knife months ago. He'd always admired it. It wasn't...it didn't have anything to do with the murder?"

She felt the tension coiled inside him and quickly shook her head. "No, but the sheriff considers it evidence that you were there."

Shelby thought of Mama Royce. The old woman had loved three things—the swamp, Billy and Shelby. If Mama were alive now, she would encourage Shelby to help Billy. There were powers at work here, more than just a debt to a dead woman, more than the remembered passion shared in a single night of youth.

This was the kind of case she'd only dreamed about. Billy Royce already had a dozen strikes against him just in the mere accident of where he was born, where he had grown up. Without a good defense lawyer, Billy was as good as a dead man.

She looked at him, seeing the aura of danger that surrounded him, the mocking half smile, the arrogance that would make it difficult for him to find any other adequate representation. No good lawyer liked an uncooperative client, and she had a feeling Billy could be very uncooperative. "Yes. Yes, I'll represent you," she finally agreed.

He nodded, as if he hadn't expected any other answer. "Then we can discuss the particulars at our meeting in the morning."

"And I don't want you spying on me anymore." Shelby moved toward the door. "I'll see you in the morning." She started to open the door, but hesitated as he called her name. She turned back to look at him.

"You haven't asked me." His voice was soft, but filled with a repressed energy.

She frowned. "Haven't asked you what?"

"If I'm guilty or not."

She looked at him for a long moment, then sighed. "Maybe that's because I'm afraid of your answer." Without waiting for a reply, she slipped through the door and into the house.

Chapter Four

"So, the rumor is true. You've finally come home." Big John Longsford looked at Shelby expectantly as she walked into the living room where the whole family was gathered.

"Hello, Daddy."

He sat on the sofa like a king, the rest of the family gathered around like loyal subjects. She walked over to him and kissed him on the cheek, then did the same to her mother, who sat in a nearby chair.

"What will it be, sis?" John Junior grinned at her from behind the bar. He had the slightly glazed look of somebody who had already reached his limit of alcohol but would never admit it.

"Just a club soda." Shelby walked over to the bar and took the beverage from her eldest brother. It was amazing how in the past twelve years he had become a young replica of their father. He carried himself with the same arrogant assurance, parted his hair carefully on the left. His chest, although not quite as barrel-like as Big John's, was emphasized by the tailored cut of his expensive dress shirt.

"Sit down, Shelby. I was just telling the family about our success in New Orleans."

Shelby tamped down an edge of resentment that flared at the command in her father's voice. Big John never

asked. He demanded, and expected immediate compli-
ance. She slid onto a bar stool, feeling as if she'd been
thrust back in time. Big John had always liked family
meetings with all his children gathered around him as he
drank bourbon straight up and held court.

"You should have heard Junior's speech. It was brilliant." Big John looked at his namesake proudly.

Junior grinned and poured himself another drink. "Of
course it was brilliant. You wrote it."

Big John's laughter filled the room, robust and deep
from years of bourbon and cigarettes. As he rehashed the
speech and Junior's performance, Shelby studied the
members of her family.

The years hadn't diminished her father, rather he seemed
bigger, bolder, more colorful than Shelby's memory. Time
hadn't been as kind to her mother. Celia Longsford had
faded, her features blending and becoming indistinct, like
a watercolor painting left out in the rain. It was as if Big
John sucked all the oxygen out of the air, not leaving
enough for his wife to flourish.

Olivia sat next to Big John on the sofa, rapt with attention as he spoke. Beneath her caustic wit and hard crust,
Olivia had always adored Big John, despite the fact that he
often treated her with a casual cruelty.

In truth, Big John had always had little use for the
women in his life. A fact Shelby had long ago accepted but
Olivia continued to try to change.

She looked over at Michael, who winked at her like a
coconspirator, as if he read her thoughts and commiser-
ated with them. Again Shelby realized how much she had
missed having Michael in her life. When she'd left Black
Bayou so many years before, she'd left a lot of good behind in her attempt to flee her own confusion and misery.
Another strike against Billy Royce, she thought irritably.

''Shelby hasn't told you yet what brought her home,'' Olivia said to Big John, then smiled archly at Shelby, obviously aware of the can of worms she opened. ''She's come back to defend Billy Royce.''

Celia gasped, a hand shooting up to cover her mouth.

''The hell you say.'' In an eye blink, Big John was transformed. His features grew taut, the warmth of his brown eyes hardened to cold, hard speculation as he looked at Shelby. ''Is that true?''

''It is.'' She met his gaze steadily, her heart taking up a beat from childhood.

''And what if I tell you I don't want you to do that?'' The silence in the room was deafening as Big John confronted his youngest child.

''Then I'd tell you that I'm sorry you don't approve, but nothing changes. I intend to defend Billy.''

''And what if I told you that you aren't welcome here if you're going to defend that man?''

Celia gasped again and Shelby shrugged. ''There are several adequate hotels in Black Bayou. I'm sure I could find accommodations.''

''Now that would sure as hell give the gossips a field day.'' It was Big John who finally broke their eye-contact battle. He stared down into his glass. ''Damn it, Junior. My glass is empty.'' As Junior hurried forward to refill the glass, Big John looked at Shelby once again. ''This is my house. I won't have that trash here.''

Shelby nodded curtly. She would respect his wishes even though she hated his prejudice. At times she wondered if that wasn't what had first prompted her to befriend Mama Royce, some kind of childish rebellion against the strong prejudice her father had always entertained against the people from the swamp. However, in those years of visiting Mama Royce, mingling with the people who embraced the wildness as their home, Shelby had developed a respect for them far greater than she would ever have for members of her own family.

Big John finished his bourbon in one deep swallow, then stood. "Been a long day. I'm ready to turn in." Celia rose also, as if connected by wires to her husband. It had always been that way. When Big John was tired, Celia also slept. When Big John was hungry, Celia ate. Shelby had never seen her mother as anything but a shadow. Big John's shadow.

"Some things never change," she said the moment Big John and Celia had left the room.

"Things have changed," Olivia protested. "Mother used to wait until cocktail hour to have her first drink. Now she starts far earlier."

"Mother hides her pain in a bottle," Michael observed. "And you hide yours in flirting."

Olivia smiled at Michael. It was not a pleasant smile. Shelby's stomach tensed. "At least I don't hide behind a clerical collar."

"That's enough, Ollie," Junior admonished. He smiled at her fondly, then stifled a yawn with the back of his broad hand. "Guess I'll head to bed. Being charming and intelligent all day has worn me out. Shelby, good to have you home."

"I'm out of here, too," Olivia said, rising from the sofa with the languid elegance of a large cat. She gazed at Michael and Shelby in wry amusement. "I'll leave you two to pontificate on why we're all the way we are."

Junior laughed, and together brother and sister left the room. A moment later the back door opened and closed, signaling Olivia's departure from the house.

"I don't know about you, but the last thing I want to do is pontificate," Michael said with a grin.

Shelby laughed and moved to sit on the sofa. "I'm with you. I have too much on my mind to take on the quirks of my relatives."

"Billy?"

She nodded. "In my heart I can't believe he would ever be capable of killing anyone. I spent a lot of time with Billy and Mama Royce, and I know she's the one who raised Billy. I can't believe she'd raise a man capable of murder."

"That time you spent with them was a long time ago. Mama Royce has been dead for years and Billy has been left on his own without her influence. Things change, Shelby. People change."

"I know. That's what frightens me. As a defense lawyer his guilt should be relatively unimportant to me. I'm sworn to give him the best possible defense no matter what. But as a woman, there's a part of me that knows whoever committed that crime deserves to spend the rest of their life in prison."

"Follow your heart, Shelby. It rarely steers you wrong."

She leaned over and kissed Michael on his cheek. "Thanks, big brother. And now I think I'll go to bed. It's been a long day and I have a feeling the days are only going to get longer."

"I WOULD LIE FOR YOU."

Billy turned away from the window at the sound of the low, melodic voice. She stood framed in the doorway between the kitchen and living room of the small shanty. She was tall and slender, her features etched with fierce pride and generations of misery. She was of an indeterminable age, with the unwrinkled skin of a teenager but the eyes of old wisdom. Angelique Boujoulais had been Billy's closest friend other than Tyler LaJune since his grandmother's death.

"I can't let you do that." He sank onto the sofa.

"You need an alibi, somebody who saw you, spent time with you on the night of the murders." She sat next to him, bringing with her the scent of roots, herbs and the black earth of the swamp floor. Although the familiar smell comforted him, it couldn't compete with the memory of Shelby's perfume. "I could tell the sheriff you were here all night with me."

"I won't let you lie for me. Besides, nobody would believe you." He smiled humorlessly. "You're the Gypsy Queen."

"Bah, if I was as powerful a gypsy as they all think, I would make a special charm to protect my people who meet the swamp serpent." Her dark eyes narrowed, and Billy knew she was thinking of the family members she'd lost.

First her sister, then her husband. Each had fallen victim to the swamp serpent, their bodies found where they had fallen in their own blood.

With each subsequent swamp serpent murder, Billy had felt Angelique's rage growing until it was a festering wound eating her from the inside out. It was a fury of loss, the anger of a lifetime of prejudice and a town's seeming nonchalance over the lives lost. Billy knew her anger, had its kin inside him. It had exploded only once, and the results had been devastating.

He stood. "It's late." He started toward the door that led to one of the bedrooms.

"Let him sleep," Angelique said softly. "There's no sense in waking him up and dragging him out in the middle of the night. Besides, he and Rafe can play in the morning, then you can come by for him tomorrow after his lessons."

Billy hesitated, then nodded. Rafe, Angelique's son, was Parker's best friend, and Billy knew Parker was in good hands with Angelique. Still, he went into the bedroom and stood over the sleeping child. This child, Parker Royce, was the only good that had come out of his marriage. Initially he'd hoped the child would make Fayrene settle down, be a real wife and mother, but it wasn't to be. Fayrene had the maternal emotions of a stump in the woods.

He leaned down, studying the cast of dark lashes on childish cheeks, the little mouth puckered in sleep. He breathed in deeply, like an animal identifying its young, knowing he would recognize the scent of his child in any crowd.

There was no hint of Fayrene in the child's features. It was as if Parker had been fashioned from Billy's rib, a miniature clone without the emotional baggage and soul scars of his father. And Billy was determined that the child would not be scarred by the same forces that had tormented him. Everything Billy had done, he'd done for the welfare of this child. He was ruthless when it came to Parker.

After pulling the sheet up closer around the little boy's neck, he turned and left the room. Angelique still sat on the sofa but she stood as he walked toward the door. "You'll be all right?"

He hesitated a moment, then shook his head and grinned. "No swamp serpent would have me, Angelique. I'll be fine." He bent over and kissed her on the cheek. She held him for a moment, one hand pressing tightly on his back, the other raking through his hair. He pulled away, touched her cheek softly. "I'll see you tomorrow."

Angelique watched him as he left the porch, disappearing into the dense, dark swamp. He moved like the wind, swiftly, silently, not a twig snapping, just a soft rustle of underbrush.

She crossed her arms over her breasts, hugging her shoulders tight. She ached. A deep, abiding ache that had been with her from the moment Remy's body had been found. Losing her sister had been horrible, but four years later when Remy had been killed, Angelique had fought the invasion of madness.

She knew the panacea for that throbbing emptiness was Billy, knew she could find the sweet peace of mindlessness in his embrace. She'd been patient through his ill-fated marriage to Fayrene, knowing it wouldn't last, knowing sooner or later he'd be free once again.

What she hadn't counted on was Shelby Longsford. She'd felt his distance as he'd spoken of the woman lawyer. Shelby Longsford. Although Angelique didn't personally know Shelby, she knew the family. The Longsford power in the area was wide and far-reaching.

Angelique smiled. But she had some power of her own. She'd never before used a charm to bind Billy to her, had wanted his heart to be hers uncoerced. Perhaps it was time for a change.

Holding her hand up toward the silvery crescent moon, she saw the single dark hair between two fingertips. She would not lose Billy. She would do whatever it took to get him. Whatever it took.

Chapter Five

Silence greeted Shelby the next morning as she descended the stairs to the dining room. There were no signs of breakfast, although a silver coffeepot remained on the serving buffet. She helped herself, then sat down at the large table.

She was surprised by how deeply, how long she had slept. There had been no nightmares, no dreams, just the wonderful oblivion of sleep. She felt refreshed, ready to face whatever the day might bring.

"Good morning, Ms. Shelby."

"Suellen." Shelby smiled brightly at the broad woman who'd entered the room.

"Welcome home." Suellen's fat face was wreathed in a smile that plumped her cheeks and caused her dancing brown eyes to nearly disappear in folds of flesh. "How about some breakfast? I can get cook to fix you something."

"No, thanks, coffee is fine." Shelby looked at her wristwatch. "Besides, I have to leave in a few minutes for an appointment in town. Where is everyone else this morning?"

"Your daddy and John Junior left for Washington, D.C., and won't be home till the weekend." The old woman frowned, her lips pursed slightly in disapproval. "And your mama and Ms. Olivia are still in bed. They don't never see the day before noon. Besides, Ms. Olivia's husband came home late last night."

Shelby nodded and took a sip of her coffee. She'd almost forgotten Olivia was now a married woman, having tied the knot six months before. "What's Roger like?" she asked, having only vague memories of the man who had at one time been mayor of Black Bayou and now was her brother-in-law.

Suellen frowned. "Handsome, smooth as snake oil. A politician through and through."

Shelby smiled. "You don't like him much, do you?"

Suellen's face reddened. "It's not my place to like or dislike. I just don't trust a man who dyes his hair and has had a face-lift," she exclaimed.

Shelby had been shocked when she'd heard Olivia had married Roger Eaton. Roger was twice Olivia's age, and a political ally and peer to Big John.

"Shelby?" Suellen looked at her in speculation. "Heard you were defending Billy."

"You heard right." Shelby smiled as she brought her coffee cup to her lips. "I figured the town could use that little item for gossip."

Suellen snorted. "This town finds everything a matter of gossip." Her eyes darkened and she touched the gold cross that hung on the wall of her enormous breasts. "They'll have more than enough to chew on this morning. There was another swamp serpent murder last night."

Shelby sucked in her breath and set her cup back down on the table. "Where's the morning paper?"

"Your daddy took it with him, but you won't find nothing worthwhile there. It was buried on page seventeen, just a little paragraph."

Outrage swept through Shelby. "And what was the headline of the paper?"

"Something about the police still seeking evidence in the death of Tyler LaJune. Tyler's daddy is an important man. He's not about to let his son's death be forgotten." Suellen shook her head sadly. "Tyler's murder is a sad thing. But so is the killing of all those people in the swamp. There's something evil in Black Bayou...something horribly evil."

Long after Suellen left the dining room, Shelby remained seated at the dining room table. Something evil in the swamp. The old woman's words had evoked haunting images. Moonlight flowing through the trees, dancing on figures with the surreal illumination of a dream. Evil.

She rubbed her forehead, as if in doing so she could bring the vision into sharper focus, but instead it dissipated altogether. She drank the last of her coffee.

Poor Bob. He would have his hands full. Looking at her wristwatch a final time, she realized it was time she left for her appointment with Billy.

Billy. Minutes later as she drove toward town, she couldn't help but think of the boy he had been and wonder about the man he had become.

She'd been six and he'd been nine when she'd first met him. Angry with her parents, who rarely remembered she existed, stinging from a brawl with Olivia, Shelby had decided to run away. The swamp beckoned and she vaguely remembered thinking at the time that it would serve her parents right if she got eaten by an alligator, or drowned in the dark water. She didn't know how far she'd run before she sat down on a fallen log, lost in fantasies of her own funeral. In her childish reverie her mother leaned weakly against her distraught father, and Olivia threw herself on the coffin, crying her name over and over again. It was a pleasant vision, one that had comforted Shelby. It wasn't until the daydream faded that she realized day had passed into night. She was alone in the dark swamp and hopelessly lost.

She didn't know how long she cried before Billy finally found her. Even then, he'd had the unique ability of moving silently across the forest floor. He hadn't spoken to her, he'd merely held out his hand and taken her to Mama Royce's cabin.

Shelby rolled down the window of her car, allowing the hot air to fill the interior and caress away the tears that had sprung to her eyes at thoughts of Mama Royce. Billy's grandmother had been the one good, loving constant in Shelby's life, and even after all this time she still felt the hole of Mama Royce's absence in her soul.

She'd fallen in love with Billy Royce on that first night, when his hand had closed around hers with warmth and he'd led her out of the darkness and into the light and love of Mama's shanty.

Childhood, she scoffed inwardly. She was no longer that innocent girl who'd fled the coldness of her home, the dictatorial demands of her father and the inadequacies of her mother, seeking the warmth of the tiny shanty, Mama's arms and Billy's silent presence.

No, she was no longer that little girl, she thought as she parked in front of Martha's Café. She realized now that there was no way to make her father love her, no way to make her mother strong. She couldn't fix her family and she couldn't change the world. The only thing she could do was use all her legal prowess to keep Billy Royce out of prison. She prayed in doing that she wasn't making a mistake.

Gathering her briefcase and purse, she steeled herself for seeing Billy again. Even the deep sleep she'd enjoyed the night before hadn't erased the sensual feel of his fingers lingering on her ankle as he'd slipped on her sandal, the scent of him that had wrapped around her like strong, warm arms.

Did all women remember their first sexual experience so clearly? Every nuance, each caress of that moment was burned into her memory. She'd lost herself in him, could still remember her need to bury herself in his very skin. No experience she'd had since had managed to diffuse any of the power or emotion surrounding that night.

Billy had awakened her sexually, then abandoned her to find complete and lasting fulfillment elsewhere. And she had yet to find that whole fulfillment, the kind that sated not only her body but her heart, as well.

She got out of the car and headed for the café, needing to concentrate on the crime, not the man. Somehow they had to come up with a strategy for defense in the event of Billy's arrest. And, if Billy was arrested, she was going to have to hire some help. She couldn't do all the investigation that would be required alone.

As she walked in, Martha nodded toward the back room, letting Shelby know that Billy had already arrived. She felt his energy as she stood in the doorway of the back room. It filled the air, simmering like a pot about to boil as he paced back and forth in the small confines. When he saw her, he stopped all movement. However, even in utter stillness he gave the impression of perpetual motion.

"Have you heard?"

"Heard what?" She stiffened instinctively as he approached her, then relaxed as he closed the door and motioned her to a chair at the small scarred table where they'd sat the day before.

He pulled up a chair across from her, his face a study in intensity, his eyes burning with flames of anger. "Another one was killed last night." He slammed his fist down, the force shaking the table and forcing a gasp from Shelby. "Damn it, somebody is killing our people and nobody in this godforsaken town seems to care."

"I care," Shelby said softly. Without thought she reached out to cover his hand with her own.

He jerked away from her touch, his gaze cold, scornful. "Your family and their kind are half the problem."

Shelby's anger was swift to rise. "And yet it's me and my kind who you ran to when you thought you might be in trouble." Her gaze was equally cold.

A smile lifted one corner of his lips. "I'm angry, Shelby. But nobody ever accused me of being stupid."

"So, you'll throw in your lot with the devil to save your own skin?"

His grin widened and he leaned toward her. "I've seen the devil, Shelby, and he doesn't have your considerable charm."

She felt a blush sweep over her, heating her cheeks as his gaze lingered on the swell of her breasts. "Stop it, Billy." Her voice was low, but steady.

"Stop what?"

"Don't treat me like I'm one of your women. I'm not. I'm your lawyer and you're my client. I've already had the experience of sex with you, and your practiced seduction has no effect on me."

He reached out and touched the throbbing pulse at the base of her throat. "No effect?" A dark eyebrow quirked.

The sinful warmth of his fingertips awakened a shiver at the base of her spine. Before it could work itself free to shimmy up her back, she batted his hand away in irritation. "With your arrest for a double homicide pending, can you really afford to spend your time indulging in this kind of nonsense?"

He leaned back in his chair, the lazy amusement gone, usurped by emotions darker, more dangerous. "This kind of 'nonsense' is supposedly what got me in this position in the first place."

Shelby frowned, unsure she understood what he meant. "What?"

"Sex." Once again he leaned across the table toward her, so close she could see the unrelenting darkness of his eyes. "Passion. The kind that drives people wild, makes them ignore the laws of man, turns rational people into irrational animals." She could smell him, a rich male scent that stirred her senses. "Have you ever felt that kind of mind-numbing passion, Shelby?"

She shook her head. "No." Her voice was faint, her throat dry.

"Neither have I." He sat back and raked a hand through his hair in irritation. "That's why all this is a bunch of garbage. They think I killed Fayrene and Tyler in a fit of jealousy, because Tyler and Fayrene were lovers." He smiled, the sardonic twist of his lips adding to his dangerous attractiveness. "Hell, if I killed every one of the men Fayrene supposedly had affairs with, I'd cut the population of Black Bayou in half."

"She was promiscuous?"

"So I'm told. Although Fayrene wasn't above a little twisting of the truth."

Shelby rubbed her forehead thoughtfully. This information, rather than helping Billy's defense, only added to the strength of the possibility of charges against him. "They'll just say you finally snapped, that you couldn't stand it that your wife's latest lover was your very best friend."

Billy scowled and snorted in derision. "Tyler and Fayrene weren't lovers."

Shelby looked at him sharply. "How can you know that?"

"Believe me, I know. The sheriff's whole scenario doesn't play out, because I know for a fact that Fayrene and Tyler were just friends, never lovers." For a brief moment a stark pain swept over his face, the pain of grief. It was there only a moment, then gone, and he drew in a deep breath.

Shelby pulled a legal pad from her briefcase and began making notes. "Did Fayrene have any girlfriends, any confidantes? Somebody she might have told about her relationship with Tyler?" She smiled sardonically. "I have a feeling nobody is just going to take your word on their relationship. I need somebody else to back it up."

Billy frowned thoughtfully. "For the most part Fayrene didn't care for other women. Although I know she spent a lot of time at The Edge."

"The Edge?"

"A bar on the south side of town. It's a rough place, Shelby. If you decide to go there, I'll go with you."

"That isn't necessary," she replied. "I can take one of my brothers with me."

Billy smirked, his gaze indulgent. "You take a Longsford into The Edge and you'll have to carry him out on a stretcher."

"Have you forgotten that I'm a Longsford?" she asked stiffly.

Once again his gaze burned with renewed intensity. "There's not a day that goes by that I don't remember who you are and where you come from," he said softly. "I mean it, Shelby. If you go to The Edge, I come with you."

She wanted to protest, wanted to tell him that she didn't intend to spend a minute of time with him that wasn't necessary. But she'd known what to expect when she agreed to represent him. Besides, she had no intention of repeating past mistakes with Billy Royce. "Then let's go tonight."

"Fine. Things don't start hopping there until late, so I'll pick you up at ten o'clock."

"I think it would be better if I met you someplace," she said, remembering her promise to her father.

He nodded, eyes narrowed and lips thinned in studied arrogance. "We'll meet here at ten."

She focused back on her legal pad. "Where were you on the night of the murders?"

"Alone in the swamp."

Looking back at him, she frowned. "Nobody saw you?"

He shook his head. "No alibi, nobody to corroborate my whereabouts."

"You aren't making this easy for us," Shelby replied.

He smiled tightly. "Nothing has ever been easy in my life." Staring down at the knife scars on the table, he continued, "The way I have it figured, the only way to get me out of this mess is to find the real killer. God knows, the sheriff isn't even looking for anyone else."

"Billy, I wouldn't even know how to find a killer. My job is to come up with a legal defense that will get you out of this mess."

"I'm changing your job description." He reached out and tore off a piece of her legal pad. "There's somebody you need to talk to, work with." He scribbled a name then handed it to her.

"Gator Revenau?"

Billy nodded. "Don't let his exterior scare you off. Gator is something of a character, but he'd know if Fayrene was close to anyone. Gator knows a lot of things about everyone."

"What's his connection to Fayrene?" she asked curiously, tucking the slip of paper into her purse.

"None, other than the fact that for the last couple of months I've been paying him to follow her."

"Why?" Shelby's heart sank. More damning information.

His gaze was dark, enigmatic. He pushed away from the table and stood. "That's my personal business."

"Billy, you have no personal business," Shelby objected vehemently. She stood as well, frustration gnawing at her nerves. "I'm your lawyer and you have to tell me everything. We can't afford to have secrets between us."

He walked over to where she stood, standing close...too close, invading her space with his blatant masculinity. "No secrets?" He touched a length of her hair that had fallen over her shoulder, his fingers precariously close to the swell of her breast. "Then I guess I should tell you right now I intend to have you again, except this time in a bed, not on a plank wood floor."

Shelby fought against her rapidly racing heart, her palm itching to slap the arrogant smirk off his face. Despite her aversion, her head swam with a sudden vision of him in bed, his bronzed body erotically bared against pristine sheets. Making love with Billy the boy had been a remarkable experience, but she knew making love with Billy the man would be devastating.

She stepped back from him, leveling on him a look of

cool control. "Too bad for you we don't always get what we want in this life."

He smiled. "Too bad for you, I always do."

Chapter Six

"I want to know why that scum who killed my boy hasn't been arrested." Jonathon LaJune filled the sheriff's office with his anger and the sweet scent of the Swisher cigars he smoked. "Billy Royce has always been a loose cannon. I tried again and again to warn my Tyler that Billy was like a mad dog who'd bite him when his back was turned. If only that boy had listened to me. If only he'd listened."

He ran out of steam and collapsed into the chair, his grief a clawing torment inside him. He drew in on the cigar, squinting slightly as smoke burned his eyes. "I want Billy Royce arrested. What the hell are you waiting for, boy?"

"Evidence." Bob looked at him impatiently. "Jonathon, right now all the evidence we have on Billy is circumstantial, not enough for an arrest. Besides, in case you haven't heard, there's been another person murdered in the swamp."

"What the hell do I care?" Again the grief was back, rich and thick in his chest.

"Jonathon, we have a legal responsibility..."

Jonathon jumped up, felt the pounding of his blood pressure like a hammer in the back of his head. "Legal responsibility?" he roared, the ashes of his cigar flaming like a volcano about to erupt. He yanked the cigar from his mouth, dropped it to the floor and smashed it out with the heel of his boot, then looked back at Bob. "And I have a responsibility to avenge Tyler's death. I've half a mind to get my gun and splatter that sewer rat's brains to kingdom come."

Bob stood, a frown pulling his pale brows together over the bridge of his nose. "Here, now, I can't allow that kind of talk."

Jonathon snorted derisively. "You don't do something about Billy Royce, won't take long and I'll be through talking." Without waiting for a reply, Jonathon strode from the office and out into the afternoon sunshine. Bob stared after him, a bad feeling pressing tightly against his chest.

THE TRAILER SAT at the edge of the swamp. It was impossible to guess what color it might have originally been, for age had weathered it to a mottled gray. It looked as if the structure had been plopped down in the middle of a junkyard. The skeletons of several old cars were nearly hidden in the overgrown weeds, rusting in the heavy humidity.

A huge satellite dish filled one side of the yard, the gleaming piece of technology incongruous with the squalor and primitive conditions.

However, it wasn't the dismal appearance of the place that kept Shelby in her car. It was the appearance of two huge black dogs. They took positions about a yard from her car door, not barking but eyeing her with cunning intelligence and baleful suspicion.

Where in the hell was Gator Revenau? And why hadn't Billy mentioned the dogs? Shelby rolled down her window halfway. "Hello?" she yelled, then paused. One of the dogs growled, a throaty, menacing warning.

The door opened and a thin, short man stepped out on the sagging porch. He stood, not speaking, reminding her of a little blond banty rooster. Short and wiry, he nevertheless exuded belligerence with his puffed chest and wide stance. "You lost, girlie?"

"Are you Gator Revenau?"

"I am."

"Then I'm not lost." Shelby waited for him to say something more, and when he didn't, she sighed impatiently. "Mr. Revenau, would you call off your dogs? I need to talk to you."

He hesitated a moment, then muttered something and the dogs immediately joined him on the porch, lying down at his feet as he sat in an old recliner the sun had bleached to a pale pink.

Shelby opened her car door and stepped out, eyeing the two dogs anxiously. Although they remained at Revenau's feet, they stared at her malevolently.

"They won't hurt you none...not unless I tell them to." Gator grinned at her, displaying a gap where one of his front teeth used to be. His smile faded and his gaze suddenly mirrored those of his dogs. "If this is about them taxes, you'd better get back in that car and drive outta here. I'm done talking about them and nobody is gonna move me off my land."

"Mr. Revenau, I'm not a tax collector. My name is Shelby Longsford. I'm...I'm a friend of Billy Royce. He suggested I talk to you."

"Well, why in the hell didn't you say so? Come on up here and have a seat." He motioned to a wicker chair next to his recliner. At that moment Shelby noticed Gator Revenau was missing a hand.

She made her way gingerly up the stairs, onto the wooden porch that creaked and groaned beneath her weight.

Whatever Billy Royce was paying her, it wasn't enough, she thought irritably as she eased into the rickety wicker chair next to Gator Revenau.

He grinned and gestured to a large cooler that sat next to him. "How about a cold one?" She shook her head and he opened the cooler to reveal chunks of ice and can upon can of grape soda. Billy had described Gator as something of a character. She'd forgotten how Billy was master of the understatement.

Gator popped the tab, raised the can and swallowed, his protruding Adam's apple bobbing as he quickly drained the can. He crushed the can, simultaneously emitting a rolling belch, then grinned at her expectantly. "You wanted to talk...so talk."

She pulled a small notebook from her purse. "Do you mind if I take some notes?"

"You sure you aren't one of those infernal revenue people?"

Shelby smiled. "I promise. I'm a lawyer."

Gator snorted and rubbed the stump where his hand had once been. "One's as bad as the other." He cocked his head, the sun stroking the grizzled gray strands she'd initially mistaken for blond. His skin was tanned the color of bark and weathered to the texture of leather. She realized he was considerably older than she'd initially thought. And if she was to guess, nothing had ever come easily for Gator Revenau.

"How long have you known Billy?" she asked, trying not to fixate on the missing hand, which he continued to rub.

"Oh, about fifteen years." Gator reached into the cooler and grabbed another soda. He popped open the tab and leaned back. "Billy saved my life."

"How so?" Although Shelby knew this couldn't help Billy's case, she was intrigued. Besides, she could tell by the look on Gator's face that it was a story he relished telling as often as possible.

"It was a crazy moon night in the swamp," he began in a melodic, almost singsong patter. He set his soda can down and began rubbing his stump once again, as if seeking to scratch the palm of the missing hand. "You know, one of them nights when the moon shines down on the water and you can't tell which is the real one—the one up in the sky or the shimmery one dancing on the surface of the water. Anyway, I was doing a little gator gigging." He grinned mischievously at Shelby's perplexity. "Poaching," he explained. "Course, it's illegal, but at the time I didn't care much as long as it paid enough to keep me in gin." He shook his head, his grin widening. "Saints alive, but I used to love that gin. This particular night I'd been nipping a little at the bottle." He laughed, a pleasant, oddly musical sound. "Hell, I was so drunk I couldn't see straight. I decided I was going to go after Maybelline."

"Maybelline?"

He flashed his toothless grin again, then picked up his soda and took a long slug. "The biggest, meanest gator I've ever seen." He set the can next to him and rubbed his stump, his gaze drifting from hers to the distant past. "Oh, she was a beauty. When she bellowed, I swear she could be heard clear to Texas. I'd tried to get her before but never tried real hard. I hated her... but I loved her, too. I respected her." He paused a moment, his fingers caressing the blunt end of his wrist. "But this night was different. This night I was senseless drunk and vowed to get her."

Shelby knew the end of the story, could easily guess how Gator had lost his hand, but she also understood that his retelling of the tale was important to him, and so sat patiently as he gazed off in the distance, reliving the night in his mind. Besides, there was something bewitching about his storytelling ability, one that Mama Royce had possessed, also. How often Shelby had sat listening to Mama Royce magically spinning tales and legends of the swamp.

He picked up his soda and drained it, crushed it then threw it aside. "I found her in a deep pool, where the moon shone so bright on the water it was like the swamp had swallowed it whole. Maybelline flipped her tail and stared at me. She knew that night was different. She could smell the booze on me, smell my bloodlust."

A drop of sweat left Shelby's hairline and trickled slowly down the side of her face. Despite the heat, a shiver worked its way up her spine as she waited for Gator Revenau to finish his story. His body had tensed, his eyes darkened, haunted with visions of his personal demons from the past. One of the dogs stirred and whimpered, as if sensing Gator's disquiet.

Shelby swiped the sweat, her movement pulling Gator's gaze back to her. "We fought, her and me. Like two lovers bent on destroying each other. Finally, I thought I had her, thought she was dead. I went to tie her to the side of the boat and she took my hand clean off with one snap of her jaws." A grin once again danced at the corners of his mouth. "I know they heard me bellow clear to Texas." His smile faded and he swiped his hand down the length of his face, then batted at an irksome fly. "If I wasn't crazy before, I was insane then. I yanked off my shirt and wrapped it around my wrist. It was pumping blood like a derrick spewing oil. I got the pirogue over to the bank and was contemplating jumping back in the water to find my hand when Billy Royce appeared. He tried to convince me if I didn't get some help I was gonna bleed to death. But I was damned and determined I needed to go back in and get my hand." He laughed, again the musical tones oddly pleasing to the ear. "That Billy Royce, even then he didn't take nothing from nobody. He gave me a shot in the jaw and knocked me cold. I come to at his gramma's place—my stump had been cauterized and was wrapped in clean bandages. I stayed there a week. Most of that time I was pretty out of it. Billy and Mama Royce took turns sitting with me, wiping the sweat off me, spoon-feeding me. When I got well, I decided no more booze." Once again his eyes twinkled with a boyish gleam. "Ask me what happened to Maybelline."

"What happened to Maybelline?" she asked dutifully.

He stretched out his feet, displaying a pair of alligator skin boots. "She got my hand . . . but I got her hide." He looked back at her soberly. "Nowadays I don't do much poaching anymore." His gaze went to the swamp. "Not safe anymore to be in the swamp after dark, and I'm not about to git killed by no swamp serpent." He shifted positions in the chair and looked back at her. "Billy's in trouble, ain't he?"

She hesitated a moment, then nodded. "It looks that way."

"I told him years ago not to get involved with that Fayrene, but you can't tell Billy anything. He was a hardheaded, stubborn boy and he's become a stubborn, hardheaded man. He thought he was in love with her, thought he could change her wild ways. Can't change the direction of the wind, no matter how hard you try. Now, what can I do to help him?"

"You can start by telling me why he hired you to follow Fayrene."

Gator shrugged. "Hell, I didn't ask him why, but I suppose 'cause he wanted to see who she was with, what she was doing."

"How long did you follow her?"

"I started tailing her right after her and Billy separated, stopped a week before she was killed."

"What was she like?" Shelby tried to tell herself the question was important to Billy's defense, but she couldn't help but acknowledge her personal interest in the woman who'd managed to snare Billy into matrimony.

Gator whistled softly beneath his breath. "Fayrene Whitney was some piece of work. She was pretty, I'll grant you that. Had a kind of innocence about her that would fool a person...till she opened her mouth. She was the kind of woman who thrived on misery, her own and other people's. She wasn't really happy unless she was stirring things up, and there was nothing she liked more than baiting Billy." His gaze hardened.

"During the time you were following her, did you see her with any other men?"

Gator snorted. "Fayrene liked to party. She liked her drinks strong and her men plentiful."

"Anyone in particular?"

Again he batted at a fly, frowning thoughtfully. "Nah. She spent a lot of time with lots of men, but most nights she ended up at her apartment alone."

"Any women she seemed particularly close to?" Shelby asked as she scribbled notes on her pad.

Gator frowned. "Not really, although there was one waitress she seemed pretty friendly with at The Edge. They'd huddle up and talk every time Fayrene was there."

"You know the waitress's name?"

"Winnie. Winnie Mae Ralston." His face flushed slightly and he grinned. "She's a mighty fine woman, Ms. Winnie is."

Shelby smiled, wondering what kind of woman Gator Revenau would consider mighty fine. He stirred restlessly against the faded cushion of the chair and Shelby realized his interest in her questions was waning. "Just a few more questions, Mr. Revenau," she promised. "Do you know of anyone other than Billy who might have wanted Fayrene dead?"

He frowned thoughtfully. "I dunno. Fayrene was always sticking her nose where it didn't belong. Tyler's daddy might have wanted her dead if he thought Tyler was getting involved with her." He shook his head ruefully. "But it don't make no sense that he'd kill Tyler, too. I just don't know. Fayrene managed to make a lot of people mad when she was alive." He held out his good hand in a gesture of helplessness. "I wish I could help. I'd do anything for Billy Royce. Hell, if he'd wanted Fayrene dead, I would have done it for him. All he had to do was ask me."

"The sheriff thinks Billy killed them both in a passionate fit of jealousy. What do you think?"

Gator frowned once again and kneaded his stump. "Billy didn't kill 'em. Billy didn't love Fayrene anymore. Hell, he didn't even hate her. He just plain didn't care about her anymore. But he did love Tyler like a brother. He couldn't have cut Tyler up no matter how mad he got."

Shelby shoved away a sense of helplessness, realizing that Gator had told her nothing new, nothing useful in Billy's defense that she hadn't already known. "One more question. Why did you stop following Fayrene when you did?"

"Billy told me to. I suppose he had all the information he needed to fight Fayrene for Parker."

"Parker?" Shelby's heart began beating a dull dread.

"Billy and Fayrene's little boy. Fayrene had threatened to get custody, but there was no way Billy was going to let that happen. That's why he hired me."

Shelby mentally reeled. Billy had a son. A little boy. Why hadn't he told her? Dear God, didn't he know that this more than anything was the strongest motive for Fayrene's murder?

Chapter Seven

Billy knew Shelby was angry the moment her car roared down Main Street and pulled into the space next to his pickup in front of Martha's Café. She threw the car into Park before it had completely stopped its forward motion. The grinding gears made him wince.

"Damn you, Billy," she exclaimed as she got out of the car and slammed the door with more force than necessary.

He remained leaning against the side of his pickup, watching as she approached, blue eyes flashing fire as short, clipped footsteps brought her within inches of him.

"Damn you," she repeated, the fire in her eyes only intensified as she drew nearer. "I thought I'd made it crystal clear to you that if I'm going to help you, you have to tell me everything that's pertinent to this case."

Billy stifled the impulse to grab her, touch her, drink the self-righteous fire that flamed from her. It bothered him how badly he wanted her. They had shared one experience, a single moment in time twisted by grief, but Billy had never been able to forget it or diminish it to the kind of unimportance other experiences had in his life.

"What are you yammering about?" he asked, summoning his own irritation to mask the intensity of his desire for her.

"Yammering?" Her eyes widened in outrage. "I'm yammering about saving your life. Don't you realize that if you're arrested for those murders it's possible they could ask for, and get, the death penalty?" She took a step back from him and eyed him incredulously. "Do you have a death wish, or what? Why are you withholding important information from me? I'm trying to help you."

"And what important information have you learned I've supposedly kept from you that has you so riled up?"

"Why didn't you tell me about Parker?"

"Because he has nothing to do with any of this." He strode around the other side of the pickup and opened the door. "You wanted to go to The Edge. Let's go." He stared at her, could see more questions forming in her eyes but wordlessly dared her to continue the conversation. Parker was the one piece of his heart he would never share with anyone.

Shelby hesitated another moment, then climbed into the pickup. "Parker is—"

Billy slammed the door, effectively cutting off whatever she had been about to say. He walked back around and climbed in behind the steering wheel. He started the engine with a roar and backed out of the parking space.

As he drove down the deserted Main Street, he could feel Shelby's gaze on him. He could smell her. It was a soft, feminine scent that stirred his blood and evoked a renewed defensive irritation.

He'd grown up being told that the Longsfords and their social ilk were not for him. "They might invite you to dinner, they may even take you into their bed, but they'll never welcome you into their heart." Everyone in the swamp told him the same thing . . . everyone but Mama Royce. She just smiled and told him to follow his heart.

Before his marriage he'd dated plenty of them, knowing they thrived on the novelty and danger of sneaking out with a swamp beast. But that single night with Shelby had been something different . . . something frightening.

She'd told him she loved him. And he'd hated her for it, hated her for the momentary hope the words had instantly evoked. The words had come from the passion of the moment, not from the depths of her soul. What could an eighteen-year-old virgin know about love?

Her flight the next day had proved it. Having sex with him had driven her not only away from him, but out of Black Bayou. And he'd been left with an odd regret, and the feeling of something left unsettled between them.

Again his irritation reared its head. He gazed at her once more, noting the way the pale pink cotton shirt clung to the outline of her breasts, how the jeans she wore molded themselves to her slender curves. Her hair was bound at the nape of her neck and his fingers itched to release the dark tresses, allow it to spill over his palms. She was wearing those damnable glasses and, despite the fact that he thought she wore them to hide behind, they hid nothing. The stark frames only emphasized the blueness of her eyes, the sweet femininity of her full lips, the soft curve of her jawline. His body responded, tightening against the crotch of his jeans.

He smiled, able to imagine Mama Royce's voice in his head. "You got your butt in a tight wedge and all you can think about is sex. Heaven help you, Billy Royce, 'cause the devil sure as hell got a hold on you."

"I'm so glad you can still find something humorous in this situation," Shelby said thinly, letting him know she'd seen the smile that had crossed his lips at thoughts of Mama Royce.

"Ah, darlin', you don't know the half of it," he returned.

"And that's exactly what has me so angry." She turned on the seat to face him, her features illuminated by the glow of the dash lights. "Billy, I thought I'd made it clear to you that you have to tell me everything that might have a bearing on the murder."

"Parker has no bearing on the murder."

"He does if a custody battle was going to ensue. That's a motive for Fayrene's murder. A strong motive."

"That's nonsense." Billy frowned as he thought of the woman he'd married. At the time he'd thought he loved her, believed they were two of a kind, understood each other and could make a good life together.

He'd wanted children, a family, and Fayrene had made so many promises, mouthed so many lies. His hands tightened on the steering wheel. "Fayrene threatened to seek custody, and that's why I hired Gator to follow her. Why would I pay him to do that if I was going to kill her and solve the issue myself?" He frowned. "Besides, Fayrene didn't want Parker. Even when we were together she had a nanny she used all the time." Again he thanked goodness for Angelique's friendship. Angelique had spent more time with Parker than Fayrene ever had. "Fayrene just used him to try to get at me."

"And people will say she did get to you, to the point that you lost all control and killed her."

"I've only lost complete control once in my whole life." He looked at her pointedly. "And that wasn't with Fayrene."

She flushed and looked away. Damn him, he was trying to unsettle her. She'd noticed that whenever the conversation cut too close, he turned it into sexual innuendos intended to unsettle her and change the topic. He seemed hellbent on self-destruction, alienating the one person who was trying to help him. She should get out of the whole mess, let him take his chances with a public defender. But even as she thought this, she knew she wouldn't follow through. She was determined to help Billy in spite of himself.

She wasn't doing it because of any lingering affection for him. Those adolescent emotions were gone, buried beneath too many years and the memory of his hateful words on that night. No, she wasn't sticking by Billy for any reason other than her intense love and gratefulness to the grandmother who had raised him and made a special place in her life for a lonely little girl.

Staring out the window, she watched as they left town, turning onto an overgrown, pothole-riddled dirt road she'd never been on before. A plethora of greenery encroached on the road, and the air was cooler, the night darker.

"Are you sure you're going the right way?" she asked, seeing nothing but darkness and overgrowth around them. There was no sign of civilization, no twinkling lights or noise to indicate the presence of a bar in the vicinity.

He grinned. "What's the matter? Afraid I'm taking you out to the swamp to have my wicked way with you?" He laughed, a flat, mirthless sound. "Don't worry, Shelby. I already told you, the next time I have you it's going to be in the comfort of a soft bed."

"And what makes you so sure there's going to be a next time?" she asked, trying to ignore the rapid beat of her heart, the sudden dryness of her mouth.

"Because sooner or later you're going to want me." His utter certainty raked through Shelby like rain on a tin roof, discordant and maddening. He looked at her again, his eyes shining their wickedness. "Sooner or later you're going to want to find out if that one night we had was really as explosive as you remember."

"You're one arrogant piece of work," she retorted with a shake of her head.

He laughed again, this time a genuine sound of amusement. "I'm only arrogant about those things I have a right to be. Sooner or later you'll want me to show you."

"You're disgusting, and you can show me when hell freezes over." It felt wonderful, flinging his words back in his face, and she smiled smugly.

His laughter filled the cab of the truck and made a tingle of warmth creep up her spine. Drat the man anyway, drat him for his sinful attractiveness and wicked laughter. And damn him for being so sure she would eventually succumb to the desire to physically be with him again.

She sat up straighter in the seat as they broke into a clearing and The Edge came into view. It was a large metal shedlike building with a neon sign on top that flashed the name in spastic fashion. The parking lot, little more than a cleared-off dirt area, was packed with pickup trucks, souped-up cars and motorcycles.

Billy parked and they got out. Raucous music poured from the open door, and Shelby found her heart echoing the drumming throb in anticipation. Perhaps in the bar she would find the key piece of evidence that would absolve Billy of any guilt in Fayrene's and Tyler's deaths.

She started toward the door, but gasped as Billy grabbed her arm and pulled her close against his side. "We're going to set some ground rules here," he said, not releasing his hold on her despite her attempt to wrestle her arm free.

"What kind of rules?" she asked as she stopped struggling and stood still, offended by his high-handed manner.

"When we get inside, you stick close to me. You don't speak to anyone without checking it out with me first."

"Don't be ridiculous," she snapped irritably. "I can't operate like that."

He grasped her arm once again. "Then you don't operate at all." The amusement that had lightened his eyes moments before was gone, replaced by a dangerous gleam that taunted her to contest him. "You're in my world now, Shelby, and you have to play by my rules."

"Are you trying to frighten me?" she asked softly.

"This isn't a game, Shelby. You're out of your league here and I'm talking about survival."

She searched his face, unsure whether he was playing macho mind games with her or was honestly warning her for her own good. At that moment a man came flying through the open doorway of the bar, landing in a heap on the ground near where they stood.

He stood, brushing the seat of his filthy pants with one hand and flipping the middle finger of his other hand toward a tall figure silhouetted in the doorway. "You'd better watch your back. I'll get you when you least expect it." The brawler jumped on the back of a gleaming, chromed motorcycle and roared off into the night.

Shelby looked back at Billy. "Okay, you win," she conceded. "We'll play by your rules."

It was his turn to smile smugly. "I thought you'd see things my way." As they walked toward the door he kept his hand firmly beneath her elbow, leaving no doubt in anyone's mind that she was with him.

When they stepped into the bar, Shelby reluctantly admitted to herself that he was right. She was out of her world here, and she was grateful for Billy's strong presence beside her.

Nowhere Shelby had ever been in her life prepared her for the interior of The Edge. Smoke hung in a noxious layer, deepening the gloom that even the neon-lit beer signs couldn't pierce. The din was earsplitting, a combination of violent curses, rowdy shouts and breaking bottles. The smell inside was nauseating—the scent of sweaty bodies and cheap booze underscored by the more unpleasant odors of urine and vomit.

Looking at the patrons, Shelby could have sworn she recognized half a dozen from FBI posters in the post office. Everyone looked as if their face could easily adorn a Most Wanted list from any law enforcement agency in the world.

Billy was obviously no stranger. As they walked toward the bar at the far end of the huge room, he was greeted by men and women, their easy familiarity letting Shelby know Billy was a frequent visitor to The Edge.

"What do you want to drink?" Billy asked as they reached the bar. Shelby slid onto a stool and he stood just behind her, one hand resting casually yet possessively on her shoulder.

"A club soda."

"Two specials, Pete," Billy yelled to the bartender, who grinned and flashed a thumbs-up sign.

Shelby raised an eyebrow. "Club soda is the specialty?"

"Shelby, if you drink a club soda in this place, somebody will think you're an undercover cop. If you want to rub shoulders with the bad boys, you're going to have to drink like the bad boys."

At that moment the bartender plopped two glasses down before them, a grin on his face as his gaze lingered on Shelby. "Two of those and he'll snort like a stallion all night long," he exclaimed. "I guaran-damn-tee it." He slapped the wooden surface of the bar, then walked away, cackling like a half-possessed demon.

Shelby felt the blush that began at her neck, warming her face to the tips of her ears. She heard Billy's husky chuckle and resisted the impulse to elbow him in the ribs.

"Who, exactly, did you want to talk to in here?" he asked.

"Gator told me Fayrene was friends with a waitress here, Winnie Mae Ralston. Do you know her?"

Billy nodded, his gaze darting around the crowded room. "There she is." He gestured to an older woman who was serving drinks to a group of men surrounding one of the three pool tables. "You sit right here and I'll go get her. Don't move from this chair," he warned, then left her to weave his way through the crowd.

Shelby picked up her drink and took a tentative sip, gasping as the alcohol content exploded in the pit of her stomach. She couldn't discern what kind of alcohol the drink contained, only knew it was exceptionally strong.

"Hey, sweetcakes," a voice purred right next to her ear.

She turned to look at the man leering at her, his eyes glazed with the effects of too many drinks and not enough brain. He was clad in leather, with a filthy bandanna twisted around his head to hold back stringy blond hair. A hoop earring dangled from one pierced ear, the shine competing with the gleam of a gold front tooth.

"How about you slide over here and sit on my lap and we'll talk about the first thing that comes up." He laughed uproariously, his fetid breath hitting Shelby full in the face.

"I'm waiting for somebody," Shelby replied curtly, looking back to where Billy had reached the waitress.

"Aren't we all? Why don't you dance with me?" He placed a hand on her arm and Shelby noticed the dirt crusting his fingernails.

She jerked away from his touch. "I told you I'm waiting for somebody," she said coolly.

"Ah, be nice," he protested, the glaze in his eyes hardening as his gaze brazenly lingered on her breasts. "Don't be so uptight." There was an ugly sneer in his words. "Maybe I should teach you some manners."

"How's it going, Louis." Billy's voice caused a shudder of relief to sweep through Shelby. "You bothering my woman?"

"Your woman?" Louis frowned drunkenly and tugged on the gold hoop at his ear.

Billy grabbed the back of Shelby's hair and tilted her head back. Before she could protest, his lips covered hers, possessing them in a kiss that spread fire through her veins as effectively as the sip of her drink had done only moments before. She was vaguely aware of Louis's hoots and other catcalls as the kiss lingered, his tongue slipping into her mouth to ignite more flames. When he removed his lips from hers, she gasped for air, eyeing him resentfully.

"Billy, you know I wouldn't have messed with her if I'd known she was with you." Louis backed away from them, his hands held out in front of him to indicate no problem, no foul.

Billy watched the man until he'd moved to the other end of the bar. "That was completely unnecessary," Shelby hissed angrily.

His eyes glittered with entertainment. "Perhaps," he agreed indolently. "Winnie is going to take a break in about ten minutes and will come over and talk to you."

Shelby nodded, still reeling from the kiss and angry that he appeared so unmoved by it. However, one thing was certain—she was grateful she wasn't here alone, that Billy was with her. He'd been right. She was definitely out of her world. She belonged in a courtroom, not in some sleazy bar chasing down leads for charges that hadn't even been officially pressed.

For the first time Shelby realized how impulsive it had been for her to drop everything and come back here to help Billy. It had been more than just the promise of a big case. She'd been pulled back by the provocative thought that

Billy needed her. It had been a power trip, and after his initial phone call to her she'd felt a sense of poetic justice that now somehow shamed her.

She cast Billy a surreptitious glance. As always, even standing still he radiated a vital energy that seemed to pulse in the air around him. Although his stance suggested lazy relaxation, on closer assessment she recognized the coiled muscles, the darting gaze as those of a man prepared for anything.

His strength and masculinity both comforted and unsettled her. She liked having him standing so protectively close to her, yet hated that she could feel the furnace of his body heat, smell the evocative scents of his spicy cologne and maleness.

He was the only man she'd known in her life who struck her on such a gut physical level. What made her more angry than anything was that he'd been right when he'd said that eventually she would be curious about making love with him again. There was a small part of her that wanted to experience making love with Billy, this time as a grown woman.

She took another swallow of the drink, welcoming the warmth that exploded in the pit of her stomach and overwhelmed the heat of thoughts of Billy.

His fingers softly touched the nape of her neck, just to the side of where her hair was clasped with a barrette. "You doing all right?" he asked.

"I'm fine," she snapped, swatting his hand away.

He grinned lazily. "While we wait for Winnie Mae, you want to dance?"

Shelby looked out to the dance floor, where several couples gyrated in X-rated fashion to the beat of the jukebox. She instantly imagined Billy holding her, his hips pressed insinuatingly against hers. "Not with you," she replied.

He laughed, a low, wicked sound that coiled more heat through Shelby. She took another deep swallow of her drink, repressing a shudder as the alcohol swirled down her throat.

Gratefully she saw the waitress she'd come to talk to approaching, her bright red hair gleaming like a beacon in the dismal environment. "Billy said you wanted to talk to me. I just got a few minutes, so make it fast," she snapped, slapping her serving tray on the bar next to where Shelby sat.

"I understand you and Fayrene Whitney were friends," Shelby began, thankful as Billy moved away and started talking to another nefarious-looking older man.

Winnie frowned and plucked nervously at a gray eyebrow. "I wouldn't call us bosom buddies. She was in here a lot and we talked most evenings during my breaks." Winnie sat down on the stool next to Shelby and pursed her ruby lips. "Fayrene was an odd one, not much for sharing confidences. Damn shame the way she died."

"Did she ever talk to you about men?"

Winnie snorted. "Wasn't much else Fayrene liked talking about."

"Anyone in particular?"

Winnie's heavily lined eyes darted to Billy. "Him. Fayrene was crazy when it came to Billy."

"Crazy how?"

Winnie grinned and shook her head ruefully. "I wouldn't be surprised to find out that Fayrene killed Tyler, then stabbed herself just to get Billy's butt thrown in prison. There's nothing worse than love gone bad, and Fayrene was ate up with bad love for Billy."

"But Fayrene didn't inflict those wounds on herself. When was the last time you saw her before her death?"

"She was in here the night it happened. I told the sheriff all this," she said impatiently.

"I don't work for the sheriff," Shelby explained. "I'm just trying to find out what happened, who killed Fayrene and Tyler."

"You ain't never gonna find out. Billy is going to go down for this sure as I'm sitting here." She nodded sagely. "When this town needs a fall guy, it's always one of us from the swamp that takes the fall. And before it's all said and done, they'll probably have him guilty of the serpent murders, too." Laughing wryly, she stood and grabbed her serving tray. "Mark my words, missy. There's some in this town who'd love nothing better than to see Billy Royce behind bars. He's spent a lot of time sticking his nose where it don't belong, getting a lot of the town people mad at him."

Shelby pulled off her glasses and rubbed her forehead. If everyone in town hated Billy Royce, how was she supposed to find the person who'd killed Fayrene and Tyler? How was she going to find out who would be happy if Billy took the fall for a crime he didn't commit?

"Just a couple more questions," she said as Winnie looked at her watch. "On the night of her murder, when Fayrene was in here, did she say anything about anyone giving her problems, or being afraid or involved in something that had her frightened?"

Winnie shook her head. "Nah, she was her usual self, laughing and drinking, dancing up a storm. Fayrene wasn't scared or worried about nothing."

"Did she leave alone that night?"

"No, that pretty boy Tyler came in and got her. They talked for a few minutes, then they left together." Winnie looked at her watch once again. "Look, it's a damn shame, the way Fayrene died, but I don't know anything about it and I got to get back to work."

The moment Winnie moved away, Billy reappeared next to Shelby's side. "Did you get any answers?"

"I'm not even sure I know the right questions to ask," she admitted, rubbing her forehead once again. She'd drunk just enough and that, combined with the smoke and noise, had created the beginning of a headache that pulsed behind her eyes. "Let's get out of here." She slid off the stool and walked toward the door, eager for fresh, clean air to take away the stench she feared permeated her very pores.

She didn't stop walking until she reached the pickup, where she leaned against the polished side, closed her eyes and drew in deep breaths of the sweet-scented night air. "You okay?"

Opening her eyes, she looked at Billy. "No, I'm not okay." She sighed, then folded her glasses and dropped them into her purse, her mind racing with everything Winnie had said, most of which was no use to Billy's defense. But one thing stuck in her mind. She drew in another deep breath, then looked back at Billy. "I want you to make a list of all the people you've had angry words with in the last year."

"You've got to be kidding." Billy stared at her a moment, one corner of his mouth curving up in a smile. "Might be easier to make a list of the people I haven't had words with."

He moved to stand before her, an arm braced on either side as he captured her against the side of the truck. "Enough about that. I have something else on my mind." He stepped closer and trailed a finger down the side of her jaw then slowly, languidly ran his fingertips across the fullness of her mouth.

Shelby remained unmoving beneath the sexual onslaught, although her heart skipped erratically, letting her know her body responded to him despite her attempt at control. "Move that finger any closer to my teeth and I'll bite it off." He laughed and dropped his hand. Shelby sighed. "Billy, you've got to stop thinking with your crotch and start using your head."

"Ah, but don't you know that the mind is the most sexual organ in the body?"

"Billy, I don't care about your sex life. I'm trying to find out the truth of who killed Fayrene and Tyler. Isn't it possible somebody set you up? Somebody who knew the odds were good that you'd be charged in these murders?" She pushed away from him. "Just make a list."

A loud crack resounded. A searing heat instantly exploded in Shelby's shoulder. She gasped as Billy tackled her. Together they hit the ground, a grunt escaping her as Billy's body covered hers. As her head cracked against the hard earth she momentarily saw stars.

"Are you all right?" Although he didn't move, she could feel his tension as his gaze focused on the thick brush and trees that lined the parking area.

"Yes, but—"

"Shh," he hushed her, his head cocked alertly as he scrutinized the area where the shot had come from.

Moments stretched into minutes and they remained unmoving. Apparently the sound of the shot had not been heard over the commotion in the bar, for nobody came running out.

"Whoever it was, I think they're gone," he finally said. He rolled off Shelby and sat up. "Well, darlin', you can't say I'm not an exciting date."

"Do all your 'dates' end the evening with a trip to the hospital?" she asked, gritting her teeth against the nause-ating pain that ripped through her shoulder.

She started to sit up, but a wave of darkness swept over her. Vaguely, she heard Billy curse as she gave in and fainted into sweet oblivion.

Chapter Eight

Billy knew the bullet that had pierced Shelby's shoulder had been meant for him, and for the first time he realized the depth of passion stirred in Black Bayou by Tyler's and Fayrene's murders. Fayrene's loss was insignificant; it was the death of Tyler that had summoned fury, stirred fear. The good people of Black Bayou were accustomed to bad things happening to the swamp people, but Tyler had been one of their own.

The truck bounced and careened over the back roads, unconscious groans escaping Shelby with each jolt. She was slumped against his side, her breath warm against his neck. His right arm held her steady as his left hand worked the steering wheel.

He could tell her wound wasn't life threatening. He'd immediately ripped her blouse aside and had seen that the bullet appeared to have grazed the top of her shoulder, rather than pierced it. There had been an initial burst of blood, but by the time he'd gotten her in the truck, the bleeding had nearly stopped. Still, his heart beat an unsteady rhythm as he thought of how close she had come to being killed.

"Damn it." He slapped the palm of his hand on the steering wheel, a whisper of rage building in the pit of his stomach. He wasn't angry that somebody had attempted to shoot him. He'd half expected something like this. But his rage was built on the sloppiness of the shooter, who'd missed his target and instead hit Shelby.

One thing was certain. As far as this particular case was concerned, Shelby was finished. He'd take his chances with another attorney. He wouldn't risk her life to save his own.

He wheeled into Doc Cashwell's place and parked the truck in front of the back door that led to the office and examining room. Shutting off the engine, he got out of the truck, then leaned back in to scoop Shelby up in his arms. Her face nuzzled against his shirtfront, muffling another soft groan against his beating heart.

Doc Cashwell must have heard them drive up, for he met Billy at the door. "What have we here?" The old man gestured for Billy to follow him through the small waiting room and to an examining room, where Billy placed Shelby gently on the paper-covered examination table.

"Gunshot wound to the shoulder," Billy said tersely, stepping back so the doctor could perform his magic. "She fainted almost immediately."

"How long has she been out?" Doc Cashwell quickly cut the blouse away from the wound.

"Just a few minutes, as long as it took me to get her here from The Edge."

The old man paused in his ministrations and cast Billy a curious glance. "Did you shoot her?"

Billy leaned against the doorjamb and grinned indolently. "No, Doc, there's no way anybody can pin this one on me."

"Git out of here so I can clean this up. If she doesn't come to soon, I'll bring her around when I'm finished."

Nodding curtly, Billy went back into the waiting room and sat down on one of the plastic chairs. The bullet to

Shelby's shoulder changed everything. When he'd first realized he was the number-one suspect in the murders, he'd talked to several lawyers in New Orleans. None of them seemed willing to take on what they considered a losing case. It had shocked and surprised him when one of them recommended Shelby. The lawyer had told him Shelby had a reputation for tenacity, especially when defending an underdog. God knew Billy was an underdog.

For Billy, it had seemed right that he would be the reason for her coming back home. Especially since he'd been the reason for her leaving in the first place. But somebody had just raised the stakes and made this a deadly game. That bullet, a couple of inches one way or the other, could have been lethal. He couldn't consciously put Shelby in harm's way.

He'd have to take his chances alone, and if things didn't go his way then he'd take Parker and disappear so far into the swamp nobody would ever find him again. He'd do whatever it took to keep Parker mentally well and physically safe. Hell. He raked a hand through his hair, a rueful smile curving his lips. That particular sentiment was what had gotten him in this predicament in the first place.

SHE WAS EIGHTEEN years old again. The humid, thick night air embraced her as she tried to walk off the anger that always appeared after spending an evening with the family. As usual, her father had spent the family time raging at each child for some imagined sin. None of them had been spared vicious verbal lashings as Big John recited his litany of complaints and disappointments. He'd finally run out of steam over dessert and had left the house, slamming the back door with enough force to shake the foundation. One by one the children had drifted out as well, unable to stay in the oppression of the house with only their drunken mother as company.

As always, Shelby sought the comfort of the swamp, intent on ending the evening in a visit with Mama Royce. Mama Royce always made Shelby feel safe and warm... loved.

As she walked through the woods she practiced trying to be as silent as possible. Billy had told her that in order to walk with the stealth of a wild animal she had to become an animal, but she remained mystified by Billy's skill in traversing the wooded area without making a single noise.

It was a crazy moon night, the kind where the moon shone so full on the water it looked as if the swamp had swallowed the lunar globe whole.

She wasn't far from Mama Royce's shanty when she heard a soft whimper followed by hoarse, guttural, but unintelligible words. Confused by voices this deep in the swamp, disturbed by the fear-filled whimpers, she parted the brush in front of her, searching for the source of the noise.

For a moment she didn't understand what she saw. Figures locked in a macabre embrace, shadows and slivers of moonlight splashing them in surreal lighting. She was too far away to see their features, but could tell it was two figures. As she watched one of them transformed, features blurring as skin turned reptilian. Suddenly it was no longer human, but rather an alligator. Maybelline. Clutched in her massive grip was Gator, his wrist spurting blood as he whimpered like a child.

Consciousness came abruptly. Shelby sat straight up and batted a hand under her nose, fighting against the strong ammonia scent that pulled her from the strange nightmare and into the real world of pain.

"Welcome back."

She stared blankly at the white-haired old man, who looked vaguely familiar. "Wha...what happened?" She gasped as a fiery pain arrowed through her shoulder, bringing with it the memory of the sound of the gunshot, the grit of the gravel beneath her and Billy's animal-like watchfulness as he eyed the surrounding woods.

"You've been shot, dear. Do you remember what happened?"

She nodded and reached for her shoulder, her fingers encountering a bulky bandage and the unfamiliar material of a hospital gown. "Is it serious?"

"About as serious as a splinter." The old man grinned, and instantly Shelby recognized him. He was older, his hair no longer the sandy brown she remembered, but the smile was the same one that had graced his face when Shelby had been a child and had been brought to him for a variety of childhood ailments.

"It's just a flesh wound," Doc Cashwell continued. "The bullet grazed the top of your shoulder. It will be sore for a couple of days, but should heal up without complications. Unfortunately, your blouse is beyond my medical expertise." He held up the pale pink blouse, the shoulder ripped and bloody.

Shelby swung her legs over the side of the examining table and eased herself to a standing position. Clutching the edges of the hospital gown together, she felt as if she'd been run over by a semi. Her body ached and her ribs felt bruised. "Is Billy all right?" she asked.

"Fit as a fiddle and out in the waiting room." The doctor walked with her to the door. "Keep the bandage clean and check back with me in a couple of days."

He opened the door, and Shelby walked out into the waiting room just as Bob entered the small room from the back door. "Shelby." He rushed to where she stood. "Are you all right?"

"I'm fine," she assured him, her gaze going to where Billy stood motionless at one end of the room. "What are you doing here?" she asked Bob.

"Doc called me, said you'd been shot."

"I'm duty bound to report all gunshot injuries," Doc interjected.

"What the hell happened?" Bob demanded. He raised a hand and touched Shelby's cheek softly. "Are you sure you're all right?"

Shelby moved away from his hand, uncomfortably aware of Billy's dark gaze. "I'm fine. I'm just tired and I'd like to go home."

"Somebody needs to tell me what happened." Bob turned and looked at Billy. "What do you have to do with this? Why is it every time there's trouble, you're around?"

"I'm just lucky, I guess." Billy's voice held ill-disguised sarcasm. "We were leaving The Edge and somebody shot at us. If I was to guess, the bullet that hit Shelby was probably intended for me."

"Oh, I have no doubt of that," Bob replied. For a moment the enmity between the two men shimmered in the room. It was Billy who finally broke the moment. "Shelby, I'll wait for you out in the car." He spun on his heel and went out the door.

Bob sighed and raked a hand through his hair, his gaze focused on the spot where Billy had stood. "Someday somebody will put a bullet through his thick head." He looked back at Shelby, his features softened. "Shelby, I told you this was ugly, and promises to get uglier. Tyler's death has stirred emotions and there's no way I can police everyone's passion." He sighed again and pulled a small notepad from his pocket. "You want to tell me exactly what happened so I can make out a report?"

Shelby leaned against the wall, exhaustion suddenly overwhelming her. "Bob, would it be all right if I come into the station tomorrow and make a report? I'm really tired and my shoulder hurts."

"I think that is an excellent idea," Doc Cashwell replied. "Shelby has had a nasty shock, and needs to go home and get some rest." He looked at the sheriff. "Surely the report can wait until tomorrow."

Bob closed the notebook and put it back into his pocket. "Okay, I can get the details tomorrow. You want me to drive you home?"

She shook her head. "Billy can take me. I'll be fine," she added as he frowned. "I'll see you tomorrow."

He hesitated a moment, as if wanting to say something else to her. She saw the worry in his eyes, a worry coupled with emotions too personal for Shelby's comfort. She had a sudden memory of her junior high school friends teasing her about big-eared Bob's crush on her. Bob had grown into his ears, but she had a feeling he hadn't quite outgrown the crush.

"Shelby, I want to give you some pain pills before you go." Dr. Cashwell broke Bob's inertia. With a final goodbye he left the office.

Minutes later, clutching a handful of sample pain pills and a package of sterile bandages, Shelby left the office and joined Billy in his pickup truck. "Just take me back to my car. I can drive the rest of the way home from there."

"You sure?" He started the engine and pulled out of the doctor's driveway. "I don't mind taking you all the way home."

"I'm positive, just take me to my car." She leaned back in the seat and closed her eyes, momentarily lulled by the silence and the gentle movement of the truck. She didn't open her eyes until the truck pulled to a stop and she realized they were parked next to her car.

"I want you to go back to Shreveport." Billy broke the silence between them, his dark eyes glowing in the illumination from the dash lights.

"Pardon me?"

"You heard me. I don't want you working on this anymore. Pack your bags and go back where you belong." His tone was curt, harsh, and evoked in Shelby an anger that overwhelmed her battered exhaustion.

"Don't be ridiculous," she snapped. "I'm not about to allow some coward hiding in the bushes with a gun to scare me off."

He shut off the engine, then twisted in his seat to confront her, his face stern and forbidding in the play of shadows from the dim lighting. "You don't understand. I'm firing you. I don't want your help any longer."

"I really don't care what you want," Shelby returned. "This has gone beyond you and become something personal. I'm not quitting this case and I'm certainly not leaving town."

She opened the car door and started to step out, but gasped as he grabbed her, his fingers curling around her wrist in a tight grip. He pulled her toward him, close enough that she could see the wicked flare of his pupils, smell the odor of soap and male sweat that emanated from him.

"I don't want you here," he whispered. "It was a mistake for me to call you, a mistake to drag you into this mess. Go home, Shelby. Go back to Shreveport where you belong."

"I've been pawed by a drunk, thrown down to the ground and shot all in a single night." She wrenched her wrist out of his grasp. "The last thing I need right now is for you to give me crap." She got out of the truck and glared back in at him. "If and when I decide to go back to Shreveport, it will be my decision, not yours. I'm finished running, Billy Royce. I ran from here years ago feeling powerless and alone. Nobody, not you, not my dysfunctional family and not some fool hiding in the brush is going to make me run again."

She bit her bottom lip, having said much more than she had intended. Realizing her emotions were at a fever pitch and veering dangerously out of control, she slammed the door and got into her car, thankful that Billy didn't get out of the truck and try to continue the argument.

As she drove home, her shoulder throbbed, a constant reminder that something was dreadfully wrong in Black Bayou. She was more determined than ever to get to the bottom of it. Fayrene and Tyler were dead, and if Billy went to prison for that crime it would be an enormous miscarriage of justice.

People were being stabbed, their bodies left to rot in the swamp that was their home, and the public outcry was but a whisper.

She frowned, remembering the nightmare she'd been suffering while in the darkness of her faint. Parts of it had the disturbing elements of a distant memory, and yet other pieces had been absurdly nightmarish. Crazy, obviously a mixture of her outrage over the swamp murders and a lingering disquiet about Gator and his colorful rendition of his war with Maybelline.

Still, there was no doubt about it. There was a core of rot here that far surpassed dirty politics or good-ole-boy networking. Black Bayou harbored a couple of monsters. One had killed Fayrene Whitney and Tyler LaJune. And somebody horribly disturbed was killing innocent people. Shelby knew she wouldn't be satisfied until the monsters had a face, until she knew the monsters' names.

Chapter Nine

"What happened to you?" Michael arose from the dining table as Shelby entered the room the next morning, her shoulder bandage apparent beneath the light cotton blouse she wore.

"An evening with Billy." She grinned wryly, then winced as she sank into the chair opposite where he'd been sitting. "It seems Billy isn't very popular, and I got in the way of somebody's bullet."

"My God, Shelby." Michael moved to the sideboard and motioned to the coffee. Shelby nodded and he refilled his own cup, then poured hers and returned to the table. "I assume you've seen a doctor?"

"Dr. Cashwell fixed me right up." After she explained the previous evening's events, she looked at her brother curiously. "What are you doing here so early?"

"Twice a week I volunteer my time at the community center. I stop by here for coffee before I go. My coffee always tastes like tar sludge."

"What do you do at the community center?"

"Whatever needs to be done. It's been one of Big John's pet projects since its inception."

Sipping her coffee, Shelby raised an eyebrow. "Father has never been particularly interested in projects that don't benefit him."

Michael nodded, a wicked grin curling one corner of his mouth. "It benefits Junior, who receives positive publicity every time Big John gives a check or one of us volunteers time there. Even Mother spends one afternoon a week there reading to the children. It's all part of the major campaign to make the Longsford family look like they care about the 'little people.'"

"I should have known Big John never does anything that doesn't reap him large rewards." She smiled. "Tell me, Father Michael, is there a place in Heaven for a man like him?"

The smile fell from Michael's face. "I think there's probably a special place in Hell for Big John." He grinned again. "But even there, I imagine Big John will be running the show."

They fell into silence. Shelby sipped her coffee slowly, discovering that the simple act of swallowing caused sore muscles and bruised ribs to ache. She'd slept poorly, haunted by disturbing visions of the swamp and dreams of Billy. The throbbing heat of her shoulder had awakened her several times, and each time she'd been grateful for the interruption of those dreams.

"Are you going back to Shreveport?" Michael interrupted her thoughts.

"You think I should?"

He looked into his coffee cup with a rueful smile. "Shelby, I'm not our father. I would never tell you what you should or shouldn't do. I want you to stay here, but I want you to be safe, and it's obvious those two things might not be possible."

Shelby touched her shoulder thoughtfully. "Billy told me to leave, to go back to Shreveport. He tried to fire me."

"He's obviously concerned for your safety, too."

It was her turn to smile ruefully. "Billy is concerned with Billy. He knows if I'm accidentally killed, he'll be skinned alive." She frowned and sipped her coffee once again. "I'm not leaving, and I'm not going to stop digging into Fayrene's and Tyler's deaths. I know Billy is innocent."

Michael reached across the table and covered one of her hands with his. "I'm glad, Shelby. I'm glad you're going to stay. God help me if something happens to you, but I want you here. You give me strength."

She grasped the warmth of his hand lovingly. "I've always thought of you as the strong one."

Michael laughed ruefully. "Why? Because I didn't do as Big John wanted and go into politics?" He released her hand and touched the collar around his neck. "I'm not strong, Shelby. We have become a family of professional hiders." He looked at her, his blue eyes darkened in thought. "You're the only one who didn't find a place to hide."

"Yes, I did," Shelby countered. "While I was living here, I hid at Mama Royce's shanty and then I ran away and hid in Shreveport." She stared down reflectively into her coffee cup. "I realized last night that my life in Shreveport isn't real. I wasn't really living...I've been biding time, waiting to come back here where I belong."

"Why did you leave, Shelby? What drove you away so suddenly?"

She frowned, wondering exactly how to answer. She couldn't tell him that the depth of her passion for Billy had frightened her away, although that had certainly played into her decision to leave. Nor could she tell him grief for Mama Royce had caused her to run. Although both those things had been partially responsible, there had been something else...a fear...an undefinable need to escape. How could she explain what she still didn't understand? She looked at Michael helplessly and shrugged. "It's too complicated to explain. Let's just say I knew it was time for me to leave, give myself a chance to see something of the world beyond Black Bayou. But now it's time to stay here where I belong."

Michael's hand covered hers once again. "I'm just glad you're back, Shelby." He finished his coffee and stood. "Why don't you come with me to the community center? Let me show you some of the good things that are being accomplished there."

"I'd like that," Shelby agreed, also rising from the table. "Besides, I promised Bob I'd stop by the police station and give him a statement."

They decided Shelby would drive her own car and follow Michael. Minutes later as Shelby rolled down her car window to allow in the warm morning air, her thoughts turned to Billy and the kiss they'd shared in the bar the night before.

It was still there. Whatever powerful force had exploded between them on the night of Mama Royce's death was still there, simmering with intensity, volatile and unpredictable. She wished it wasn't. She could pretend it didn't exist, deny it to Billy, but she couldn't fool herself.

He touched her like no other man, but she knew it would be foolish to follow through on the attraction. He needed her legal prowess, nothing else. She'd survived one bout with Billy; she wasn't at all sure she could survive another.

She would keep their relationship firmly on a professional level. Although she knew there were times when lawyers got intimately involved with their clients, she'd never considered it a smart move. She smiled and reminded herself that as of last night, according to Billy, she no longer worked for him.

She'd sort that particular detail out later. As far as she was concerned she wasn't off his case until she decided. Pulling in to a parking space next to Michael's car, she turned her attention to the building before her.

The community center was a large, nondescript, one-story building. On one side a fence surrounded a playground full of colorful playground equipment and on the other side was a basketball court. Behind the building the edges of the swamp encroached, filling the air with the scent of exotic flowers, dense greenery and always the underlying scent of something rotten.

Michael met her as she got out of her car. "It's not much to look at, but it's a beginning," he said. "We provide before- and after-school care for the kids around the area, we've got a teen program and are working now to provide some services for the elderly." His gaze went toward the dark marshlands. "At least this is one place the people from the swamp can come and be safe." Michael shook his head sadly. "There isn't a family in that swamp that hasn't been touched by the serpent murders. They say at night you can hear the mournful cries of the bereaved."

Shelby shivered at the haunting image his words evoked. "Bob says there have been no clues, nothing to indicate who might be responsible."

"No clues, no pattern to the timing of the murders, no motive tying them all together. I have little faith the killer will ever be found. Whoever is responsible for the crime is smart and evil."

"And so people will just continue to die? What a horrifying thought. And the worst part is that nobody seems to care."

Michael smiled at her. "Your Don Quixote syndrome is showing." He took her arm as they walked toward the front door. "You always did joust at windmills. Honey, you aren't going to change the prejudices of this town overnight. We're making a start here, but we've got a long way to go."

He opened the front door and together they walked into a room filled with chaos. More than a dozen children were seated at tables on one side of the room, uncooked elbow macaroni, bottles of glue and colorful construction paper providing their entertainment.

"Father Mike." Several of them left their table and ran toward him, their arms outstretched. Michael bent and embraced each one, laughing as they chattered, each vying for his attention. It was easy to tell these were children from the swamp. Although clean, their clothes were faded and ill fitting. The children were thin, their faces already weathered by nature's elements, poverty and a hint of distrust.

Michael patted them each on the back, then sent them back to their places at the table. He straightened and smiled at Shelby. "The young ones are the purest. Their hearts haven't been hardened yet by their circumstances and this town's hatred."

"Father Mike, you should have married, had children of your own," Shelby observed, noting the loving expression on his face as he watched the children at work.

He shook his head. "No. I knew from a very early age that marriage wasn't for me." He grinned ruefully. "We didn't exactly have the best example of a healthy marriage with Mother and Father. Mother had her bottle, and Father had his other women."

Shelby looked at him sharply. "Big John had affairs?"

Michael grimaced. "Sorry, I just figured you knew."

She smiled ruefully. "Ah, another ideal shattered beneath reality."

"I remember one spring night years ago when I overhead Mom and Dad fighting about his latest mistress. It scared me because I was certain he was going to leave all of us for her. Funny, I think it was the year you left home."

"I'm really not surprised," she replied thoughtfully. "Makes you wonder, doesn't it?"

"Wonder what?" he asked curiously.

Shelby grinned. "How we turned out so normal and well adjusted."

They both turned as the door opened and in walked a tall, dark-haired woman and a young boy. "There's Angelique and Parker Royce," Michael murmured, then went to greet the two.

Shelby would have known Billy's son in any place, among any crowd. His paternal stamp was all over the child, in the shiny dark hair that covered the boy's head, in the stubborn thrust of his chin and in the overwhelming darkness of his eyes. He had his father's eyes, only in Parker's there was still a wealth of hope, a childish trust that had yet to be betrayed.

He smiled at her, a shy, sweet smile that arrowed right through to her heart. Shelby knew if Billy went to prison it wouldn't be the memory of Mama Royce's eyes that haunted her dreams. It would be Parker's.

Her gaze moved from the child to the woman. Whoever she was, she was beautiful, with the proud carriage of a queen. Her multicolored skirt and blouse only added to her exotic allure. She spoke with Michael only a moment, then released her hold on Parker's hand and gently pushed him toward the other children. She headed for the front door, then hesitated and turned, her gaze locking with Shelby's.

Shelby's breath caught in her chest as she fought an impulse to step back, to escape the powerful hostility that radiated from the woman's eyes. It was there only a moment, then masked beneath passivity. Shelby didn't breathe until the woman went through the doorway and disappeared from sight. She exhaled and turned to Michael, who'd rejoined her. "Who's that woman?"

"That's Angelique Boujoulais. She's a friend of Billy's and supposed to be a powerful woman in the swamp community."

"Powerful how?" Shelby wrapped her arms around herself, warding off a chill as she thought of the brief eye contact.

"She's reputed to be a powerful healer. Even Doc goes to her for help in herbal cures. Some say she dabbles in magic."

The chill that Shelby had tried to ward off shivered up her spine as she once again remembered that moment when their eyes had locked and Angelique's had radiated malevolence. Terrific—as if she didn't have enough to worry about, she'd somehow managed to garner the gypsy woman's animosity.

She wondered if Angelique and Billy were lovers, and was surprised when the thought brought with it a tinge of jealousy. Once again her head filled with the memory of his kiss, so seductive, so provocative.

"Shelby, you okay?"

She jumped when Michael touched her arm. "I'm fine." She shoved thoughts of Billy aside and smiled at her brother. "Why don't you show me the rest of this place and introduce me to the children?"

IT WAS NEARLY NOON when Shelby left the community center and drove to the nearby police station, anxious to give Bob a statement about the shooting the night before, then get back home for a nap. Her shoulder throbbed, and her restless night was catching up with her.

"Shelby, I was just going to send my deputy after you," Bob greeted her as she walked into the station. "Jonathon LaJune is in the back." He gestured toward a closed door. "He's spilling his guts. He's the one who shot you last night."

"Tyler's father?" Shelby looked at him in surprise.

Bob nodded. "He's convinced Billy is responsible for Tyler's death. He decided to mete out his own brand of justice last night, but his aim isn't as good as it used to be. I'll need your statement so we can press charges."

"I want to speak with him before I give a statement."

Bob hesitated, then shrugged. "I suppose it would be all right." He ushered her through the door, down a hallway and into a small interrogation room.

"I'd like to speak to him alone," she said before going in.

Again Bob paused, then nodded. "Okay, I'll give you five minutes. He's grieving, Shelby, but he's also a very angry man."

Shelby had childhood memories of Tyler's father, memories of a man as vivid, as powerful as Big John. But the man who was seated at the table in the small interrogation room held little resemblance to the man of her memories. He seemed to have shrunk, his shoulders slumped forward as he rested his head between his hands.

He looked up when she closed the door behind her, and his eyes filled with tears. "Shelby, I'm a foolish old man," he said, his voice full of the tears his eyes couldn't hold. "I could have killed you."

"Yes, you could have," she agreed, and sat down across from him at the table.

He swiped at the tears angrily and glared at her. "I wish I'd hit him. I wish I'd killed him. I'll dance on his grave when he's gone."

Shelby sucked in her breath at the intensity of his hatred for Billy. "Mr. LaJune, I don't believe Billy is responsible for Tyler's death."

He leaned back in his chair and studied her for a long moment, his expression alternating between profound loss and simmering rage. "I heard you came all the way here from Shreveport just to defend that killer." He leaned forward, allowing Shelby to smell the scent of cigar smoke and grief that clung to him. "You were Tyler's friend. How can you let yourself be taken in by Billy Royce?"

"I'm not being taken in by anyone," Shelby countered. "Right now all I'm looking for is the truth. Tell me about Tyler. I've been gone from Black Bayou for a long time. Where was he working? Who were his friends?"

Jonathon leaned back once again in the chair, his gaze losing some of its intensity. "Of course, I'd dreamed of him coming to work for the family business, but you know Tyler, always writing, scribbling stories and keeping journals. For the last seven years he worked as a reporter at the *Black Bayou Daily News.*"

"How long had he been seeing Fayrene?"

The rage came back, filling his eyes and twisting his features. "I don't know. If I knew he was tied up with that swamp scum, I'd have had his hide." A vein pulsed in the side of his neck and his breathing was rapid and uneven. "Tyler was a victim of circumstance. He was in the wrong place at the wrong time. That was his only crime... accidentally getting in the middle between Fayrene and Billy. He was the victim of a madman's rage."

His pain was a palpable force in the tiny room. He slumped farther down in the chair, as if the rage had been all that held him erect, and with it momentarily expended he was left with only exhaustion. "I'm sorry I hurt you, Shelby. It was an accident, the failing eyesight of an old man. Tyler was my only child, the only heir to the LaJune name. Billy Royce not only killed my child, he killed the hope of future LaJunes."

"Mr. LaJune." Shelby reached across the table and touched his hand, wanting to convey her own sorrow, her grief at the loss of Tyler. "I grew up with Tyler and Billy. Billy couldn't have murdered Tyler. Billy loved Tyler."

Jonathon LaJune smiled, an ugly gesture that had nothing to do with joy. "Ah, Shelby, you're a fool if you think so. Don't you know that Billy Royce loves no one? That man doesn't know how to love."

Bob opened the door and stepped in, preempting any further conversation. "Shelby?" He motioned her out into the hallway. "We'll go sit down in one of the other rooms and I'll take your statement."

"I'm not giving a statement. I'm not pressing charges."

Bob raked a hand through his hair. "Are you sure?"

She nodded. "It was an accident, Bob. The act of a man consumed with grief. I don't think he'll try anything like it again."

"Okay, it's your call." He suddenly looked sheepish. "I've got some other news to break to you."

"What?"

"A warrant was issued for Billy's arrest. A couple of deputies brought him in just a few minutes ago. He's being charged in the double homicide of Fayrene Whitney and Tyler LaJune." Bob's voice was stilted, the voice of the sheriff speaking to a lawyer.

"Damn it, Bob, you could have warned me," she snapped, her fatigue suddenly gone as adrenaline pumped through her. "Where is he? I want to see him."

"He's in one of the holding tanks. The judge is out of town for the night. The arraignment is scheduled for first thing tomorrow morning, so he'll be our guest at least for the night. Come on, I'll take you back."

As Shelby followed Bob, her mind raced. She'd hoped to have more time. She'd hoped to be able to investigate more, come up with some reasonable doubts to present to a jury. Now the wheels of justice were turning too fast, and unless she came up with something quickly she feared Billy would be crushed.

"Just knock on the door when you're finished with him," Bob said as he unlocked the steel door and motioned her inside.

If she expected Billy to be subdued or humbled by his arrest, she was mistaken. He sat on a chair in the corner of the small room, his hands cuffed together before him.

He smiled as she came in, the same bold, sexy grin he might have offered to her had they met in a smoke-filled bar. "Ah, my lovely counsel has finally arrived."

"Last I heard you fired me," Shelby replied.

His gaze drifted from her face to where the bandage showed through the thin material of her blouse. "How's your shoulder?"

"It's fine. Jonathon LaJune confessed to being the shooter."

"So I heard." He gestured her into the chair next to him. The chains of the handcuffs jangled discordantly with his motion.

"Billy, before we go any further, I need to know that you're committed to me acting as your legal representative. I can't have you firing me whenever the mood strikes or when things get tough." She sat down in the chair, her gaze locked with his. "I'm not a little girl anymore, Billy. I no longer need you to hold my hand and lead me out of the

darkness of the swamp. Now it's you who needs me.'' She
held up a hand to still his protest. "You need me, Billy, to
see you through the intricacies of the legal system."

He reached out and took her hand in his. His eyes were
dark, unreadable, but a smile curved the corners of his lips.
"I have a feeling before this is all over and done with, we're
going to need each other.''

Shelby drew in a deep breath, unsure what terrified her
more: the battle ahead to keep Billy out of prison, or the
thought that she might ever need him again.

Chapter Ten

"We've got to set some ground rules here," Shelby said the next morning as she walked with Billy into the courtroom for his arraignment. "You don't speak with anyone without checking with me first. You answer the judge respectfully and only when I tell you to." She eyed him harshly. "This isn't a game, Billy. You're out of your league here and I'm talking about your survival."

He nodded, his eyes mocking her, telling her he realized she was repeating his words from The Edge back to him. "You're the boss, Ms. Longsford."

"Let's try to keep it that way, at least until the end of these proceedings," she said, nerves taut as a fiddle string as the district attorney, Abner Witherspoon, entered the courtroom.

"Shelby." He greeted her with a wide smile that reflected off the spit shine on his patent leather shoes. "I couldn't believe it when I heard that little Shelby Longsford was going to be my adversary in this particular case. I still think of you with pigtails and freckles."

"I never had freckles, nor did I ever wear pigtails," Shelby returned, knowing the mind games had already begun. Good old Abe would try his best to intimidate her before the case even began. "I must confess, I was a little surprised to realize you were presenting the state's case. I thought you were dead.'' Shelby smiled sweetly, aware of Billy's rumble of laughter as Abe turned on his heel and went to his table.

"Do you think that was wise?" Billy asked as Shelby sat down next to him and they awaited the arrival of the judge.

"What? Baiting Abner? Probably not, but I had to let him know in no uncertain terms that he won't intimidate me." She unlatched her briefcase. "It's part of the game lawyers play."

"What other kinds of games have you learned to play since you've been gone?" Billy asked, his voice soft and insinuating.

"All rise," the bailiff said, preventing any response Shelby might have made.

The proceeding took thirty minutes, and in that time Shelby managed to convince the judge to set a bail. Although she knew Abner only agreed because he was certain Billy would never be able to raise the appropriate percentage of the hundred-thousand-dollar amount. However, both Abner and Shelby were surprised when Gator stepped forward and posted bond, leaving Billy free to walk out of the courthouse, his court date set for the next month.

"We've got a lot of work to do in a short amount of time," Shelby said as they walked out into the brutal humidity and midmorning heat. "I can't believe the judge refused to give us more time."

"Everyone in town is eager to get the crazed killer behind bars," Billy replied dryly. "Why don't we start by going over to Martha's and getting a bowl of her gumbo," he suggested. "I don't have much to say for jail food."

"If we don't come up with some reasonable doubt as to your guilt, you'll be eating jail food for a very long time to come."

He grinned. "Ah, Shelby, a man could get lost in your sweet talk."

They fell silent as they walked down the sidewalk toward the restaurant. Shelby felt the curious stares of the people they passed and knew word was out that Billy had been arrested and charged. The gossip mill in Black Bayou was apparently as healthy as ever.

"Where did Gator get the kind of money it took to bail you out of jail?" she asked, breaking the silence between them.

"I gave Gator that money to hold in the event of my arrest."

"Where did you get that kind of money?" She looked at him curiously, trying not to notice how the sunshine played on the darkness of his hair, highlighted the sharp angles of his face.

"Don't worry, it's not stolen or ill-gained," he replied. "When Mama Royce died she left me a healthy nest egg. I've made some investments that have been quite profitable. I've learned how to play money games with Wall Street. There's nothing I like better than to legally rob from the rich and give to who needs it." He paused as they came to the restaurant door. "To tell the truth, Shelby, I'm one of the wealthiest people in this town, but everyone sees me as just another swamp rat." His eyes darkened in intensity. "Money can buy you lots of things, but in this town it can't buy you out of the swamp."

"Is that what you want?" she asked softly. "To buy your way out of the swamp?"

"No. I don't ever want to forget where I came from and the community of people who embraced me. The people who live in the swamp are good people, whose only fault is being poor and having to fight prejudice. They begin their lives with a curse on their heads. Swamp rats." He spoke with a passion that stirred Shelby.

"But that's changing, isn't it? Now there's the community center, and at least it's a beginning."

He nodded. "Yes, it's a beginning, but in the meantime somebody is trying to clean up the town by killing off the swamp community."

"Billy, we can't solve all the murders in Black Bayou. At the moment the top priority is to figure out who is responsible for Tyler's and Fayrene's deaths."

"At the moment my top priority is a bowl of Martha's seafood gumbo." He opened the restaurant door and ushered her inside.

They went to the back, into the same small room where they'd sat before. Shelby would have preferred the more open, less private area of the main dining room, but knew here they would both be safe from curious stares.

As she slid into the chair across from him, she tried to ignore how he filled the air with his scent. The walls of the room seemed to close in as if attempting to quell his overwhelming presence, contain his vibrating energy.

She should be thinking about the case. She shouldn't be thinking about how his lips had felt on hers. She shouldn't be remembering the taste of his skin, the feel of his bare flesh beneath her fingertips.

She sighed in relief as Martha entered, order pad in hand. "Heard you was in jail," she said, giving Billy a nudge with her elbow.

"I was, but I have a good lawyer." Billy's gaze was warm as it lingered on Shelby. It was a look devoid of sexual insinuation, instead holding a touch of respect. Heat exploded in the pit of her stomach, making her realize she wanted Billy's respect, knew it was something he didn't give lightly.

She schooled her thoughts back to the matter at hand, aware that Billy's respect wouldn't be worth much if he wound up spending the rest of his life in prison.

Once Martha had departed with their lunch orders, Shelby leaned back in her chair, turning the facts of the case as she knew them around and around in her head. "There has to be something we're missing in all of this," she finally said. "Everyone has said this was a crime of passion, that you killed Tyler and Fayrene in a jealous rage. If we take away that motive, then who wanted Fayrene dead?"

"If we knew that, we'd know who killed her and we wouldn't be here having this conversation," Billy said wryly.

"Maybe we're approaching this from the wrong angle," Shelby said. She paused as Martha returned with two cold sodas and steaming bowls of gumbo with chunks of thick corn bread on the side.

When Martha departed once again, Shelby continued her thought. "Jonathon LaJune said Tyler was a victim of circumstance, simply at the wrong place at the wrong time. Everyone is assuming the killer was after Fayrene, and Tyler merely happened to be in the way. But what happens if the intended victim wasn't Fayrene at all and instead was Tyler?"

Billy stared at her. "That definitely puts a different spin on the situation." He broke off a piece of the corn bread and popped it into his mouth, chewing thoughtfully as he continued to stare at her.

It was difficult to concentrate on anything except the fact that his days of freedom were now numbered unless Shelby could somehow pull a rabbit out of a hat. A night in jail had brought home the reality of his situation, and he was suddenly struck with the sweetness of his present freedom and a frantic need to experience everything possible before he went to trial.

Billy had no illusions about himself. If the unthinkable happened and he was found guilty, he would die in prison. Whether from the heartbreak of being without Parker or from a homemade knife in the back because he'd smarted off to the wrong tough guy, he knew within a year he'd be dead.

And who would mourn his passing? Not Parker, who was too young to understand the finality of death. Certainly not anyone in the town of Black Bayou would grieve for him. He looked at Shelby, wondering if she'd shed a tear at his funeral. Surely not. Longsfords didn't cry over swamp rats.

"So how are you going to get me out of this mess?" he asked, irritated by his thoughts and finding her an easy target.

She glared at him in unconcealed aggravation. "I was attempting to do a little brainstorming here, but you appear to be brain-dead."

He smiled. "Okay, let's try it again and I promise to do my part." She'd grown strong while away, and he was surprised to realize he was drawn to her strength, just as he was drawn to her softness.

He leaned back in his chair, trying to focus on the question she'd raised moments before. "I can't imagine why anyone would want to kill Tyler. Tyler was friends with everyone. He didn't know how to have cross words or create enemies."

"But he's dead, and there has to be a reason for his death."

"And that brings us full circle. Tyler was at the wrong place at the wrong time," Billy replied.

She sighed and focused on the meal. They ate in silence. Billy knew Shelby was still silently brainstorming. She ate slowly, methodically, her eyes holding the distance of deep preoccupation.

He didn't mind. It gave him an opportunity to study her, to catalog the ways she'd changed in the passing years. Physically she hadn't changed much. Her eyes were just as blue, her hair the same cloud of darkness that had occasionally haunted his dreams. No, the changes he saw in Shelby had nothing to do with her physical appearance. They were subtle, more profound.

There had once been an untainted innocence in her eyes, but that was no longer there. Had he taken that from her on the same night he'd taken her virginity? He shoved this thought aside, not wanting to be responsible for that. He had been her first lover, and he found himself wondering how many she'd had since. He'd guess few.

One thing was certain. He wasn't about to risk a lifetime in prison without making love to Shelby one last time.

"CAN YOU TELL ME what kind of stories Tyler wrote for the paper?" Shelby asked Martin Winthrop, editor in chief of the *Black Bayou Daily News*. She and Billy had parted after lunch with the agreement that she would meet him later should she learn anything important.

"Since Mrs. Wilmington's death three years ago, Tyler mostly took care of the society news," Martin said as he led Shelby back to Tyler's desk. "I kept promising him that sooner or later I'd find somebody else to do the society pages, but with his name and connections he had an inside track to all the parties and hoity-toity events." A flash of guilt crossed Martin's face. "He wanted to do the hard stuff, but I hated to waste his background and breeding. A dozen reporters can do hard stories, very few get invited into the inner circles of society.''

"And nobody has touched any of his things here?" Shelby asked, scanning the neat surface of the scarred wooden desk.

"Nah." Martin scratched his rotund belly. "I was gonna box it all up and send it over to his folks. Didn't know what else to do with it." He frowned and his fingers moved up to scratch absently at his chest. "Damn shame. He was a fine writer, a good kid."

"Do you mind?" Shelby gestured to the desk.

Martin shrugged. "Help yourself, but you won't find much here. Tyler did most of his work on his laptop computer."

"And you don't know where that is?"

Martin shook his head. "I assume it's at his parents' house." He looked at his watch. "Look, I gotta get back to work. You be all right?"

She nodded and waited until Martin walked away, then she sat down at the desk where Tyler LaJune had worked for the past seven years. A computer sat on one corner of the desk.

She punched the On button and while it booted up she opened the desk drawer and scanned the contents. Paper clips, pencils, small notepads, all the tools of a writer neatly organized for easy access.

She had no idea what she was looking for, knew she could be chasing her tail, but she had to follow through on the possibility that Tyler was the intended victim and Fayrene the unfortunate victim of circumstance. In that particular scenario Billy's motive no longer played, and without a motive, the state's case was weak.

The desk drawers yielded nothing of consequence and Shelby turned her attention to the computer. In the word processing files she found story after story of weddings, charity dinners, balls and gala events, but nothing that would make anybody want to murder Tyler.

It took her nearly an hour to go through all the files the directory held. Finally she shut off the computer and heaved a sigh of frustration. Nothing. There had been nothing in his files to provoke his murder. Disappointment weighed heavily on her shoulders as she left the newspaper building.

She'd hoped to find something, anything they could use as an alternative to the case Abe would build against Billy. She got back into her car and sat, waiting for the air conditioner to cool the stifling interior.

The dog days of summer were approaching, when the temperature and humidity would soar. Tempers would flare, passions would rise and the furor over Tyler's death would escalate. Jonathon LaJune had tried to mete out his own brand of justice. Who else might try to harm Billy in a misguided attempt to balance the scales of fate?

She thought again of Martin's words. Tyler had used a laptop. The obvious place for the laptop to be was at his home. She frowned, dreading another meeting with Jonathon LaJune. His grief drained her, his anger daunted her, but she hoped his guilt over shooting her would prompt him to cooperate.

The LaJune mansion wasn't far from Shelby's home. As she pulled up in front, she noted the brown, withering flowers in the pots on the porch, weeds sprouting amid the untended lawn. It was as if Tyler's death had infected this place, bringing with it an aura of sorrow that surrounded the house.

Her knock on the door was greeted by a butler, who told her Mr. LaJune was not home but she could speak to Mrs.

LaJune. As Shelby waited, she looked around the formal living room, her gaze lingering on a picture of Tyler.

Tyler and Billy. She'd never known exactly what had brought the two together. Billy was as taciturn as Tyler was gregarious. They had been seniors when Shelby had been a freshman and she could remember them walking together down the halls, the popular golden boy and the ultimate bad boy. In each other they seemed to have found a part of themselves that was missing, and the bond between them had been tangible and enviable.

She wondered if Billy had even had time to grieve for his best friend. What a tragedy, not only to lose a friend but to be charged for his death, as well.

Shivering, she remembered another night long ago when Billy had been grieving for the loss of a loved one. Had he sought asylum from his anguish in her arms? Had that been what had prompted that night of explosive passion between them? If so, in whose arms was he assuaging his grief for Tyler? And more important, why did she care?

"Shelby?"

She turned at the sound of the soft voice, her heart expanding as she held out a hand to greet Tyler's mother. "Mrs. LaJune, I'm so sorry."

Although Tyler's mother was impeccably groomed, her features were lifeless, trapped in the expression of heartache. "Thank you, my dear. They finally released him to us. We're having the funeral tomorrow. You'll come, won't you?"

"Of course." Shelby followed the older woman's lead and sat down on the sofa.

"And it is I who should be apologizing to you for my husband's actions." Mrs. LaJune looked down at her hands folded in her lap. "My husband isn't really a bad man, Shelby."

Shelby nodded. "I know that. Are you aware that I'm representing Billy?"

"I know." She looked at Shelby and for a moment a flash of life shone from her eyes. "I want the person who killed my son in prison, but I'm not convinced that person is Billy."

Finally, Shelby thought. Finally somebody else who believed in the possibility of Billy's innocence. "Do you have any idea who might have wanted Tyler dead?"

Mrs. LaJune shook her head and once again looked down at her hands. "My husband sees everything in black and white, with no room for shades of gray. He's decided Tyler was seeing Fayrene and Billy killed them both. But I know my son, and he would never be interested in a woman like Fayrene." She sighed, a deep, weary sigh. "I know my son had secrets. Tyler was hiding something before his death."

"How do you know?"

She placed a hand over her heart. "There are things a mother just knows. He was staying away more, sometimes not coming home for a day or two at a time. He told me he was working on an important story and was staying at the newspaper office, but that wasn't true. Unfortunately, I don't know what the truth is."

"I understand Tyler did most of his work on a laptop computer? Do you have it here?"

Mrs. LaJune frowned. "No...no, I haven't seen Tyler's little computer. It must be still at his desk at the paper."

Shelby shook her head. "I just came from there. It wasn't there."

"That's odd. Perhaps it's in his car." She stood and motioned for Shelby to follow her through the house and out the back door to the detached garage. "The police towed the car here the day after..." She let her words trail off, and Shelby felt the pain of the unspoken.

The laptop was not in the car, nor was it among any of Tyler's things. Shelby left the LaJune mansion mystified, entertaining the hunch that the laptop could provide the key to Tyler's murder.

She drove back to her house, parked her car, then took off walking across the expanse of lawn. She and Billy had made plans to meet to discuss what she'd learned in the course of the afternoon. Somehow she hadn't been surprised when he'd told her he was staying at Mama Royce's shanty. Although she knew he had an apartment in town, she understood his need to escape back to a place where he'd been happy and life had been less complicated. Or had life always been complicated for Billy Royce?

She left the manicured grass of the lawn, the air cooler as she entered the dense swamp. As if it had been only yesterday, she moved instinctively, her feet remembering where to step, when to jump to avoid pools of water or soggy marsh.

A rustling of the thick brush behind her shot a burst of adrenaline through her. Was somebody following her? Who was it? What? Evil. Evil in the swamp. Visions danced in her head...indistinct visions of a full moon and two figures. Blood in the water and the glint of a knife in the moonlight. A cry of rage...a muffled scream. Evil. Evil.

Shelby ran, blinded by terror, operating solely on animal instinct. She clattered across the rickety bridge that led to Mama Royce's shanty, her fear choked in her throat.

The door to the shanty flew open and Billy caught her in his arms. "Shelby? What's wrong? Are you all right?"

She pressed her face against the hollow of his neck, trembling uncontrollably with residual, irrational fear. "I'm...I'm fine," she said, confused by her fear and not yet ready to release her hold on him. "Something frightened me…rustling in the woods." She tried to reach back, to capture the mental images that had provoked her fear, but they were gone, crowded out by the sharper reality of Billy's arms around her.

The collar of his cotton shirt smelled of the sun, the swamp and the heady scent that belonged to him alone. His arms held her securely, banishing the shivers that had chased up her spine.

"You sure you're all right?" His voice was soft, low in her ear. She nodded and reluctantly moved out of his arms.

"I'm fine. I don't know what happened. I heard something, probably an animal in the brush. I just suddenly got scared."

"Come inside." He touched her arm and she followed him into the shanty where years before she and Billy had shared an eruption of passion that had changed Shelby's life forever.

She was surprised and relieved that the interior of the shanty no longer looked the same. Although it still had plank wood floors, electric lights had taken the place of the kerosene ones Mama Royce had used. A ceiling fan overhead stirred the air, cooling the room with a slight hum of the motor.

The furniture was different, except the chair in the corner. The sight of Mama Royce's rocking chair brought an ache to Shelby's chest. It sat empty, the shawl she'd always worn folded across the back as if awaiting her return.

Shelby walked over to the chair and ran her hand lovingly across the wool of the knitted shawl. "Do you still miss her?" she asked.

Billy nodded. "Not a day goes by that I don't think of her, hear her voice in my head giving me hell about something or another."

Shelby smiled. "I used to envy you, having somebody like her in your life. She was so wonderful, so loving. Thank you for sharing her with me."

"She would have been proud of you, Shelby. She would have been proud of the woman you've become. She loved you."

Shelby nodded, for a moment her throat too full for words. She moved away from the chair, surprised to see a door to a room that hadn't been there years before. "What's this?" she asked curiously.

"Parker's bedroom. He's taking a nap." Billy sat down at the table and motioned her into the chair across from him. "I added it on the year he was born. Fayrene hated this place, but I wanted Parker to know it, think of it as his home away from home."

Shelby sat down across from him and relayed to him the events of the afternoon, explaining about the importance of the laptop. "I know it's a long shot," she said. "But Tyler's boss at the paper told me he wanted to write hard-hitting stories. What if he was secretly working on something that put his life at risk?"

Billy frowned thoughtfully. "I suppose it's possible. Tyler hated writing the society news. He always told me he intended to write a story that would force Martin to take him off the society pages and make him front page material." Billy sighed and pulled a hand through his hair. "He made the front page, all right, but not in the way he'd hoped."

"The problem is the laptop is missing. It's not at the newspaper offices and it isn't at Tyler's home."

"I know where it might be," Billy said.

"Where?"

Billy's gaze moved to the closed door to Parker's room. "I'll have to take you there, but it will have to be tomorrow."

"Tyler's funeral is first thing in the morning," she reminded him.

"Then I'll meet you after the funeral and we'll go from there."

A plaintive childish cry from the bedroom interrupted any further conversation. Billy jumped up from the table. "He often has nightmares," he said, then disappeared into the bedroom.

Although Shelby knew she was intruding on his privacy, she couldn't help herself. She got up from the table and moved to the doorway of the bedroom.

The room was small, but cozy. A twin-size bed was against one wall, a long dresser against the opposite wall. On top of the dresser were shiny rocks and colorful leaves, bird feathers and other treasures of boyhood. But what captured Shelby's attention was the vision of Billy sitting on the edge of the small bed, the little boy curled in his arms. He spoke softly to the child, his words indistinct to Shelby, but his tone reassuring.

He stroked Parker's hair and looked up, his gaze meeting Shelby's. In his eyes she saw an emotion so intense it stole her breath away. She knew in that instant that Jonathon LaJune had been wrong. Billy wasn't a man who didn't know how to love. Billy was a man who loved deeply, passionately and, God help her, for just an instant she envied Parker for possessing Billy's love.

Chapter Eleven

"Ah, good, you're home." Big John greeted Shelby as she walked into the living room. "Your mother has gotten it into her head that we're having a family dinner this evening. We were just about to sit down."

Shelby nodded. "Let me run upstairs and clean up a little then I'll be right down."

Once in the bathroom, she washed her face and hands and ran a brush through her hair. As she stared into the mirror, it wasn't her reflection she saw. The vision of Billy holding his son remained etched in her mind.

He was a man of many facets, a wealthy man living in a small shanty, a suspected murderer cradling a child in his arms.

She'd left while he was still in the bedroom with Parker. Whispering to him that she'd see him tomorrow after the funeral, she'd left the shanty. She wished she'd had an opportunity to ask him where he thought Tyler's computer might be, where he intended to take her to find it. But in that moment of seeing Billy vulnerable, his love for his son shining so intensely from his eyes, she'd felt the need to escape...run before she fell beneath the bewitching allure of him.

Taking one last look at her reflection, she shoved away thoughts of Billy, focusing instead on the family dinner ahead. She hoped Michael would be in attendance. His presence would certainly make the event more enjoyable.

When she went back down to the living room, Olivia and her husband, Roger, were seated on the sofa. Roger stood as Shelby entered, his smooth, tanned features curving into a smile as he reached out a hand to greet her. "Shelby, good to have you home where you belong."

"Thank you, Roger." Shelby released his hand and stifled the impulse to wipe her palm down the side of her skirt. Suellen had been right. Yes, Roger was smooth as snake oil, but Shelby knew it was a politician's smoothness. She wondered if Olivia had consciously set out to marry a younger image of their father or if it had been a subconscious choice.

"Can I get you a drink before dinner?" Roger asked as he walked over to the bar.

"Saint Shelby rarely drinks," Olivia said. "In fact, I don't think Shelby has any vices at all, unless you consider being the champion to underdogs a vice."

Shelby sank onto the sofa next to her sister and gave her a wry grin. "It's a tough job, but somebody's got to do it."

"Are you sure it's wise for you to get involved in this mess of Tyler and that woman's murder?" Roger asked. "The whole town is in an uproar. A messy business, what with your brother campaigning for a seat in Congress. I've thrown my hat into the ring for the state legislature and I'd hate for this to turn away votes."

"You think my defending Billy Royce will hurt your and John junior's chances?" She looked at him incredulously. "I hardly think that's going to happen."

"What's going to happen?" Michael asked as he entered the room.

"Roger is just speculating that my defending Billy Royce might harm the political aspirations of this family," Shelby answered.

"Somebody needs to defend him," Michael observed as he eased down into one of the chairs. "I understand he was officially charged this morning." Shelby nodded. Michael sighed and rubbed his forehead. "There are times I think the swamp serpent is performing an act of mercy. At least the victims are put out of the misery of their lives."

"Personally, I think the serpent should be given a medal for ridding us all of *those* people," Roger replied.

Shelby gasped, surprised by the ugly sentiments being expressed. "I find the whole subject boring and tedious," Olivia said before Shelby could speak. "I'd much rather talk about the Whalens' party this weekend. I heard Madge Whalen is flying in caterers from Europe."

"It's going to take more than caterers from Europe for Madge to catch a husband for that horse-face daughter of hers," Roger said, causing Olivia to laugh appreciatively.

At that moment Big John and John junior came into the room and the talk, as usual, turned to politics. Shelby was grateful when Suellen announced that dinner was ready and they all seated themselves at the big table in the dining room.

With Big John at one end of the table and Celia at the other, it was like dinners from years past. Shelby had forgotten how entertaining her family could be despite all their problems. Big John roared his laughter at Olivia's acerbic humor. Even Celia seemed to enjoy herself, smiling often like a mother hen proud of her brood.

As the dinner progressed, Shelby found herself studying her sister and her brother-in-law, wondering what it was that had drawn the two together in marriage. Certainly they didn't seem overly affectionate with one another, and

Shelby had gathered from Michael's comments on the night she'd arrived that Olivia wasn't faithful to her husband.

If Shelby was to guess, the marriage was based on several things. For Roger, marrying into the Longsford family could only help him in his political aspirations. She looked at her sister thoughtfully, wondering what Olivia might gain from a marriage to the older, ambitious man. It was obvious Big John liked Roger, apparently approved of the marriage.

Was this another pathetic attempt on Olivia's part to gain favor with Big John? The thought saddened Shelby, who knew Olivia would never be able to get the love she so desperately needed from her father. Big John was simply incapable of connecting with his daughters in a positive manner, a fact Shelby had accepted long ago.

Over dessert, the talk once again turned to the murders. "Heard you got Billy Royce out on bail this morning," her father commented as he finished the last of his apple dumpling.

Tension welled up inside Shelby. "That's right. His court date is less than a month away. We've got lots of work to do before then."

"You better talk to brother Michael here. He's the resident Longsford in charge of miracles," Olivia said. "And if you think you're going to convince a jury Billy is innocent, you'd better be looking for a miracle."

Michael touched his collar and smiled at Shelby. "I'm afraid those kinds of miracles are far beyond me."

"I'm not looking for a miracle. I simply want justice," Shelby answered. "Besides, I'm checking into the possibility that the deaths had nothing to do with Fayrene and Billy, but perhaps were the result of a story Tyler might have been working on." She bit her lip, instantly realizing she'd made a mistake. "Of course, that's just one possibility. There are certainly many more,'' she said, trying to cover herself.

Big John snorted. ''What kind of story would that boy have been working on that would have made somebody kill him?''

''Maybe he wrote an article about how horrid the food was at the Jeffries gala last month and the caterers retaliated,'' Olivia said. ''Perhaps the knife that killed Fayrene and Tyler was the same one that sliced up fruit in pretty little designs.''

Celia frowned and shoved her dessert away. ''Must we talk about this over our meal? It's been years since we've had a dinner where we've all been together. Can't we talk about something more pleasant?''

For the rest of their time at the table the discussion revolved around neighbors, parties and upcoming social events. Shelby sat quietly, as always fascinated by the dynamics of her family. Her mother deferred to her father, John junior emulated Big John and Olivia entertained, obviously preening each time she drew a smile from her father. For as long as Shelby could remember, the world had revolved around Big John, and that was something that hadn't changed in the years she'd been gone.

Only Michael seemed relatively inured to Big John's presence, and he and Shelby exchanged several warm, supportive looks.

Finally the meal ended and the family members parted for different directions of the house. Shelby went up to her room, wanting to review her notes and work on the case looming ahead.

Before sitting down at the small desk, she walked over to the window and stared out at the thick, dark jungle of the distant swamp. The sun had set and twilight reigned, casting a gloomy cloak over the area. Billy had been raised in the darkness of the swamp, and that darkness had invaded his pores, making it difficult to separate the darkness from the man.

Yet in that single instant of seeing Billy with his son Shelby had realized Billy was more than darkness, had a core of love in his heart that shone through despite his attempts to hide it.

Up until this moment she hadn't been sure of her motives for defending Billy. There had been a small piece of her that hadn't been sure her motives weren't ignoble. There had been a tiny part that wondered if she'd come back to seek revenge against the man who had passionately made love to her, then callously cast her aside.

She no longer worried about that. She intended to defend Billy wholeheartedly, with all the skill and passion she could muster. He deserved nothing less, and she could give nothing less.

She started to turn away from the window, then paused, something catching her attention at the edges of the swamp. A figure walking toward the darkness. Squinting, she cursed the encroaching night as she tried to identify the person. Michael? Or it could be Roger. Both were approximately the same build and both had worn dark slacks and a white shirt at dinner.

The figure disappeared from view and Shelby left the window. Sinking down at the desk, she wondered what on earth either man would be doing entering the swamp as night approached.

SHELBY LOOKED at her watch as she hurried to the courthouse, hoping the appointment with Abe wouldn't last long. She didn't intend to miss Tyler's funeral.

She'd been surprised when Abe had called and asked her to meet him for an early-morning appointment. Her stomach knotted in apprehension as she entered the courthouse and looked for the room where Abe had said he'd meet her. She hoped Abe didn't have more surprises for her where Billy was concerned. She'd had more than enough bomb-shells in this case.

She found the antechamber where Abe had said he'd be, and knocked briskly. A deep, gruff voice bade her enter. Drawing a deep breath, she opened the door to see Abe sitting at a table. "Shelby." Abe stood with the courtliness of a true Southern gentleman and gestured her to the chair opposite the table from his.

"Good morning, Abe." She set her briefcase on the tabletop, then slid into the folding chair and looked at him expectantly, wondering what had prompted his phone call.

"Can I get you a cup of coffee?"

"No, thanks." She looked at her watch again. "I don't have a lot of time this morning. What's up?"

Abe sat back down and leaned back in his chair, his pale eyes gazing at her in bemusement. "I still remember you as a ragamuffin, running the swamp in spite of your parents' admonitions. It's hard to believe you're all grown up and now my adversary."

"We don't have to be on opposite sides. Drop the charges against Billy and find the real killer."

Abe laughed and swept a hand through his thin white hair. "Actually, that's exactly what I wanted to discuss with you."

"You're dropping the charges against Billy?"

"With all the circumstantial evidence against him I'd be a fool to do that. However, since the case is looking so bad for you, I thought you might be interested in a plea bargain. Instead of murder in the first degree . . . man-slaughter."

Shelby restrained her snort of derision. "Why would an innocent man plea-bargain and agree to a charge of manslaughter?"

"We could save the taxpayers a lot of money by agreeing to a plea," he continued.

Shelby's snort escaped. "Since when has saving taxpayers money been a priority of yours?"

He flushed, his features tightening in frustration. "I take it you aren't interested in my offer?"

Shelby stood and grabbed her briefcase. "I'll take it to my client, but I wouldn't hold my breath."

Abe stood as well, a challenging light in his eyes. "I'll destroy both you and Billy in court. I'm one of the best at what I do."

Shelby flashed him a quick smile. "So am I," she retorted, then turned and left the office.

TYLER LAJUNE'S FUNERAL was attended by nearly everyone in the town of Black Bayou. The sun shone brightly and the humidity was as heavy as the grief that etched Jonathon and Laura LaJune's faces.

Billy arrived at the end of the service, standing in the back of the crowd of mourners gathered around the elegant, flower-bedecked casket.

As the minister intoned his eulogy, Shelby worked her way through the throng of people to where he stood. "Is it wise for you to be here?" she asked, aware of the venomous glares he drew from the others.

"Probably not." A muscle ticked in the side of his jaw. "But I have as much right as anyone to mourn the passing of a friend." His eyes darkened. "And God help the person who tries to stop me."

Shelby fought the impulse to touch his arm, offer support, knowing he would rebuke a gesture that implied sympathy or pity. "I heard Fayrene was buried earlier this morning. I would have come had I known."

The muscle in his jaw worked again. "It was well attended by the swamp community, a simple, small ceremony." He shoved his hands in his pockets, seeming unaffected by the hostile frowns he garnered.

Shelby looked around the crowd, recognizing neighbors and townspeople she hadn't seen since coming back to Black Bayou. Was one of them the murderer of Fayrene and Tyler? Was it possible that one of them might be the swamp serpent?

Black Bayou had always been a town of secrets and sins, of prejudice and intolerance. Had Tyler uncovered a secret? Had his quest for a good story led him to his death? Or had the intended victim indeed been Fayrene, as most of the town seemed to believe?

Her gaze lingered on a young woman standing some distance from the rest of the crowd. Obviously pregnant, she displayed strength and pride in her posture despite the tears that ran freely down her face. Shelby moved closer to Billy. "Who's that?" she asked softly, gesturing with a tilt of her head toward the young woman.

"That's Sissy LaJune. Tyler's wife."

"Tyler's wife?" Shelby exclaimed.

"Shh," Billy hissed, and pulled her farther away from the crowd of mourners. "She and Tyler were secretly married months ago. That's where I was going to take you this afternoon. That's where I suspect Tyler's laptop computer is."

Shelby stared at him, shocked by the information she'd just received. Tyler had secretly married? And from the appearance of Sissy, Tyler LaJune had married himself a swamp girl.

The thought opened up a whole new area of speculation. Had his father found out? Had Jonathon LaJune
discovered his son's secret marriage to Sissy and exploded? Or had somebody else killed Tyler because of his
marriage? With each new piece of information that re-
vealed itself, things got more and more complicated.

One thing was certain—if Tyler was married and loved
his wife, there was no way he'd compromise that love by
having a fling with Fayrene. This new information destroyed the prosecution's scenario of an affair between Tyler and Fayrene. A surge of hope filled her at this thought.
Finally she had something substantial to use to poke holes
in the crime-of-passion theory.

The minister conducting the solemn ceremony finally
finished, and Shelby touched Billy's arm. "I don't think it's
a smart idea for you to linger here." She looked to where
the young widow had been standing. She was gone. "Take
me to Sissy's place."

"You can't use this," Billy said when they were in his
truck and headed toward the swamp.

"What do you mean?"

"You can't tell anyone that Tyler and Sissy were married."

Shelby stared at him. "You've got to be kidding. That
information is dynamite. It blows apart the prosecution's
whole case."

Billy shrugged. "Doesn't matter. I served as Tyler's best
man, and I made a promise to keep the ceremony quiet until he was ready to let people know."

"But Tyler's dead," Shelby protested.

Billy cast her a heavy-lidded gaze. "But my word to him
isn't."

Shelby settled back in the seat. "I didn't give my word to
anyone and this information is vital to your case."

Billy didn't answer. He pulled the truck off to the side of the road and parked it, then turned to her. "It's a vital piece of information you won't use because I won't allow it. How long do you think the LaJunes will allow Sissy to keep the baby she's carrying once they discover it is Tyler's? And that's the end of this particular discussion." He opened the truck door. "Come on, we walk from here."

Frustrated, Shelby got out of the truck and slammed the door. Damn him and his particular code of ethics. A promise to a dead man was more important than his defense against a murder charge. Surely she could talk sense into the LaJunes if she decided to use the fact that Tyler was married. She swallowed hard against a lump of doubt. In honesty, she wasn't sure she could talk sense into them. Jonathon LaJune was a difficult man, and she wouldn't be able to live with herself knowing she'd been responsible for Sissy losing her baby to the LaJunes.

They left the gravel road and followed a nearly imperceptible narrow path. "Abe asked to meet with me this morning. He offered us a plea bargain," Shelby said as she followed close behind Billy.

"A plea bargain?" He stopped and turned back to look at her.

She nodded. "He said he'll drop the first-degree charges if you'll cop to manslaughter."

"Not in this lifetime." Once again he started down the path, with Shelby following.

As they walked deeper into the tangled growth the sunlight disappeared, unable to filter through the thick brush and trees around them.

Insects buzzed and clicked a cacophony of sound, a reminder to Shelby that she was an intruder in this world of dark coolness and mystery. She used to pretend that she had been born in the swamp. In her childish fantasies Billy's grandmother had been her mother and the swamp shanty had been her home. There had been a sense of belonging there she hadn't found within the bosom of her own family.

She hurried to catch up with Billy, whose long legs strode with confidence through the thick brush. As they entered the dark heart of the swamp, Shelby's throat tightened convulsively as haunting visions filled her head. What was it? What dreams plagued her? Or were they half memories trying to be retrieved from the bottom of her subconscious?

Her steps faltered and her heart pounded faster, fighting beneath the burden of claustrophobia that tightened her chest. Moonlight on still waters, two figures dancing in the shadows... a grunt followed by a muffled cry... evil in the swamp.

"Shelby? Are you all right?"

She gasped, the visions disappearing as she focused on Billy, his forehead furrowed with concern. "Yes... I'm fine." She swiped a hand across her forehead, realized her skin was sticky with a sheen of perspiration. "Can we rest just a moment?"

He nodded and she leaned against the trunk of a cypress tree, waiting for her breathing to return to normal. But as Billy stepped closer and gently touched a strand of her hair, her heart resumed its frantic beat. Where before it had been the rhythm of fear, this was something different. Evoked by the touch of his fingers, elicited by the intimate nearness of his body next to hers, the heat of desire pumped her blood in hot, heavy waves.

He stood so close to her his scent surrounded her, infused her with its wicked wildness. His fingertips left her hair and trailed down the side of her cheek across the vulnerable hollow of her throat.

She fought the impulse to lean her head back, give him full access so he could place his lips against her flesh. She knew how easy it was to get lost in him, to forget everything but the heat of his touch, the pleasure of his hard-muscled body against her own.

She pushed off the tree and stepped away from him. "How much farther is it to Sissy's?" she asked, wishing her voice didn't sound so breathless.

"Not far." He smiled, the confident smile of a man who knew what his touch did to her, who enjoyed making her heart pound frantically.

She wanted to tell him to stop touching her, stop making love to her with his eyes, but to speak of these things was to acknowledge the power he had over her. It angered her, how his most simple touch made her blood sing, caused her heart to surge in anticipation.

With a softer smile still curving his lips, he held out a hand to her. In that single gesture her anger died and she was once again a frightened girl being led through the darkness of the swamp by Billy Royce.

She placed her hand in his, and as it warmly enfolded hers she knew she would do anything possible, whatever it took, to keep him out of prison.

Within a few minutes they broke into a clearing where a small wooden house had been built on piers, keeping it high above the swamp water below.

Although it was nearly noon, here the dense greenery and trees made it appear to be perpetual twilight. Birds called from a nearby tree, as if signaling their approach.

The front door opened and Sissy stepped out, a figure of pity in her faded navy dress and with her swollen stomach and red-glazed eyes.

"Hi, Billy." Although she spoke to him, her gaze remained on Shelby, curious yet wary.

"Sissy, this is Shelby Longsford, a friend of mine. Can we come up and talk to you for a few minutes?"

The young woman nodded, then disappeared back into the house. Billy and Shelby climbed the stairs and entered the small shack.

Immediately Shelby felt that this was a place where love had dwelled. The walls were lined with pictures. Photos of Tyler as a boy, as a teenager and as a man, images of him and Sissy in various poses, their faces filled with joy and laughter, with love and dreams of a future.

"Please, sit down." Sissy gestured toward the table and offered them a glass of iced tea. As she fixed their drinks, she moved with a fluid grace despite the bulk of her pregnancy. When she'd placed glasses before them both, she joined them at the table. "The funeral was nice, wasn't it? Tyler had so many friends." She caressed her stomach, and Shelby felt an aching sorrow for her.

"Sissy, I'm so sorry for your loss," she said, knowing the words were inadequate, but needing to say them nevertheless.

Sissy nodded, her fair hair falling over her shoulder in a heavy curtain. Again her hand moved across her swollen belly as if to comfort the child within. "We'd made such plans, Tyler and me. He said all he needed to make him happy was me, our baby and his writing." She closed her eyes for a moment, her features radiating a quiet dignity, an inner strength. She opened her eyes and this time looked at Shelby. "We should have known better. Angelique told us it was a mistake, that swamp and town don't mix. That's why Tyler died, 'cause he was with me."

"Sissy, that's not true," Billy said, a gentleness to his tone Shelby had never heard. "Tyler's death had nothing to do with him marrying you. In fact, we think his death might be the result of a story he was working on. Somebody told Shelby that Tyler worked a lot on a laptop computer, but we haven't been able to find it.''

"It's here," Sissy said. "Tyler knew he was going to meet Fayrene at The Edge and he was afraid to take it with him that night. You know that crowd at The Edge is rough. He was afraid somebody would steal it from him.''

"Did he say why he was meeting Fayrene?" Shelby asked.

"He was working on something important and he said Fayrene might have a missing piece of the puzzle . . . that's what he said, but I didn't really understand. Tyler never talked about his story-writing to me." She held her hands out in a gesture of helplessness.

"Sissy, could I borrow Tyler's laptop for a couple of days?" Shelby asked. "I promise I'll bring it back to you, but I think it may be very important in helping us catch Tyler's killer.''

Sissy rose from the table and disappeared into a back room. While they waited for her return, Shelby looked around with interest. Though small, the place was meticulously clean. Curtains hung at the window, hand stitched with lace trim. A vase of wildflowers brightened the end table and stood next to a book of Shakespeare's sonnets.

Shelby wondered if Tyler had read the sonnets to his wife in the quiet of the night, with the rhythm of the swamp surrounding their home. Her heart ached for Sissy, who would now rock her fatherless child alone, with only the rhythm of the swamp as company. She realized there was no way she could use the information about Tyler and Sissy. She couldn't risk hurting Sissy.

"You can keep it as long as you want," Sissy said as she reentered the room, the laptop in hand. "I don't know much about computers, so there's no hurry.''

Shelby cradled the laptop, aware that it might hold the key to Tyler's murder and Billy's redemption. "You going to be all right?" Billy asked Sissy.

She nodded, a sad, resigned smile curving her lips. "You know me, Billy. I'm a survivor." She sighed, and tears sparkled on her long lashes. "I just wish Tyler hadn't wanted to wait till the baby was born to tell his parents about us. Now it's too late . . . too late for all of us."

Moments later, as she and Billy walked back to his truck, Shelby asked, "What's going to happen to her?"

"She'll be all right. The swamp takes care of its own."

"How did Tyler and Sissy meet?"

"Tyler never told me." Billy paused to hold a low-lying branch out of Shelby's way. "I just know he came to me one night and asked me if I'd be his best man at his wedding. I'd never seen Tyler so happy. He'd dated around quite a bit but never seemed to make a real connection with anyone until Sissy." For a moment he looked almost wistful. "Seeing Tyler and Sissy together you couldn't help but know they were meant for each other . . . soul mates." He frowned, as if irritated with himself, then turned and walked on.

Shelby followed more slowly, wondering if Billy truly believed in the concept of soul mates. Had he once thought Fayrene was his? Or was he still seeking the woman who would bond to him heart and soul?

She shoved these thoughts aside, cradling the laptop closer to her chest. She had to remain focused on her job as his lawyer; otherwise he'd be seeking a soul mate in prison.

By the time they got back to Billy's truck, Shelby couldn't contain her curiosity any longer. "If the battery is charged, I should be able to boot this up right now," she said as Billy started the truck.

Punching the power button, she felt her excitement grow as the motor whirred and the miniature screen lit up. She quickly scanned the list of files, unsure what she sought, but somehow believing she'd know it when she saw it. File names flew by, none of them ringing a bell of premonition. Then there it was. The file was marked simply Serpent.

She called up the file, unmindful of the bumps and jolts of the truck, her attention completely riveted to the machine in her lap. Notes. The file contained pages of notes on the swamp serpent murders. "This is it. This has to be it."

"What?" Billy slowed the truck, his attention obviously torn between driving and the computer.

"Tyler was working on the swamp serpent murders. He's got page after page of notes in here. Police reports, newspaper accounts, interviews with surviving family members..."

"That explains how he met Sissy. A couple of years ago her older brother was a victim of the swamp serpent."

"That poor girl," Shelby said softly, then refocused her attention on the screen. Scanning quickly, she went through page after page of information, amazed at the mass of material Tyler had compiled.

She leaned back against the seat and stared at Billy, suddenly overwhelmed by the daunting task ahead of them. "Billy, do you realize what this means? If what I suspect is true, then we're no longer only looking for who killed Fayrene and Tyler. We're looking for the swamp serpent."

Billy sighed, but didn't speak. Shelby looked back at the computer screen. Her fingers tingled as she paged down and across the top of the screen flashed the words *Potential Suspects*.

Chapter Twelve

Potential Suspects. The words shimmered, luminescent against the computer screen's dark background. Shelby drew in a deep breath and read the first name. Malcolm Waylon. She vaguely remembered him, the weasel-faced pharmacist whose only son had been badly hurt in a bar fight when a group of town kids had jumped a gang of swamp kids. His name was followed by several others she didn't recognize, but she gasped as she found another name she did know.

"What?" Billy asked, apparently responding to her gasp of surprise.

"Tyler made a list of potential suspects...people he thought might be the swamp serpent. My God, Billy, his father is listed here as a potential perpetrator. Tyler suspected his own father."

"Jonathon LaJune has never been particularly secretive in his prejudices toward the swamp community," Billy replied. "Tyler was too good a newspaper man to let his heart rule his list of suspects."

Shelby nodded and looked back at the list. More people she didn't know or barely remembered from her childhood. As she reached the last three names, her blood turned frigid. Impossible. The word reverberated in her head. Absolutely impossible.

She closed her eyes and rubbed her forehead, as if in doing so she could obliterate the names shining on the screen. But even with her eyes closed she could see them in her mind. Roger Eaton. Michael Longsford. Big John Longsford.

"My God, Tyler even suspected my father," she said faintly. "And Michael and Roger." She shut off the computer, overwhelmed by Tyler's suspicions and speculation. She drew in a deep breath. "Well, that's obviously ridiculous. Tyler was really reaching to include my family."

"Was he?" Billy pulled the truck to a stop next to her car in the cemetery parking area. He shut off the motor, then turned to look at her. "Shelby, the members of your family, like Jonathon LaJune, have never been particularly quiet in their distaste for the swamp and its people. Your house is the closest to the swamp and the murder scenes."

"Yes, but it's one thing to be prejudiced, it's another to be a crazed murderer," Shelby exclaimed. She rubbed her forehead once again, the heat of the day and the jumble of her brain producing the beginning of a tension headache.

"Don't make the mistake of assuming the swamp serpent is crazy. This is a murderer who has killed a lot of people over a long period of time without leaving behind any clues or evidence. This is not a nut. The swamp serpent is a shrewd, cunning killer."

Shelby forced a rueful smile. "Then certainly that lets out the members of my family. I don't consider any of them particularly shrewd or cunning."

Billy reached out and gently touched her cheek. The pads of his fingertips weren't soft and yet the touch was pleasant, too pleasant. "I'm sorry I dragged you back here, into this mess. I should have left you alone, let you keep living the good life in Shreveport.''

She shook her head, both glad and disappointed when his hand dropped back to the steering wheel. ''No, I'm glad I came back. It was time. The years in Shreveport were just an interlude, like an extended vacation. But my home is here, my heart is here and I'm going to stay no matter what happens.''

Billy's gaze remained dark, enigmatic. ''This could get very difficult, Shelby. As you just stated, Tyler had members of your own family listed as potential suspects in the swamp murders.'' His features remained inscrutable. ''I wonder what you'll do if in order to save me you have to sacrifice one of your own family members?''

''That's not going to happen,'' Shelby stated firmly. ''The swamp serpent might be many things, but it's not a Longsford, by blood or by marriage. My family may be dysfunctional, prejudiced and riddled with faults, but we are not monsters.''

Billy smiled at her, a gentle expression that caused a twist of her heart. ''Shelby, monsters come in all shapes and sizes.'' His smile fell away and in his eyes she saw the haunting of monsters past and present. ''Sometimes they hide within the people we love.''

Shelby suddenly remembered the stories she'd heard about Billy...stories about his father killing his mother, then hanging himself from a tree deep in the heart of the swamp. She had never known for sure if the stories were true, had at one time dismissed them as dark fantasies and more swamp myths, but now she wasn't so sure.

''I've got to go,'' he said, breaking their locked gaze by looking at his wristwatch. ''I promised Parker we'd spend some time together this afternoon.''

"And I want to thoroughly read through the material on this computer. If Tyler was killed because he got too close to the swamp serpent, I need to know what he knew." She started to get out of the truck but was stopped when Billy's hand closed around her arm.

"Shelby, whatever you learn from that computer, you bring the information to me. We're in this together and there's no such thing as heroics."

"Of course," she said automatically, but still his hand held her in place.

"And don't share the information with anyone else . . . especially the members of your family."

She hesitated a moment, remembering that she'd already said far too much to her family. She nodded. He released his hold on her and she got out of the truck. He watched as she got into the car, her dark hair sparkling in the afternoon sunshine. Even in funeral black she looked good.

As she drove out of the cemetery, Billy slumped in the seat, exhausted by the events of the past several days. The murders, his arrest, now the link from Tyler to the swamp serpent all swirled around in his head, and beneath it all a simmering passion for Shelby demanded to be acknowledged.

He hadn't been surprised by the revelation that Tyler had suspected members of the Longsford family. It made sense. The Longsford mansion was close to the swamp and the family had always harbored vehement intolerance toward the people who lived in the nearby marsh. It wouldn't surprise him if the swamp serpent was one of the Longsfords, although it wouldn't surprise him if the murderer was one of the other suspects on Tyler's list, either.

Black Bayou seethed with secrets and sins, both past and present. It was a community built on bigotry and steeped in the tradition of hate. Tyler had been one of the few jewels among the grit of gravel. He'd overcome his privileged background, his breeding and had accepted each person on their own merits, no matter where they'd come from. He'd accepted Billy, first as a boyhood friend, then man to man.

Billy's chest ached at thoughts of his friend. When Tyler was killed, something shining had left Billy's life. Tyler had filled Billy with hope, made him believe in dreams. And when Tyler had fallen in love with and married Sissy, he'd made Billy realize anything was possible.

Billy smiled, remembering Tyler's joy when he'd told Billy that Sissy was pregnant. "I know it's going to be a boy," Tyler had said as he'd paced the floor of Billy's shanty. "When he's born, Dad will forgive me for marrying Sissy. Surely he won't care where she came from, only that she makes me happy and that our son is a LaJune."

They had celebrated long into the night, two friends, brothers despite their parentage and backgrounds. And now Tyler was gone. And buried with him was Billy's hope that things would ever change between the people of Black Bayou and the people of the swamp.

He started his truck and drove out of the cemetery, shoving away thoughts of Tyler. And as always when he consciously emptied his head, thoughts of Shelby filled it.

All those years ago when she'd first left Black Bayou, he'd hated her. First for running away rather than facing him again, but mostly because she was the only one in the world who had seen him weak, seen him completely out of control, his emotions raw and aching with Mama Royce's death.

Over the years he'd rarely allowed thoughts of that single night of love to haunt him. It was a night that should never have happened, a night that had just briefly allowed him to forget who he was and where he was from.

With Mama Royce dead, Fayrene, Tyler...Billy couldn't afford to care anymore. Other than Parker, he couldn't let his heart ever be vulnerable again. He could desire Shelby, he could want to possess her physically, but he could never afford to love her.

Besides, if he found out that one of the Longsfords had killed Tyler, was the culprit responsible for the murders, and for the grief of the swamp community, Billy wasn't sure what he would do. His hands tightened on the steering wheel as he wondered what Shelby would think of him if he avenged Tyler's death by killing one of her own.

SHELBY STOOD at the window in her room, her head reeling with information from Tyler's computer. She'd read through only half the files, but enough to fill her head with gruesome murder facts for a lifetime of nightmares. Tyler had documented information on fifteen murders, beginning the year Shelby had left Black Bayou. Fifteen murders in twelve years. Fifteen people viciously stabbed to death. Fifteen lives lost forever. If Fayrene and Tyler were counted into that, the number of victims rose to seventeen.

Without anything more to go on than gut instinct, Shelby knew the information she had in her possession was what had gotten Tyler killed. If it had been a crime of passion, it had been the passionate survival instincts of a madman. A madman she had to find if she wanted to save Billy.

She turned and looked back at the computer on her desk, the screen glowing eerily in the waning daylight of the room. She hadn't read anything other than Tyler's reports of each of the murders. She had consciously stayed away from the page that listed his potential suspects, but the names she'd seen briefly while in the truck still burned in her brain.

How could Tyler suspect any of the members of her family? It was crazy...ridiculous. The Longsfords might have plenty of faults, but the idea that any of them might be crazed killers was preposterous.

Turning away from the window, she rubbed her forehead. The headache that had begun in Billy's truck hadn't abated, but had instead grown more persistent. Time to call it a night, she thought. She punched off the computer and turned on her bedside lamp. Even though it was relatively early, she'd go to bed and read for a little while then hopefully drift off into a dreamless sleep and start fresh in the morning.

It took her only minutes to peel off her clothes and pull on a cotton nightgown. She pulled down the blankets on the bed and slid beneath the covers. A scream clawed at her throat and escaped as her foot encountered something alien.

She jumped out of bed at the same time Olivia burst through her doorway. "Shelby. I heard you scream. What are you trying to do, raise the dead?"

"There's something in my bed." Shelby yanked down the covers and there, looking grotesque against the pristine sheets, was a bouquet of dead flowers. "What on earth?" Shelby picked it up, repelled yet perversely fascinated by the blackened, withered nosegay.

"Oh, Shelby, what on earth?" Olivia's eyes were round with fear. Gone was Olivia's usual arrogance, hidden beneath a veil of terror that instantly permeated Shelby, as well.

"Why would somebody do this? What is this supposed to mean?" Shelby stared first at her sister, then back at the bouquet.

"It's obviously a threat," Olivia said, visibly shuddering. "Put it away someplace. It gives me the creeps."

Shelby opened a dresser drawer and dropped the flowers inside, then sank onto the edge of the bed. "Who on earth would put something like that in my bed?"

Olivia sat down next to her. "I don't know, but you must have made somebody very angry."

"I've been back home less than a week and already I've been shot at and received a bouquet of dead flowers."

"You're stirring things up, Shelby. You should have just let Billy go to prison and left things alone."

"But he's not guilty," Shelby exclaimed. "And what's more, we believe that whoever killed Tyler and Fayrene is probably the swamp serpent, as well." Shelby bit her bottom lip, realizing she had done exactly what Billy hadn't wanted her to. But she had to make Olivia understand that Billy wasn't guilty, that this was much bigger than the murder of two people. "And please don't repeat that to anyone," she added.

Olivia stared at her in disbelief. "But what makes you think Tyler's and Fayrene's murders are in any way tied to the swamp serpent murders?"

Shelby waved her hands, unwilling to expand further on her mistake. "Never mind, it's just a theory we're working on."

Olivia cast her an amused gaze. "Sounds to me like a legal eagle grasping at straws to save a doomed client."

"Do you really believe Billy is guilty?" Shelby asked.

Olivia smiled. "My dear sister, in this town anything is possible."

"Speaking of endless possibilities, I have to confess I was surprised when I heard you'd married Roger."

"What surprised you more?" Olivia stretched out on the bed like a sleek kitten. "The fact that he's so much older than me, or the fact that he's an incredible bore?"

Shelby laughed, as always half amused, half appalled by her sister's irreverent honesty and slight naughtiness. "I was just surprised, that's all." She studied her sister thoughtfully. "Do you love him?"

"What's love got to do with marriage? I married Roger for lots of reasons, but love wasn't one of them." One of Olivia's finely penciled dark brows rose upward. "Oh, honestly, Shelby, I can see by your expression that you're one of those hopeless romantics who think marriage is some sort of legal soul-bonding between lovers." She laughed, a harsh, cynical sound. "You don't really believe Mother and Father have remained together all these years because they love each other, do you?"

She laughed again and looked at Shelby pityingly. "Good marriages are built on needs. Daddy had new money but no background. Mother knew politically he would go places, but he needed the cushion of her breeding and the good name of the St. Clairs behind him. Roger will probably someday be governor of this state, but he can't do it without the Longsford political machine supporting him." She pulled a slender hand through her sleek, shorn hair and smiled at Shelby. "I intend to be the sexiest governor's wife this state has ever known. Even Big John will be proud if we make it to the governor's mansion."

"There are people who marry for love," Shelby observed.

"Only fools." Olivia got up off the bed and sauntered toward the doorway. "So, what are your plans for getting Billy off the hook?"

Shelby shrugged. "If I intend to catch the killer, then I'm going to have to retrace Tyler's steps, talk to the people he spoke with, go to the places he went while searching for the story."

"Just be careful that in following Tyler's footsteps you don't wind up a companion in his grave." With these words, Olivia turned and left the room.

FOR THE NEXT TWO DAYS Shelby scarcely left her bedroom. Hours upon hours were spent reading, assessing and reassessing Tyler's notes and files on his computer. She took her meals in her room and slept in erratic spurts, completely absorbed in pulling together a defense for Billy, a defense built on reasonable doubt.

The list of suspects haunted her. Ten names, three of which were members of her family. Tyler had also discovered that four of the people on the list had airtight alibis for many of the murders. That left six people, three Longsfords and three others, as the most viable suspects.

Finally, with dusk falling on yet another day, she shut off the computer and stretched with arms over her head. Her back ached and her eyes burned from the long hours of reading the computer screen. Physically she was drained, but mentally she was disturbed by the information Tyler had compiled. The more she had read, the more she realized why Tyler had placed Roger, Michael and Big John's names on his list.

The murders had several things in common. First and foremost, none of the victims had shown signs of any struggle, implying that they knew their assailant. Everyone knew Big John, and Michael often ministered to the people in the swamp. Even Roger would be known to the victims. And she couldn't forget the night she had seen somebody go from the house into the swamp. Who had it been? And what had they been doing? Granted, no murder had taken place that night, but why would any member of her family venture into the swamp at night?

"Enough," she said aloud, knowing what she needed was a break from thinking about it all. Something about what she'd read in Tyler's notes bothered her, like the socket where a missing tooth should be. She knew the only way to bring whatever it was into focus was to get some distance from the whole mess.

As was usual in the late evenings, when she walked down the stairs the house was quiet. For as long as Shelby could remember the members of her family had sought separate spaces after the evening meal. It was as if the act of sitting together for supper created a suffocating need for privacy.

She found Roger in the library, sitting in one of the easy chairs, a book open in his lap. She waved as she passed the door. What she didn't need was to be cooped up in a room with her pompous brother-in-law. Instead she headed for the door in the kitchen that led to a back porch facing the swamp.

The outside air was heavy, humid and thick with pungent scents. Although it was still light, a half-moon was visible, peeking over the tops of the cypress trees as if waiting the sun's departure.

Shelby leaned against one of the wooden pillars, breathing deeply of the fragrant air. Shreveport had smelled much the same way, of mimosa and magnolias, and fresh grass and sweet mint. The difference was that here the scents were mixed with the ever-present smell of the swamp, of wildness and mystery, of shady cool and algae ponds. Shreveport had smelled Southern. This smelled like home.

A sound coming from the end of the porch drew Shelby's attention. She was surprised to see her father sitting on one of the wicker chairs, his gaze focused on the swamp. It was obvious he hadn't heard her step out of the house, apparent that his attention was absorbed in the dark, tangled growth in the distance.

For a long moment Shelby didn't move, but took the opportunity to study the man who had sired her. Did she love her father? It was difficult to sort out her snarled emotions where he was concerned. When she was younger he'd frightened her, with his booming voice and piercing eyes. She could still remember her childish need to please him, to gain a smile from him, a kind word of praise. She no longer feared him, nor did she feel the need to please him, and it saddened her that she felt so little connection to him.

She stirred as disconcerting thoughts filtered through her head. What was he doing out here in dusk's glory staring at the swamp? His face was devoid of expression, making it impossible to guess his thoughts. Was he simply observing the beauty of the moon rising over the cypress trees or was he planning somebody's murder?

She shivered, the motion drawing her father's attention. "Shelby." He stood and walked over to stand next to her. "You've been pretty scarce around here the last couple of days."

"I've been busy working on the case."

Big John grunted, as if to express his disapproval of the entire mess. "Why in the hell did you ever decide to be a defense lawyer? With my connections I could have seen to it that you were district attorney."

Shelby shrugged and tensed, a remnant childlike reaction to her father as she fought against a lingering need to please him. "I decided to do something I believe in rather than please my father." She raised her chin and met his gaze.

Big John laughed, and she felt herself start to relax. "You always had your own mind, I'll grant you that." He looked at her with an expression remarkably akin to respect. "I think you're the only one who realized all along that my bark is worse than my bite."

Shelby smiled. "Your bark has always been frightening enough. However, I'm just doing what you taught us all to do, stick with our convictions and be the best that we can."

"Yes, but you were supposed to stick to my convictions, not develop your own."

Shelby was surprised to see a twinkle of humor in his eyes. Her heart twisted as she realized this was a side of her father she'd never seen before, a self-denigration and sense of humor he rarely displayed.

"Your sister tells me somebody put dead flowers in your room," he said, the twinkle gone, his expression somber once again.

"Yes, although I have to admit, I haven't lost much sleep over it. I have enough to worry about without being concerned about somebody's sick joke. The only thing that bothers me is how it got into my room."

"Huh, it's probably Angelique's doing. She's got long arms and wields a lot of power. Most likely she got one of our maids to put it there."

Shelby looked at her father in surprise. "You know Angelique?"

"Mostly through reputation." Once again Big John's gaze drifted back to the swamp, and Shelby could have sworn a flash of wistfulness crossed his features before he turned back to her. "I knew her sister, Marguerite. She worked over at Martha's restaurant, a cute little lady with big eyes and a spitfire temper. She died years ago at the hands of the swamp serpent." His face and voice were expressionless. He turned back to look at the swamp one last time, then, murmuring good-night, he went into the house.

Alone on the porch, Shelby sank onto one of the wooden steps and drew in a deep, cleansing breath. What had Marguerite meant to her father? She frowned, remembering Michael speaking about Big John's affairs. Had Marguerite been lover or victim? Was Big John guilty of infidelity or murder?

Shelby stared at the swamp, where night now reigned and no remnant of the day lingered. The moon was brilliant, fully risen and casting eerie silvery strands of light dancing on the tops of the trees. She remained seated for a long time, playing over her conversation with her father, mulling over Tyler's computer notes.

Marguerite Boujoulais. The name was familiar from the files Shelby had been reading for the past two days. The young woman had been the second victim of the swamp serpent. As with the other victims, she'd been stabbed twice, once in the stomach and again in the chest.

The first victim had been Layne Rocharee, a forty-six-year-old man whose body had been found on May 13, a week after Shelby had left Black Bayou so many years before.

Two figures dancing in the moonlight…indistinct voices, a cry of pain. She closed her eyes and rubbed her temples as images continued to flicker in her mind. Moonlight through trees, reflecting off a nearby pool. Then a sole silhouette lying in the light of the moon. Blood in the water. Death in the swamp.

"Oh, no." Shelby shot up off the step, a chill rocketing up her spine and setting the hairs at her nape on end.

Layne Rocharee's body had been found on May 13, but the official report stated he'd been dead at least three or four days.

Shelby knew exactly when he had been killed. It had been on the night of May 6, the night Mama Royce had died of a heart attack, the same night Shelby had made love with Billy Royce. She had to tell Billy.

Without pause, she took off running toward the swamp. She had to tell Billy what she now knew. That's what she'd seen in the swamp. The flashes of images weren't nightmares. They were pieces of memories...memories of murder.

Chapter Thirteen

Shelby ran like the wind, her thoughts as tangled as the vegetation around her. Memories pressed heavily, a jumble of images and sensory details she'd forgotten or repressed until this moment.

With her nightmares so close to the surface, the swamp suddenly seemed alien and malevolent. Spanish moss, instead of draping from the trees, attempted to shroud her in its cobweb finery. Vines normally curled lovingly around the base of trees now reached out tendrils of green to trip her, impede her as she raced to Billy.

Evil...evil in the swamp. The very air around her seethed with it. The cloying scent of foliage rot and a distant memory of the coppery smell of blood filled her head. Evil in the swamp—her heart pounded the rhythm of the words. She'd seen the evil, had been an innocent voyeur to madness and murder. As Billy's shanty came into view, a beam of light slicing through the surrounding darkness, Shelby increased her pace and cried out his name.

Her footsteps echoed as she raced across the wooden walkway that led to his front door. As she reached the door it flew open and Billy stepped out, catching her as she catapulted into his arms.

"Shelby, what's wrong? What is it?" His voice rang low, urgent as he held her against his bare chest.

For a moment she didn't answer. She wanted to hide in the warmth of his skin, pull him over her and use him as a shield against her thoughts. Wasn't that the same thing she had done years ago? Pulled him over her and hidden in him?

Drawing in a deep breath, she stepped out of his embrace and leaned against the wooden railing. She stared into the murky swamp waters below. "I saw a swamp murder. The night that Mama Royce died I saw the swamp serpent murder Layne Rocharee."

She heard Billy's swift intake of breath, felt his presence as he moved to stand directly behind her. Around them the swamp seemed to grow and swell with a life of its own, as if the evil of murder had animated it with energy.

"Are you sure?"

Shelby shivered despite the sweltering heat of the night air. Turning around, she rolled his question around in her head. Was she sure? All she had were pieces, fragments of a nightmare that had haunted her for years. "No...yes...I don't know."

"Come inside." He touched her arm. "It's cooler there and it sounds like you need to talk."

She followed him into the shanty, where the ceiling fan stirred the air but offered only a small measure of relief against the outside heat. "How about something cold to drink?" he asked as she sank onto the sofa. He opened the refrigerator and peered inside. "I've got colas, iced tea and grape soda." He flashed her a quicksilver smile. "Although I usually save the grape for one of Gator's visits."

"A cola is fine."

"Can or over ice?"

"Can is fine," she said, knowing the mundane conversation was his effort to give her an opportunity to calm down. She drew in several deep breaths as Billy joined her on the sofa and handed her the drink.

She closed her eyes and rolled the can across her forehead, the cold aluminum a welcome relief against her fevered brow. She jumped as the can was pulled from her hands. As she opened her eyes Billy popped the top and handed it back to her. "Take a drink, then talk," he said, his eyes darker than she'd ever seen them.

Dutifully she took a sip of the soda, then set the can on the coffee table before them. Before speaking, she glanced over to Parker's bedroom door. "Is Parker asleep?" she asked, not wanting to talk of murder and mayhem where a child might be able to hear.

Billy shook his head. "He's not here. He sometimes spends the night with Angelique and her son."

"Speaking of Angelique, do you know any reason why she might want to frighten me?" Shelby felt ridiculous even asking the question.

"Frighten you?" Billy's eyebrows danced upward.

Shelby flushed and picked up the soda can once again. "I found a dead floral bouquet in my bed the other night. I'm assuming it was supposed to be some kind of a threat."

Billy frowned. "I can't imagine why Angelique would do something like that. She doesn't even know you, does she?" Shelby shook her head. "But that's not why you're here," he reminded her.

"You're right. That's not why I'm here." Shelby took another sip of the soda, knowing she was stalling, not wanting to dredge up the horrors her memory held. Once again she placed the can on the coffee table, her hand trembling slightly as she focused on the memories that had brought her here.

"For years after I left Black Bayou, I had nightmares...strange nightmares of the swamp. It was always the same dream. I'm walking through the swamp and something draws my attention." She slumped deeper into the couch cushions, mentally reaching out to capture the nightmare that had haunted her on so many nights.

"Tell me, Shelby," Billy said. He reached out and took her hand in his. Once again, as in the days of years past, with her hand in his she felt safe...able to face whatever horrors the swamp and her mind held.

"It's all confused in my head." She closed her eyes, trying to pull into focus images she'd consciously kept at bay for years. "The moon is almost full, and I see two silhouettes in a small clearing. Voices murmur. Something glints in the moonlight. The two dance and one falls to the ground." Shelby's chest tightened and she squeezed Billy's hand. "Blood on the water. Evil in the swamp." She gasped and opened her eyes. "I thought it was just a nightmare, but I don't think it is. I think...I'm afraid it's a memory. Dear God, I saw...I saw."

"Shh." He released his hold on her hand and used his thumbs to softly swipe away the tears she didn't even know were falling. He pulled her against his chest, and willingly she went, needing his warmth, craving the security of his arms around her. "Let's see if we can sort out the memory and separate it from the nightmare. Tell me everything you can of that night, beginning with dinner that evening."

As Billy stroked her hair, Shelby reached back into the past, dredging up the memories of a night she'd spent half a lifetime trying to forget. "Dinner was traumatic. Big John was on a tear, angry with all of us kids for crazy reasons, yelling at mother as if all the world's faults were hers. By the time dessert was served, I felt sick to my stomach. The tension was too much and I asked to be excused. I went up to my room and stretched out on the bed.''

She frowned, trying to remember everything, every moment of that night. "I guess I must have dozed off because the next thing I remember is it being dark and me wanting to talk to Mama Royce.''

Shelby's thoughts jumped ahead to what had happened between her and Billy that night. As their lovemaking unfolded in her mind, she suddenly found the caress of his hand through her hair too evocative, too breathtaking. Moving away from him, she stood and tried to focus on those moments before she'd reached Mama Royce's shanty, the minutes preceding the explosion of passion between them.

"The house was quiet. I didn't see anyone as I slipped out the back door and ran toward the swamp." She paced back and forth before Billy, her sandals slapping hollowly against the wooden floor. "I hadn't walked very far when I heard something and saw the two people." She frowned and paused in her movement. "I saw the moon glint off the metal of a knife, and one person stabbed the other." She closed her eyes, trying to separate nightmares from reality. "I—I must have passed out or blacked out or something because the next thing I remember is the moon having moved in the sky and only one figure lying on the swamp floor. I could see his face in the moonlight . . . still and frozen in a death mask.''

"Then what did you do?" Billy's voice made her jump and open her eyes. For a moment she'd forgotten his presence, forgotten everything but that moment in the swamp when she'd seen the man lying on the ground, the front of his shirt soaked in blood. "I . . . I ran home. Mama was on the porch, drunk. I tried to tell her what had happened but she was out of it." Shelby winced, remembering the gin on her mother's breath, the drunken wildness in her eyes. "And then she told me Mama Royce was dead. I didn't believe her. I ran here. And you were here and we..." Her voice trailed off and she averted her gaze from him. She wasn't sure which was more traumatic, remembering the murder or the power of Billy as he'd made love to her. Each memory had haunted her in its own way.

"Shelby." Billy stood and approached her, stopping when he was so close she could see the gold flecks in the irises of his eyes. "If you were close enough to see the man who was murdered, you were close enough to see the murderer. Think, Shelby. Who was it? Who did you see that night in the swamp?"

"I...can't...I don't remember." Her body trembled, her heart feeling as if it might explode at any moment. She gasped as Billy grabbed her by the shoulders, his fingers biting into her skin.

"Damn it, try harder," he roared, his eyes flaming with anger as his fingers pressed harder.

Tears sprang to Shelby's eyes and with a muttered oath Billy pulled her into his arms. "I'm sorry," he whispered into her hair. "I didn't mean to lose my temper. I'm sorry. It's just so frustrating." He stroked her hair, her back, his touch not sensual but rather an effort to comfort.

Slowly Shelby's sobs subsided, leaving her exhausted and wrung out. Willingly she allowed Billy to lead her back to the sofa, where they sank down with her still in his arms. The only sound in the room was the whisper of the ceiling fan, the muted chorus of the insects outside and the beat of Billy's heart against Shelby's cheek.

She didn't want to think anymore, was exhausted by the effort to remember something buried deep in her subconscious. She simply wanted Billy to continue to hold her. She felt safe in his arms.

His skin smelled of wildness, of sweet clean winds and hot endless nights. Shelby fought a sudden, crazy impulse to flick out her tongue and taste him, lick his chest and swallow the flavor of him. For years the events of that night so long ago had melded together in her head, making it difficult for her to separate the emotional shock of seeing a murder and the momentous event of making love to Billy.

Now, with the two events separated in her mind, she was able to remember the splendor of Billy taking her, possessing her, and she realized he'd been right when he'd said he would have her again. She wanted him again, somehow felt she needed to make love with him again and bring things full circle.

Only this time she wouldn't be a starry-eyed youth expecting love forever more. She was a grown woman, willing to accept that she wanted Billy, desired him on a physical level, needed to make love to him one last time to banish the power of the memories of that first time.

Her hands knew the way of her mind and slid across the broad expanse of his chest. At the same time she pressed her lips against his skin, giving in to her need to taste him. She felt his immediate response, a tightening of his muscles as the pace of his heartbeat accelerated.

"Shelby." It was a warning, his voice low and husky.

She knew he was giving her a chance to think ... to stop what she was starting. She didn't want to stop. Again she moved her lips against his bronzed chest, tasting the slight saltiness of his skin.

"Shelby." This time it wasn't a warning, but rather a whispered, deep-throated moan. His hands, which moments before had been caressing to comfort, now moved differently—slower, languid and sensual.

She raised her head, her gaze meeting his, wondering if her eyes reflected the same kind of want, of need that his did. She'd thought it impossible that she'd ever want to make love to him again. Now she realized it was impossible not to. He'd been under her skin for twelve long years, like a chigger burrowing deeper and deeper. Surely as a woman making love to Billy she could finally put the act, the passion in its proper perspective rather than building it to bigger-than-life proportions as she had so many years before.

His eyes flamed into hers, smoldering promises of passion as his lips descended to claim hers in a kiss of fire. It was not a kiss to tantalize or cajole, but rather one to possess and consume.

Shelby returned the kiss fully, this time not afraid of his hunger but rather reveling in it, a responding hunger throbbing inside her. As the kiss ended, once again her gaze sought his. "Billy, make love to me," she said softly. It was important that this be her decision, a conscious choice, rather than an uncontrollable explosion as it had been before, where she felt she'd had no will.

If possible, his eyes appeared to darken at her request. "Are you sure, Shelby?" He trailed a finger down her cheek, following the curve of her jaw. "From what you've told me about the night of Mama Royce's death, you came here seeking comfort and instead got me. You came here tonight to share your memories with me. I don't want you to be confused about what you want. What we did years ago was a mistake, two kids lost in their grief reaching out to each other in a way neither of us knew how to handle. I don't want this to be a mistake."

Shelby frowned, knowing he was right. Making love to him years ago had been a mistake, an experience neither of them had anticipated or completely understood. She'd come to him then, needing him to banish her fear, bury her memories of something heinous. But now the horror was separate from the desire and she knew exactly what she wanted. "Billy, it's not a mistake."

Eyes still darkened, features unreadable, he stood. "Not here," he said, and bent over and scooped her up in his arms. "I want you in my room. I told you the next time I have you will be in my bed."

Heat suffused her as she wrapped her arms around him and pressed her lips against the shadowed hollow of his neck. There was a sense of rightness, an inevitability, as if in her heart she had known from the moment she'd heard his voice on her phone that this was what was destined to happen between them.

In all the years she'd visited the shanty, she'd never been in Billy's room. It had been his private space, a sanctuary even Mama Royce had respected. As he carried her across the threshold, she had a vague impression of stark masculinity. Like Parker's room, this one held a dresser and a bed, only the bed was a double one covered in navy blue sheets. A low-wattage lamp sat on the nightstand, the glow softening the starkness of the room. A four-blade ceiling fan stirred the warm air.

As he placed her in the center of the bed, she realized the sheets smelled of him, the wonderful, mysterious scent she found so intoxicating. He didn't join her, but rather stood at the side of the bed, his gaze as potent as a caress.

"Billy?" She raised her arms toward him, beckoning him to come to her.

He shook his head. "Just let me look at you for a minute," he said, his voice deep, husky with desire.

Shelby had never known the power of a gaze, but as Billy's lingered on her, she felt her body responding. Muscles weakened, nerves tingled and heat coiled within her.

"Shelby, you are so beautiful." He leaned over and touched her lips with his. This kiss was different than any she'd shared with him before. Soft and tender, his lips made love to hers, and when he finished with her mouth, he moved to her ear, then down her jawline, evoking fire where he touched.

As his mouth caressed her, his fingers worked the buttons on her blouse, stopping only when the last one had been unfastened. At that moment Shelby realized there would be no violent eruption of passion this time. He intended to take the time to seduce her slowly... completely. This thought sent a shiver of anticipation rippling through her.

It seemed it took him forever to remove her clothing. Each inch of skin that was bared immediately was covered by his mouth and hands. By the time he removed his jeans and joined her on the bed, Shelby was at a fever pitch. Never had she felt so alive. Never had she wanted a man more. But when he moved to position himself above her, she shook her head and pushed him aside. "Not yet," she said, wanting to kiss him, caress him, drive him insane as he had just done to her.

Shelby pushed him down on his back, then explored his body in awe. Sleek muscle beneath warm skin, a broad chest covered with soft hair, his strength and masculinity sent her own desire winging higher as she touched, caressed and kissed him.

With a low, deep groan, he rolled her over on her back, hovering above her for a single second before sinking slowly into her. Shelby wrapped her legs around him, wanting to keep him locked inside her forever. Tears filled her eyes as she felt his heart beating the same frantic rhythm as her own. As he moved against her, her breaths quickened, matching his as he took her spiraling out of control.

Afterward they sprawled side by side on the bed, the ceiling fan cooling their heated bodies as their breathing slowly returned to normal.

"If you say I told you so, I'll slap you," Shelby said, turning on her side to gaze at him.

His lips curled up in a sexy smile that sent a shiver of delight dancing through her. "I won't say I told you so because I wasn't sure this would happen again."

She propped herself up on her elbow and stared at him in surprise. "You certainly acted sure. In fact, you were quite arrogant on the subject."

His grin widened. "Ah, there you go again, Shelby, turning my head with all your sweet talk."

"That's one thing different this time from the last time," she said thoughtfully.

His smile fell away. "What?"

"This time I won't make the mistake of confusing sex and love." For just a moment Shelby felt a swift arrow through her heart as she remembered the innocent she had been when she and Billy had first made love.

Billy reached out and caressed her face then cupped her chin with his hand. "I didn't handle things very well that night." He remembered at the time he had needed to distance himself from her, make her understand he could never be anything in her life.

She was a Longsford and he was swamp scum. And if he had any notion that any relationship could grow between them all he had to do was remember Tyler, cold in his grave. Swamp and town didn't mix, at least not in Black Bayou. He moved his hand away from her face, realizing that touching her rekindled a flame inside him.

"We were children, Billy, both of us grieving for a woman we loved." She placed a hand on his chest, her fingers twirling strands of hair. "I was angry with you for a long time after that night. I felt as if you'd taken something from me, but now I realize my bad feelings had nothing to do with what happened between us." She sighed, her expression troubled. "Every time I thought about that night, I'd get a sick feeling in the pit of my stomach and I blamed that on you. Now I know it wasn't you at all, it was repressed memories of what I saw in the swamp." She shivered, her eyes taking on a haunted glaze.

Unable to help himself, Billy pulled her into his arms, wishing he could erase that night of horror from her mind, take her back to the innocence she'd once possessed. As she nestled against him, her cheek against his chest, he felt an odd surge of guilt. "I used you to ease my grief the night Mama Royce died."

She raised her head and smiled at him. "And I used you to hide in, to escape from what I'd seen earlier. We're even, Billy." She pressed her lips against his neck and his response was immediate. He wanted her again.

This time there was little foreplay. She was as ready as he and arched against him with an abandoned splendor that stole his breath from him. It was madness, sheer madness to want her so, and the fact that she was a willing participant in the madness only increased his hunger.

Later, sated momentarily once again, he held her against him as she slept. Her body curved against his in complete trust and he felt a flare of protectiveness that tightened his arms around her.

Since the time he'd met her so many years before, Shelby Longsford had held his fascination like no other person. She'd been the fairy princess living in the castle, and as a youth he'd never been able to understand what drove her out of the castle and into the swamp.

It was only as he had grown older that he'd realized he'd been far more wealthy than her in areas unrelated to power and money. Mama Royce had been Billy's wealth, one he'd shared with the little princess. Secretly it had filled Billy with pride, that despite her family's wealth, her beautiful home and expensive toys, he'd had something she didn't, he had something she needed.

He was glad he'd shared Mama Royce with her, knew the connection with his grandmother had helped mold and shape the woman Shelby had become. He hoped some of Mama Royce's inner strength had been passed on to Shelby. He had a feeling before this was all over, she was going to need every ounce of inner strength she could find.

SHELBY AWOKE SUDDENLY, unsure what had pulled her from sleep. A whisper of light seeped in through the window, letting her know dawn was just starting to break. Billy slept next to her, his body warmly surrounding her. For a moment she didn't move, merely savoring the feel of him so close to her.

She shifted her position, turning so she could see him as he slept. Even in sleep there seemed to be a tensed wariness about him. No hint of vulnerability softened his features. Such a solitary man. A man who kept his feelings secret, shared his soul with nobody. If she hadn't seen him with Mama Royce years ago, and more recently with Parker, she would have easily believed Jonathon LaJune's assessment that Billy didn't know how to love.

Frowning, she eased away from him. She had to get home. Besides, it was sheer foolishness to be fantasizing about love and Billy. She'd made that mistake once. She would never make it again. What she and Billy shared was a curious physical attraction, a strong chemical pull that was based on lust. She'd finish this case, then go on with her life, and she'd have two memories of making love to Billy, pleasant memories to warm a cold wintry night. She grabbed her clothes from the floor and dressed, her back turned toward the bed.

"You aren't thinking of sneaking out of here, are you?"

She whirled around and finished buttoning her blouse. "I've got to get home."

He sat up and ran a hand through his hair, his smile as sexy in the purple of dawn as it had been in the shadows of the night. "Why not stay and I'll make us some breakfast...after."

Despite the intimacies they had already shared, a blush warmed Shelby's face. "I really should get home before everyone is awake at the house."

The smile died quickly. He stood and reached for his jeans. "I'll walk you back."

"That's not necessary," she protested.

"Don't be a fool. There's a murderer loose in the swamp and it's not even light yet." He pulled up his jeans and zipped them. "I'll walk you back," he repeated in a tone that brooked no argument.

They walked through the swamp toward the mansion in silence. Shelby didn't know what had caused the sudden tension that rolled off him, and so didn't know how to ease it. They didn't speak until they reached the manicured grass of the Longsford lawn.

Shelby turned to him, unsure what to say, hating that he always managed to keep her off-balance. "Thanks for walking me back," she finally said.

He bowed. "The lovely princess is successfully led through the evil forest by the troll. All is well in the kingdom." His mocking smile fell away and he leaned forward and cupped Shelby's face in his hands. "Shelby, you remembered the look on Layne Rocharee's face when he died. That means you were close enough to see the face of the monster who murdered him." He tapped the side of her head with his index finger. "The answers to everything are in there. You have the key to my exoneration buried in your memories. That makes you vitally important to me, and a genuine threat to the murderer." He kissed her forehead, then turned and, making no sound, disappeared into the swamp.

She lingered for a moment at the edge of the copse, his parting words upsetting her. Was the answer to all the murders trapped in her mind? And how much of Billy's desire was a result of that fact? She was his hope for acquittal and that meant she was a danger to somebody else.

With a troubled sigh she walked to the house and up on the porch. She jumped as she realized somebody was sitting in the rocking chair. "Mama? What are you doing out here?"

Clad in a nightgown, without her customary makeup, Celia looked older than her years. "I couldn't sleep. I often have bouts of insomnia." She gazed at Shelby, her blue eyes clear and sharp. "I saw you coming out of the swamp with that man. I hope you aren't getting in too deep with him, doing things to shame our family. The busybodies in this town would never stop talking if they could see you now."

Shelby sighed wearily. "Mama, I'm a big girl. I know what I'm doing and I don't care about the busybodies."

"Are you so sure Billy Royce is innocent in Tyler's and Fayrene's murders?" Celia's chair creaked as she rocked forward. "There's been stories about his father and mother and their deaths. They say blood will tell."

"Billy isn't guilty. He's simply not capable of that kind of crime."

Celia smiled and shook her head. "Shelby, no matter how well you think you know a man, you can never be sure you know his heart's darkness, his secret passions." She smiled again. "Men are a strange breed, darling girl." With another creak of the rocker, Celia stood. "I think I can sleep now." She started for the door, then paused and turned back to Shelby. "Make sure you shower before breakfast to get the smell of the swamp off you. You know how your father is, and I don't want to start the day off with him in one of his moods."

Shelby nodded, and her mother left the porch and disappeared into the house. Yes, she knew how her father was, and that's what frightened her. If what she suspected was true, she had seen the swamp serpent and had been so traumatized she'd repressed the memory. Seeing a murder was frightening, but seeing a murder being committed by somebody she knew would be horrifying enough to drive the memory away. She knew that's what had happened. She had seen the face of the monster, and it had been familiar... so familiar she had repressed it, unable to withstand the damage to her psyche. Somehow she had to retrieve that memory and hope that while she had been looking at the murderer, the murderer hadn't been looking at her.

Chapter Fourteen

"Bob! Wait up." Shelby ran down the sidewalk toward the sheriff, who stopped in his tracks and turned to face her. "I was just going to the station to find you," she said, pausing a moment to catch her breath.

"I was on my way to Martha's. Why don't you let me buy you some lunch?"

Shelby hesitated, aware that Bob's lunch offer was prompted by feelings less than professional. "We'll go dutch," she said, aware he got the message by the look of disappointment that crossed his face.

"How's the shoulder?" Bob asked as they walked toward the popular eating establishment.

"Healing nicely, although still a little stiff." She murmured her thanks as he opened the door to the restaurant and ushered her inside.

As usual at the noon hour, Martha's was packed with people on their lunch breaks. Three-piece suiters ate next to blue-collar workers, their chatter and clinking dinnerware creating a din. Martha waved to them as she rang up a customer at the cash register. Bob led Shelby to a just-emptied table in the center of the room. "So, why were you on your way to the station to find me?" he asked as they settled in their chairs across from one another.

"I was wondering if there were autopsy and other reports from all of the swamp serpent murders and if I could get copies of everything you have on them."

He looked at her in surprise. "Why would you want to have them? Surely they can't have a bearing on Billy's case."

Shelby shrugged, unwilling to say too much. "Until Billy is proclaimed innocent, everything has a bearing on his case."

They paused in their conversation when the waitress came to their table. Shelby ordered a salad and Bob got the daily special of Cajun chicken. When the waitress had departed, Bob looked at Shelby thoughtfully. "You've found something that ties Fayrene and Tyler to the swamp serpent, haven't you?"

He leaned back in his chair and raked a hand through his hair. "Shelby, I'm turning myself inside out to stop those murders in the swamp, but I'm grasping at phantoms. I've got nothing substantial to hold on to. If you know anything you think might help, for everyone's sake please tell me."

Shelby weighed the pros and cons in her head, aware that in not telling Bob what she suspected, she could be guilty of obstructing justice. "Did you know Tyler was working on the swamp murders?" she asked.

"What do you mean, working on them? Writing about them?"

Shelby nodded. "He's got file after file on the murders on his laptop computer and I think it might be those files that got him killed." She consciously made the decision not to tell him about her fragmented memory, knowing at this point she remembered nothing that could be of any real help. "Billy and I believe the swamp serpent killed Tyler and Fayrene. The best way to absolve Billy is to find the swamp serpent.''

Bob rubbed his chin thoughtfully, his gaze worried as it lingered on her. ''Shelby, you're in over your head. How in the hell do you expect to find a murderer who has eluded the law for over a decade?''

''I don't know. But at least I can work up a viable defense for Billy based on reasonable doubt. The jury needs to know Tyler was working on that murder case, and the night he met Fayrene he told somebody he thought she might have information as to the identity of the swamp serpent. It's a little too coincidental that they were both killed that night.''

Bob leaned forward. ''Where are you getting all this information? I don't know half of what you seem to know and I've got three deputies working the case.''

''I'll make you a deal, Bob. I'll give you all my notes, everything I have including copies of Tyler's files, if you do the same. I want crime scene and autopsy reports. I'd like the names of all the officers who worked on the swamp serpent murder cases. I want everything you've got from the first murder to the last.''

Again their conversation ceased as the waitress appeared with their orders. ''I'll have everything ready for you first thing in the morning,'' Bob said when the waitress had once again departed. ''Now, let's talk about something more pleasant. Are you going to the Whalens' party Saturday night?''

''I got an invitation, but I don't think I'm going to go. With Billy's trial less than two weeks away, I really can't afford to take off for an entire evening.''

''You know what they say about all work and no play.'' Bob reached across the table and covered her hand with his. ''Seriously, Shelby, it isn't good to work all the time.''

"Well, well. If it isn't my counsel and Black Bayou's finest."

A coil of heat unfurled in Shelby's stomach at the familiar deep voice. She looked up to see Billy with Parker at his side. Billy's gaze moved from her face to where her hand was covered with Bob's.

Shelby fought the impulse to snatch her hand away, hating the fact that Billy could make her feel guilty about anything. Still, she was relieved when Bob reared back in his chair, breaking their physical contact. "Billy… Parker," Bob greeted them. He smiled at Parker. "I'll bet you're here for some of Martha's famous chocolate pie."

"No, sir." Parker looked up at his dad as if for reassurance. "I just want a hamburger."

"And that's exactly what I'm going to get you," Billy said to his son. He started to move away, then hesitated and smiled at Shelby, a secret, knowing smile. "You look tired, Shelby. Didn't you get enough sleep last night?"

Shelby felt her face flame as visions of their lovemaking danced in her head. The man was wicked, definitely wicked. "Actually, I didn't get much sleep. I had horrible nightmares all night long."

Billy laughed, a low, deep rumble that only increased the heat inside Shelby. "I'd better feed this hungry boy," he replied. Saying goodbye to them both, Billy and Parker disappeared into the back room of the restaurant.

"Nobody can fault Billy's parenting skills," Bob observed. "Even his harshest critics can't help but admit he's a good father."

Shelby nodded and focused on her salad in an attempt to exorcise from her mind the memory of Billy's kiss, the searing of his touch, the fire of his possession.

"So, that's how it is." Bob's voice was quiet, thoughtful.

"What?" Shelby looked up from her plate.

"Billy's more than a client to you, isn't he?"

Shelby twirled the straw in her iced tea. "Well, sure, he's an old friend."

"That's not what I mean and you know it." Bob laughed and shook his head ruefully. "I don't know why I didn't realize it before. The few times I've seen you and Billy together the air positively crackles between the two of you."

"Don't be ridiculous," Shelby replied, unable to meet his gaze with hers. "Billy is a friend and a client, nothing more, nothing less."

"Are you trying to convince me or yourself?"

Shelby didn't reply, didn't even want to contemplate what he was saying. Instead she picked at her salad, eating but not tasting, trying to forget what Bob had just said.

"So, you really think Tyler's and Fayrene's murders are connected to the swamp serpent?" Bob asked, breaking the uncomfortable silence that had grown between them.

She smiled, grateful for the change in subject matter. "Why not? It makes so much more sense than Billy being responsible."

"You know, Shelby, my arresting Billy was nothing personal. He was the most likely suspect and Abe was eager to tie up the case." He popped a French fry into his mouth and chewed thoughtfully. "The people in the swamp look up to him, listen when he speaks. With the right kind of focus, Billy could really make a difference in this town."

"It's a shame anyone has to make a difference in this town," Shelby returned.

"Shelby, we're making progress. Ten years ago your family would have no contact at all with the people from the swamp. Now your mother reads to the kids and your brother ministers to some of them. I know the community center doesn't seem like much, but it's a start, a place where people from the swamp and from town can talk, mingle, learn to accept each other as equals."

"I know." Shelby sighed in frustration. She thought of Sissy, so alone, unable to share her grief with other members of Tyler's family because of Jonathon LaJune's prejudice. "I just find it sad that so many people have died and so few seem to care."

Bob smiled ruefully. "Unfortunately that's not a problem we suffer just here in Black Bayou." He looked at his watch and frowned. "I've got to get back to the station. Want me to walk you out?"

"No, thanks. I think I'll stick around until this place empties out a little. I've been wanting to visit with Martha."

"When can I expect copies of Tyler's computer files from you?" he asked as he stood.

"I'll bring them by the station first thing tomorrow morning." Shelby grinned at him. "And at the same time I'll pick up whatever reports you can get together for me."

When Bob had left Shelby settled back in her chair and sipped her iced tea, trying not to think of Parker and Billy in the next room. But her thoughts refused to be schooled away from them. What would happen to Billy's son if the worst happened and Billy went to prison? She knew Billy had no relatives. Did Fayrene? Or would Angelique take Parker?

She stood and grabbed her tea, deciding she'd rather join them than sit alone and think about them. They were seated at the small table where she and Billy had sat the couple of times they had met here at Martha's.

All the other tables in the room had people seated at them. It was the first time Shelby had seen the small private room used as overflow from the main dining area. "Mind if I join you?" she asked Billy.

"What happened to your date?" Billy asked.

"It wasn't a date, and he had to get back to the station."

Billy scooted out the chair next to him so she could sit down. "How's the hamburger?" she asked Parker.

He smiled, a curious blend of shyness and wariness. "It's good."

"Parker, Shelby is a special friend of mine," Billy said as if to alleviate some of the child's distrust. "If you ever need anything and you can't find Angelique or me, you can always go to Shelby."

"That's right." Shelby watched the play of emotions on the little boy's face and realized the child must know about his father's arrest and what might happen. Poor baby. His mother was gone, and Shelby fought the need to pull the little boy close, hold him tight against her heart. "Parker, sweetie, if you ever just need to talk you can always talk to me," she said.

Billy ruffled Parker's dark hair with one hand. "But don't worry, son. Shelby is going to do whatever she can to make sure I stay with you always."

"She's going to keep you out of jail?" Parker asked softly.

"That's what I'm counting on," Billy replied, his gaze hot as it lingered on Shelby.

Again she was reminded of their lovemaking the night before, how complete she had felt in his arms. "I asked Bob for all the reports he had on the swamp serpent. He'll have them for me first thing in the morning," she said, needing to defuse the sexual tension between them and get back on a professional footing.

"I'd like to go over them with you. I don't know, maybe I'll be able to see something you can't, a pattern, a clue...something." Billy leaned toward her. "Did you know that before Tyler went to The Edge, he ate dinner here that night? And he didn't eat alone.''

Shelby scooted forward on her chair. ''Who'd he eat with? Fayrene?'' she asked softly, hoping Parker was too involved in his meal to concern himself with adult conversation.

Billy shook his head. ''Your sister.''

''Olivia?'' Shelby looked at him in surprise. ''Are you sure?''

''That's what Martha told me. She said they ate together and left together.''

''Does Bob know about it?''

''I imagine he does. He probably dismissed it as unimportant. After all, what could she possibly have to do with Tyler's and Fayrene's deaths?''

''I don't know, but I don't understand why Olivia hasn't mentioned this to me.'' Shelby frowned, ugly suppositions running through her head. Was it possible Tyler had said something to Olivia and Olivia had passed that information to somebody else . . . perhaps Big John?

''Dad, can I have another soda?''

The childish voice pulled Shelby from her thoughts. As Billy got up to get Parker another drink, she smiled at the little boy. ''You enjoying your summer, Parker?'' she asked.

He nodded. '''Cept Angelique has me doing schoolwork all the time. Next year I'll go to school in town.'' He chewed a French fry, his gaze unwavering on Shelby. ''You gonna make sure my daddy doesn't go to jail?''

''I'm going to try my best.''

''You got any kids?'' Parker asked.

Shelby shook her head. ''I don't even have a husband.''

Parker picked up another French fry. "My dad doesn't have a wife. Maybe you guys could get married and I could be your kid."

Shelby's heart twisted as she recognized the hunger in Parker's words. It was the hunger of a child for a family. Shelby knew it well, knew that even within the confines of her own family she had suffered the same kind of hunger. "Parker, I'm just your daddy's lawyer, but I'm sure someday he'll find a wonderful woman to marry and you'll all be a happy family."

"Here you are, Parker," Billy said as he set a tall soda in front of his son.

Shelby stood, suddenly needing to be away from Billy's evocative presence and Parker's sweet need. "I'd better get moving. There's a lot of things I need to get done this afternoon."

"You're getting reports from Bob in the morning?" Shelby nodded and Billy continued. "Then why don't you meet me at the shanty as soon as you have them and we'll start going over them together." Although his words said one thing, his gaze implied another. His words said they would work on the reports, his dark, heated eyes spoke of a morning spent beneath navy sheets and a ceiling fan whispering against bare flesh.

"I'll see you tomorrow," she said, then turned and left the small dining room. And tomorrow they would discuss how foolish it had been for her to allow their relationship to be anything other than lawyer and client.

She was grateful to see that most of the lunch rush crowd had left and Martha sat at the end of the counter, enjoying a cup of coffee and a piece of her own home-baked pie. Shelby slid onto the stool next to her. "Hey, Martha, got a few minutes?"

"Sure, honey. What do you need?"

"I was wondering if I could ask you a few questions."

Martha grinned. "As long as you don't want to ask me my age or my weight."

"Marguerite Boujoulais worked for you before she was killed, right?"

Martha's smile immediately fell and sadness filled her dark eyes. "Ah, yes, Marguerite worked here for almost a year before she died. She was one of my best waitresses, sassy and full of life and so beautiful." Martha took a sip of her coffee and shook her head. "So sad when somebody so full of life has that stolen from her."

"Did you ever see her with my father?" Shelby asked, unsure how this fit into the murders, but curious nevertheless. She realized now that her home, just like the town, had been filled with secrets.

"Why do you ask?" Martha didn't quite meet her gaze.

"Because I think my father had an affair with Marguerite."

"What if he did? Ancient history. Marguerite has been dead for years. What difference does it make if your daddy had a thing with her or not?"

Shelby frowned, realizing Martha was right. What difference did it make if her father had a fling or not? How on earth could that tie in to the swamp serpent murders? "I don't know," she finally admitted. "I'll see you later." Wearily she arose from the stool and left the restaurant.

Stepping out into the afternoon heat, she wondered what she was doing, why it suddenly seemed so important that she glean all the secrets her family possessed. Was she trying to find clues to a murderer, or was she trying to piece together a portrait of a family she could understand?

Her father might have had an affair, and Olivia had had dinner with Tyler on the night he was murdered. What did it mean? Pieces . . . that's all she had, and she didn't even know if they fit at all into the puzzle of Fayrene's and Tyler's or the swamp murders.

She got into her car and waited for the air-conditioning to cool the interior. As she waited, she once again thought of Billy and how easily his gaze had stirred her. It had been a mistake to sleep with him again. By repeating the love-making she had hoped to dispel his power over her, diminish the memory that had haunted her for years. But in making love to Billy again she hadn't dispelled anything. She'd only given herself more haunting.

As she drove home she decided it couldn't happen again. She couldn't allow Billy to seduce her into wanting him again. Professionally, sleeping with him had been a mistake. Personally, it had been even worse because she knew now she was in danger of falling in love with Billy. And that was something she'd sworn she would never, ever do.

Pulling in to the driveway, she saw Michael pulling out. He waved as he passed, and she returned the gesture. He'd probably stopped by for lunch and was on his way back to his rectory. She wished she'd arrived earlier and gotten a chance to visit with him. She never tired of Michael's company.

When Shelby entered the house, she immediately saw Olivia sitting in the living room, a magazine opened on her lap. "Ah, just the person I wanted to talk to," Shelby said as she sat down next to her sister.

"What's up?" Olivia closed the magazine and looked at Shelby curiously.

"Why didn't you tell me you had dinner with Tyler on the night he was killed?" Shelby asked, trying to keep any accusation from her voice.

Olivia shrugged. "Oh, that. Because there was nothing to tell. Tyler and I ran into each other at Martha's. We decided to sit together because we were both alone. We ate, then we left. I came home and I don't know where he went."

"While you were eating, did he mention where he was going or what his plans were after dinner?"

"No, we mostly just gossiped." Olivia smiled and smoothed an eyebrow with a finger. "Being on the social scene for the paper, Tyler always had the best gossip."

"Did you discuss the swamp serpent murders?"

"We might have touched on it, but I don't remember anything specific." Olivia shivered slightly. "Why is all this so important? It makes me ill to think that a few hours after I dined with him, he was stabbed to death." Olivia sighed impatiently. "Surely you aren't still hung up on this idea that somehow the swamp murders and Tyler's are related?"

"The only thing I'm hung up on is finding out the truth."

Olivia leaned forward and smiled. "Are you sleeping with him yet?" She laughed. "Oh, I can tell by the look on your face that you are. Oh, that Billy, he's a slick one. Who else would seduce his lawyer and muddle the issue of his own guilt by tying in an old set of murders? He must be good to have you believing in his innocence. But tell me this, Shelby, would you believe him innocent if you weren't sleeping with him?"

Olivia's laughter followed Shelby up the stairs to her room. Once inside, Shelby sank down at the desk, her thoughts whirling in confusion.

Was she a fool to believe in Billy's innocence? Did Fayrene's and Tyler's murders have nothing to do with the swamp serpent? Were Billy's hungry gazes, searing kisses and seductive manner solely an effort to keep her on his side no matter what the evidence might show?

She rubbed her forehead wearily, then punched on the computer, knowing it would take her most of the afternoon to make copies of all of Tyler's files. She opened her purse, withdrew her glasses and put them on as she waited for the computer to boot up.

There was no way she'd believe Billy was guilty, and it had nothing to do with his expertise as a lover. The key to Tyler's murder was in his files, files that involved the swamp serpent murders.

Punching the appropriate keys, Shelby attempted to call up one of the files she wanted. She frowned as she received an error message. FILE NOT FOUND. Tapping on the keys, she tried again. FILE NOT FOUND. What was going on? She tried another file and received the same message. Finally, going to the root directory, she scanned the list of files. All of the swamp serpent ones were gone, as if they'd never existed.

"Damn," she muttered. Shutting off the computer, she felt cold fingers drag up her spine as she realized what had happened. While she had been gone, somebody had sneaked into her room and erased all the files. Somebody in the house...a member of her family. And there was only one reason for the files to be erased—somebody had been afraid of what she might discover.

Chapter Fifteen

"I'll be back to pick you up later this afternoon," Billy said to his son as he gave him a quick hug.

"Okay, Dad." Parker looked at Angelique. "Is Rafe awake?"

She nodded. "He's in his bedroom watching cartoons. Go on." Parker scurried down the hall and disappeared into Rafe's room.

"Walk me out?" Billy said to Angelique.

As they stepped out on her porch, the morning sun was just rising above the trees, casting a shimmering golden light on the swamp land. Angelique looked at Billy, noting how even the golden light of day couldn't dispel the darkness of his eyes.

Angelique knew it was the pervasive darkness that all people born and raised in the swamp carried with them. It was something others couldn't understand, a darkness bred in savage beauty and deepened by nature's supreme survival law. One had to be strong to make it in the swamp.

"I don't know how long it will take for Shelby and me to go over all the reports we need to read. We've got a lot of work to do."

Angelique shrugged. "You know Parker is always welcome here."

He nodded, his gaze lingering on her with a studied detachment that caused a niggle of fear in Angelique. "You've been a good friend, Angelique," he said.

"Rafe, you and Parker are the only things I've cared about since Remy's death," she answered. He smiled, but still she sensed a distance from him that frightened her. She stepped closer to him, wanting to bridge the distance, but knowing it had nothing to do with their physical proximity.

"Shelby tells me she found a dead bouquet in her bed." His eyes flashed an emotion Angelique had never seen before. "I'm not making any accusations, I just want you to know that I will kill anyone who harms Shelby." His intensity dissipated somewhat and he smiled once again. "I need her. She's the only one who can get me out of the mess I'm in, the only one who believes in my innocence."

"I believe in you," Angelique said.

Billy placed an arm around her shoulder. "Yeah, but you aren't my lawyer."

She wished she was. She wanted to be as important to him as Shelby Longsford. If she was lucky, her dreams would come true and would make Shelby's heart dead, make it impossible for Shelby to ever love Billy.

"I don't know for sure when I'll be back for Parker," Billy said. "It's going to be a long day."

"You know it doesn't matter. Parker will be fine here with Rafe and me."

He kissed her on the cheek and stepped down off the porch. "I'll see you later."

She nodded and watched as he moved through the swamp, finally disappearing into the glare of the morning sun. Leaning against the wooden railing, she drew in a deep breath. She knew Billy had meant his threat. He'd kill anyone who harmed Shelby Longsford.

With another sigh, Angelique turned and went back inside, trying to forget all the people she'd lost to the swamp serpent, how frightened she was of losing Billy to Shelby.

"I HAD TO BEG AND PLEAD with Bob to give me all this stuff after I told him I didn't have Tyler's computer files anymore," Shelby said as she slapped a stack of manila folders down on Billy's table.

"What happened to the computer files?" Billy asked. He poured her a cup of coffee, then refilled his and joined her at the table.

Shelby sighed. "Somebody went into my bedroom and erased all the files."

Billy regarded her thoughtfully. "Are you sure you didn't somehow delete them yourself?"

She shook her head. "I'm no computer expert, but I know I didn't delete them. And the hard drive didn't crash, either. All the other files were still there. Only the ones pertaining to the murders were gone. Somebody intentionally erased those. Damn it, I should have made backup copies. I can't believe I was so stupid." Her gaze met his and she wondered if her fear radiated from her eyes. "Billy, I have to face the fact that somebody in my house, a member of my family, is the swamp serpent."

He gave a quick nod. "Or somebody in your house is protecting the swamp serpent," he added.

"Who would protect such a killer?" she asked, finding little relief in his words. Although she preferred to believe nobody in her family was a killer, that one of her own would protect the murderer was just as heinous as actually committing the crimes.

"Somebody who believes in what the killer is doing," Billy answered.

An ache of harsh reality twisted in Shelby's stomach. She thought of her father and his venomous disdain of the swamp community. "All the time I was in Shreveport, I played a game with myself. I'd tell other people how wonderful my family was, how supportive my parents were, how much love there was between me and my siblings. I painted a pretty picture with words that had nothing to do with reality. Reality is somebody in my family might be a killer, and the sad thing is I can't discount anyone." She rubbed the back of her neck, where tension had built to substantial proportions. "God, to say my family is a mess is an understatement."

Billy stood and circled behind her. He put his hands on her shoulders and gently massaged. "Having a screwed-up family puts you in good company." His thumbs moved to the base of her skull, working in small circular motions to ease the tightness. "I grew up hearing about the horrors of my parents. I suppose you heard all the stories." His finger pressure increased, although not painful.

"I heard that your father killed your mother, then hung himself in the swamp," Shelby answered softly.

Billy laughed. "Ah, yes, that was the most popular rumor. The only good thing it accomplished was as I was growing up it scared the other kids into leaving me alone. I think they figured if my father was a crazed killer, who knew what I was capable of."

"So, what really happened?" she asked. She reached up and caught his wrists in her hands, stopping the massage, wanting to look at him, not have him speak from behind her where she couldn't see his face, try to read his features.

He hesitated a moment, then returned to his chair. "I heard the whispers of my father's madness and crime until I was twelve. In my heart I couldn't believe the stories were true. After all, my father was Mama Royce's son. I couldn't believe she would raise a murderer."

Shelby smiled. "That's the very reason I knew you were innocent. Mama Royce raised you and I knew she couldn't raise a murderer."

Billy sipped his coffee, a wistful sadness deepening the hue of his eyes. "I finally asked Mama Royce what had happened and she told me the truth. My mother was ill with cancer. By the time she went to a doctor it was too late for treatment. She died in her sleep, and my father found her dead one morning." He drew a deep breath and Shelby knew the emotional cost he paid in sharing with her. "Mama Royce said he went crazy with grief. They found him later that afternoon. He'd hung himself."

He stood and went back to the counter to refill his coffee mug. "What bothered me more than anything was that I wasn't enough to keep him alive." Even with his back toward her, Shelby heard the pain reflected in his deep voice . . . the pain of a little boy who believed he'd been lacking because he hadn't been enough to keep his father alive.

She got up and walked to him. She wrapped her arms around him, pressing against his solid back in an effort to assuage his hurt. "Oh, Billy." She sighed. "As children we want our parents to be perfect, and it's sad when we realize they're only human and horribly imperfect." She stepped away from him as he turned around and faced her.

Gone was the moment of vulnerability, hidden beneath a mask of strength. "I guess we'd better get to work on those files." Again a whisper of sadness darkened his eyes. "Maybe we'll get lucky and find something that will completely exonerate all the members of your family in the murders." Placing an arm around her shoulders, he led her back to the table where the files awaited them.

For a little over two hours they sat at the table, not speaking, both reading page after page of police reports, statements and notes gathered about the swamp serpent murders. After reading the autopsy reports, staring at grotesque photographs, Shelby wondered if she would ever sleep without nightmares again.

The pictures of the victims haunted her, the details of their deaths horrifying her. What kind of a person could use a knife and savagely steal life? And how could she even begin to believe that somebody in her family was capable of such a thing?

"Let's take a break," Billy said, interrupting the silence that had engulfed them.

Shelby nodded and closed the manila folder before her. "I could use a break," she admitted.

"Let's drive into town and get lunch at Martha's." Shelby readily agreed, needing not only a break from the crime reports, but an escape from Billy's closeness, as well. She'd felt his gaze on her frequently, as if questioning, probing, needing something she was reluctant to give.

She had a feeling that sooner or later she was going to have to say that sleeping with him again had been a mistake, one she wasn't going to repeat another time. She couldn't, because she knew she was at risk of losing her heart to Billy.

As they drove in his pickup toward town, she considered her relationship with Billy. That there was passion between them was certain, but Shelby knew passion was not love. They also shared a curious bond forged in childhood and their mutual love of Mama Royce. One thing that didn't concern her was the ridiculous notion that she and Billy couldn't fall in love because he was from the swamp.

One of the things she admired about him was his passion for the swamp and its people, his utter devotion to seeing to their needs, working for their futures. She'd seen his rage over the murders, knew the bitterness he held in his heart for whomever was responsible. If one of her family members was responsible for the heinous crimes, she feared that each time Billy looked at her, he'd see the faces of the victims.

"Hungry?" he asked.

She shook her head. "Not really."

"You will be when you walk into Martha's and smell some of her gumbo or jambalaya."

"Isn't it strange that Martha's is the one place in town where swamp and town people come together without conflict."

Billy smiled wryly. "There's one other place, also. The cemetery."

Shelby leaned her head back against the seat, her gaze still on him. "Did you know my father had an affair with Angelique's sister, Marguerite?"

"I think most people knew about it. But that's old news. Marguerite has been dead a long time."

"Yes, she was the second victim of the swamp serpent." Shelby sighed in frustration. "I keep trying to figure out a motive for the killings. At first I thought maybe Marguerite had broken off with my father and he killed her. But that doesn't make sense. She wasn't the first victim, nor was she the last." She frowned. "God, listen to me, attempting to tie my father to a murder."

"No, you're trying to logically think through a crime and unfortunately your father is a strong suspect."

"It's a horrible feeling, to think that your own father might be a killer."

"I know," Billy answered softly. His hand found hers on the seat and gently enfolded it in warmth. They rode that way in silence until they pulled up in front of Martha's.

Only then did he release her hand, leaving her with a momentary bereavement and making her realize how tenuous was her hold on her own heart.

"I spoke to Olivia about her dinner with Tyler on the night he was killed," she said after they'd been seated and placed their orders. "She said they just ran into each other, decided to eat together, then parted ways."

"Sounds innocent enough," Billy said.

"Yes, but I keep thinking what if Tyler told Olivia he was close to discovering the identity of the swamp serpent, then innocently she repeated that to somebody else...somebody who realized Tyler was a threat?"

"Who might she have repeated it to?"

Shelby fought a wave of helplessness. "Who knows...my father or Roger, anyone in the house." She hit a fist against the tabletop. "If only I could remember what I saw that night. It's there, trapped in my mind, but I can't get to it. I toss and turn all night long, trying to recall all the details of that night, but when I get to the face of the killer, it's blank."

Again Billy's hand covered hers, his dark gaze full of sympathy. "You're probably trying too hard. When you least expect it, you'll remember."

"Yes, but will it be too late? Billy, we don't have much of a defense for you. Sure, I can tell the jury that Tyler was working on the swamp murders and we believe that's what got him killed, but there's no guarantee they're going to take that theory over Abe's speculation that it was a crime of passion committed by you."

"Then I guess you'll just have to be sure you remember before they come back with a verdict and put me away for life," Billy said.

Shelby grinned and pulled her hand from his. "Thanks for the no-pressure approach."

When the waitress brought their orders, they fell into silence. Shelby found her mind wandering back over the files she'd been reading, reaching, struggling to find something, anything that might exclude all members of the Longsford family from any culpability.

Billy ate methodically, his gaze distantly focused on the tabletop. Shelby wondered what he was thinking, if he knew the precarious position he was in and if he contemplated running. She couldn't bear the thought of him in a prison. Shelby knew that, like a wild creature in captivity, confinement would eventually kill him. And what of Parker?

"Billy, I know you don't have any relatives, but what about Fayrene? Did she have family?"

He shook his head. "No. Like me, Fayrene had nobody. I think that's part of what initially drew us to each other."

"You loved her?"

"I thought I did." He smiled sadly. "I was lonely. I wanted to build something of my own, a family, financial security. I wanted to take the money Mama Royce left me and build something to give back to the swamp community, make a difference to those people. I thought Fayrene wanted the same kinds of things, but I was wrong. She was angry that I invested instead of spent. She'd been poor all her life and wanted baubles and nice things. She didn't want community work, she wanted luxury. I didn't realize until too late what a mistake it had been for us to marry each other."

"I'm sorry." And she was, sorry for shattered dreams and broken promises. She understood the desire to build something, the hunger for somebody to turn to in the night, to whisper shared dreams.

"What about you, Shelby? Why haven't you found some nice man and started a family?"

She twirled her straw in her soda, finding his question difficult to answer. She couldn't tell him that the single experience she'd shared with him so many years before had tainted other men for her, although that was partially the truth. "I don't know. I dated occasionally back in Shreveport, but nobody special, nobody I could imagine spending the rest of my life with."

"I have a feeling when this is all over I may have problems finding dates. Especially if the real killer isn't found and there's a lingering doubt about my innocence."

Shelby smiled. "You might be surprised. There are plenty of women who enjoy flirting with and dating dangerous men."

Billy reached out and stroked the back of her hand, the caress evoking a heat inside her. "What about you, Shelby? Are you drawn to dangerous men?" His voice was as seductive as a tongue against her ear, as beguiling as a kiss against her neck.

"Billy, what happened between us the other night was a mistake, one I don't intend to repeat. Professionally, it was a very stupid thing to do. You're my client and we need to maintain a professional relationship."

"It's a little late for that." His eyes spoke to hers in passionate whispers, igniting a flame as his gaze lingered on her lips, then on the swell of her breasts. He leaned forward and claimed her hand once again in his. "It's difficult to forget the sweet sounds you uttered when I made love to you." He raised her hand to his mouth and kissed the back of it. "You've gotten under my skin, Shelby, and I think we're going to make love again and again."

She snatched her hand from his. "You think too much," she snapped, irritated that her body had responded so quickly to his touch, his words.

Billy laughed and took a sip of his soda. "I find it amusing that years ago it was me telling you that making love was a big mistake. Now you're saying those same words back to me." His smile faded and he regarded her soberly. "I wonder if the timing will ever be right between us, when we'll make love and neither one of us will consider it a mistake."

"You'd be better off worrying about your legal position than your love life," Shelby answered. "If we don't improve your legal position, you won't have much of a love life." She busied herself with her napkin, wiping her mouth then wadding the napkin into a ball at the side of her plate. "In fact, I'd say it's time for us to get back to work on those files."

Billy nodded, and together they left the restaurant and walked out into the broiling afternoon sun. "I wonder if we'll ever get a break from this heat," Shelby said as the hot pavement burned through the soles of her thin sandals. There wasn't even a gasp of a breeze to alleviate the heavy, humid heat.

"The best thing to do on days like this is get naked and wallow beneath the air from a ceiling fan."

"Billy Royce, you are the most perverse man I've ever known," Shelby exclaimed in frustration. "If you'd spend half the energy trying to solve this crime as you do trying to seduce me, we'd have the real killer behind bars."

Billy laughed. "But we wouldn't have half as much fun. Besides, I do have an image to keep."

"Ms. Longsford."

Shelby and Billy stopped walking at the sound of the unfamiliar voice that called from the distance. A teenage boy ran toward them, a brown-paper-wrapped box in his hand. "I thought I was going to have to drive all the way out to your place to deliver this to you." He held out the package to her.

Shelby studied his face closely. "You must be one of the O'Rileys."

"Yes, ma'am." The youth smiled cheerfully, causing the freckles to dance across his nose. "I'm Jackson O'Riley."

Shelby took the package from him. "I guess your mama still runs the post office." She had a vivid memory of Emma O'Riley, who had worked the mail since Shelby had been a small child. The woman had half a dozen children and a penchant for gossip.

"Yeah, I help out during the summers, but she doesn't pay me half enough." He blushed as only a red-haired teenager could, then with a nod of his head, he went on his way.

"Secret admirer?" Billy asked with raised eyebrows.

"Who knows? There's no return address." She tucked the package under her arm as they continued toward the pickup.

It wasn't until they were driving back to Billy's that she decided to see what was inside. Carefully she tore away the brown paper to reveal a plain white box. "I can't imagine who would send me something," she said. "It's postmarked from right here in Black Bayou. Why would somebody go to the trouble to send me a package instead of just bringing it to me?"

"Maybe it's from a shy secret admirer," Billy observed dryly.

She ignored him and opened the lid of the box. As she peeled back the colorful cellophane paper inside, she stared at the contents in horror. With a startled cry, she threw the box on the floor.

"Shelby?" Billy slammed on the brakes as she bailed out of the truck. He muttered a curse as she stumbled to her

knees at the side of the road and lowered her head, drawing in deep gasping breaths of air apparently in an effort
not to be sick.

Throwing the truck into Park, Billy reached over and
picked up the box from the floorboard. He stared at the
contents, anger rolling in waves in the pit of his stomach.

Nestled inside festive paper was a full bouquet of black,
withered roses. Death in the form of flowers. He was about
to place the lid back on when he noted a folded sheet of
paper. It was a pale blue, thick sheet of stationery. And
written on it in big, bold letters was, "GO BACK TO
SHREVEPORT OR THESE WILL DECORATE AT YOUR FU-
NERAL."

Chapter Sixteen

Billy stood in the doorway of his bedroom watching Shelby sleep. He'd driven her back to the shanty, the box with the flowers in the bed of the truck, then insisted she lie down for a little while. She hadn't protested and had immediately fallen asleep, exhausted from the emotional shock she'd sustained.

He should get back to work, reading files, making notes, trying to glean a clue, any clue to the identity of the killer, but for the moment he was content to simply watch her sleep.

Her hair spilled over his pillowcase, the dark strands like finely spun silk. The laugh lines around her eyes disappeared in sleep, making her look younger. Her scent filled his room, the pleasant floral smell he would always identify with her. Just as he could be blindfolded and know his own son by smell, so it was with Shelby. Her scent was indelibly printed in his head...as was the curve of her breast against his palm, the taste of her mouth against his.

He pulled himself away from the door, irritated with his thoughts, disgusted by his very passion for Shelby, a passion more intense than any he'd ever felt for his wife. He realized now he'd been unfair to Fayrene. He'd promised to love her, without knowing what real love felt like, without understanding how all-consuming true love could be. Mentally shaking himself, he shoved these troubling thoughts away.

The box containing the ominous gift he stored temporarily in an unused kitchen cabinet. Later he would take it to Bob. It was obviously meant as a warning to Shelby, a threat that shouldn't be taken lightly.

Sinking into a chair at the table, his thoughts turned to Angelique. If he found out she was responsible for the flowers, he would personally wring her neck. It would be a long time before he managed to forget the paleness of Shelby's face when he'd helped her up off the ground, the way she had clung to him, her body shivering with fear and revulsion. Somebody would pay and pay dearly for bringing such horror to her.

Still, the dead bouquet was out of character for Angelique. Generally, Angelique was known for her healing powers; her charms and herbs were used in positive ways. There was no mistaking the message the flowers had been intended to bear, and it certainly wasn't a gift of love and goodwill.

Billy was aware of time running out, not only for himself but for Shelby, as well. There was no doubt in his mind that she had seen a member of her own family kill Layne Rocharee all those years ago. It was the only thing that made sense, traumatic enough for repression. But who?

With a deep sigh Billy focused on the files before him, somehow believing the answers to everything existed within the reports.

He'd been working about an hour, reading and taking notes, when he heard Shelby whimpering from the next room. Pitiful sounds of torment, they pulled him from his chair and to her side.

She lay on her back, her head tossing and turning, her eyes flickering beneath the lids as if she were watching a movie unfold...an unpleasant movie. A low moan escaped her and her hands flailed the air, as if warding off an assailant.

Billy reached out to awaken her, then hesitated. If she was dreaming the murder she'd seen, perhaps he was better to let the dream play out. Perhaps this time she'd see the face of the killer.

Tears oozed out from beneath her eyelids, and still he remained unmoving at her side, knowing that perhaps this time she would discover the answers they sought.

But as her moans and whimpers increased, her obvious terror pulled at his heart. It wasn't worth it. Her pain wasn't worth his vindication. He shook her shoulder gently in an attempt to awaken her, his guilt swelling as he thought of those mere moments he'd allowed her to suffer in an attempt to save himself.

"No...please stop...no," she cried. "I don't want to see, please don't make me."

"Shelby, wake up. You're having a nightmare." He shook her shoulder again and her eyes flew open. In their dark blue depths he saw the horror of her dreams. It was there only a moment, a yawning darkness that threatened to pull him in, then she sobbed and threw her arms around his neck.

"Oh, Billy, when will this end?" She clung so tightly to him he could feel her heart pounding against his chest. Her body trembled against his, like a captured bird quivering in his hand. She was so vulnerable it made his heart ache. He held her close, his hands moving up and down her back in an effort to soothe.

"You should go back to Shreveport," he said, wishing he'd never brought her back here. "Get out of Black Bayou and away from the swamp."

She pulled away from him and swiped at her tears. "And how do I run from my nightmares, Billy? How do I run from the knowledge that somebody in my family is probably a murderer?" She leaned her head against his chest and drew in a deep breath. "Shreveport isn't far enough for me to run from those things. No place is far enough."

When she raised her head again, he saw that the terror had been replaced by steely strength. "Running isn't a viable option," she said.

"Shelby, I'm frightened for you." Billy spoke what was in his heart. "Those flowers were meant as a warning. You aren't safe in your house."

"That's probably the one place I am safe," she objected. "If somebody is going to try to kill me, they won't do it in the house where the crime will be tied to the family." She uttered a bitter laugh. "Imagine the gossip if I was found dead in my own bed."

Billy pulled her against him once again, wishing he could swallow her up inside and keep her safe. It surprised him, the protective surge he felt for her, the same emotion that always humbled him when he experienced it toward Parker. He stroked her hair, listened to her heartbeat, allowed her fragrance to wrap around him.

Despite her words to the contrary, Billy knew that when the case was over she'd return to Shreveport. If what they suspected was true, her family would be destroyed when the swamp serpent was named, and there would be nothing left to keep her here. The Longsfords would be torn apart, Billy would be vindicated and the last of Shelby's innocence would be destroyed.

She moved out of his arms and got up from the bed. "If only I could remember," she said softly as she moved to stand in front of the window. "It's all there, the murder, the way the moon shone down that night, Layne Rocharee's face...it's all there, so clear, so sharp. But when I get to the face of the murderer, it's a blank."

Frustration eddied inside him. It would be so damned easy if she'd just remember. His trial date was less than ten days away and they were really no closer to catching the killer than they'd been before.

Could she not remember because she knew in her heart that for sure the memory would name her father, or her brother? Was she subconsciously making a choice, protecting her family over him? "Maybe you aren't trying hard enough," he said, inexplicably angry with her.

"Is that what you think?" She turned from the window and stared at him. "You think I'm not trying hard enough?"

"I don't know, Shelby. Are you really trying?"

Anger swelled inside her, an anger bred in frustration and fear. "I'm doing everything I know to remember that night. I relive that horrible scene over and over again in my head, hoping that the next time I'll see it all. And if you think I'm holding back, then you can go to hell." She stalked out of the bedroom and into the kitchen. She threw herself into a kitchen chair, angry with herself for not being able to remember, more angry with Billy for believing she wasn't trying hard enough.

Leaning back and staring at the whispering ceiling fan, she wondered if it was possible he was right. Was there a tiny part of her that didn't want to remember? Didn't want to shatter the last of her childish dreams where her family was concerned?

"Truce?" Billy leaned against the doorframe between the bedroom and the kitchen.

She nodded wearily. "Truce," she agreed.

"The worst thing we can do is bicker." Billy sat down across from her and reached for her hand. "I need you, Shelby. I know no other lawyer who could represent me as well as you."

She pulled her hand away, vaguely irritated by his words. She remembered Olivia intimating that Billy's desire for her was based on his need of her legal expertise. Shelby wanted him to need her, but not for her lawyering skills, and not for her memories that might solve a crime. She wanted him to need her as a woman, but she knew that was ridiculous. Billy Royce didn't really need anyone.

"I think we should just call it a day," she said, closing up the files on the table and placing them all in a neat stack.

"We need to take that package to Bob," Billy said.

"Why? What can he do with it? I'm sure whoever sent it was smart enough not to leave fingerprints."

"True, but that pale blue stationery came from somewhere."

Shelby shook her head. "I'm sure that stationery is probably sold in every discount store in the state. If you don't mind, just throw it all away. I'd rather forget about it."

"I don't want you to forget about it." Billy moved closer to where she sat. "Shelby, that was meant as a threat and you have to be on guard. I also don't want you walking alone through the swamp to come here anymore. From now on, you call me and I'll meet you at the edge of your property."

"Surely you're overreacting," she scoffed.

Billy reached out and flipped one of the murder photos in front of her. "Overreacting? Take a good look, Shelby.

This woman would have been thirty years old this year, but she died five years ago, stabbed in the swamp where nobody could hear her cries. Those bouquets, along with the note, were warnings that we're getting too close. No, I'm not overreacting, I just don't want you to become the swamp serpent's next victim.''

"I'm just so confused," she finally said, averting her gaze from the photo in front of her. "I have to admit, no matter how the evidence points to the killer being somebody in my family, there's a part of me that finds that so difficult to believe. And the worst part of all is not knowing who...my father? My brother? Roger? There has to be some way to discover the truth besides depending on my faulty memories."

Billy slid into the chair next to hers. "The only way I know to find out who's guilty is to eliminate those who aren't." He put the crime photo away and pulled out a sheet of paper. "While you were sleeping, I made a list of the murders and the dates they are believed to have happened. If your family has alibis for some of these dates, then they can't be the swamp serpent."

Shelby took the paper from him and studied it. Fifteen dates spanning twelve years—sixteen dates if the night Fayrene and Tyler were killed was added into the equation. It seemed an impossible task, trying to discover alibis for dates over that length of time. "I don't even remember what I did yesterday. How am I supposed to find out what people did on a particular night twelve years ago?"

Billy smiled at her, an obvious attempt to alleviate some of the tension that still existed between them. "I never promised you a rose garden."

She laughed, despite her edge of despair. "You've always been the kind of man who never makes promises."

He frowned, his eyes dark with the intensity that made many believe he was a dangerous man. "I promise you this. I won't rest until we find the person responsible for all the deaths in the swamp. I won't rest until I see justice done."

She heard the passion ringing in his voice, knew the depths of his abhorrence for the person responsible for the crimes. How could he not help but feel some sort of spillover revulsion for her if the killer turned out to be her father, or her brother?

"I'm done for today." She stood, grabbed her briefcase from the floor and opened it on the table. Together they placed the files inside, then she closed it and snapped it locked. "I can't think anymore."

"I hear there's a big party this evening at the Whalens'. You going?" Billy asked a few minutes later as he drove her home.

"I was invited, and I think the rest of the family is going, but I think I'll just stay home, relax and try to get a good night's sleep."

"I hope you have a lock on your bedroom door."

Shelby didn't answer, but rather wrapped her arms around herself, finding it chilling that she would have to lock a bedroom door in order to keep herself safe in her own home.

It wasn't until he pulled up in front of the house that Billy spoke again. "Shelby, I think we're getting so close the killer is getting frightened, and that makes things more dangerous. I have the feeling that somehow the situation is reaching a boiling point and there's going to be an explosion soon."

She nodded. The moment she'd stared at the withered, dry, blackened roses, she'd felt the sands of time slipping away from her, knew that before long something horrible would happen. She could only pray she'd remember what she'd seen in the swamp on that night so long ago before there was another victim.

"I'll be careful, Billy," she promised as she got out of the truck.

"Don't forget to call me before coming to my place. Under no circumstances should you be in that swamp alone."

"I won't forget." With a small wave, she watched his truck until it disappeared from sight, leaving only a layer of dust swirling in the air.

What a day. First she'd had to tell Bob about the disappearing files, then the horror of staring down into the gift box with the dead roses inside. And if that wasn't enough, Billy's unspoken accusation that she intentionally didn't want to remember the identity of the murderer, haunted her.

Was he right? Despite her family's dysfunction, she loved them all, and the thought that one of them could do something so horrible filled her with a dreadful, all-consuming sickness.

As she walked toward the house, she wondered if she was subconsciously protecting a murderer.

BY EIGHT O'CLOCK the house had grown silent. All the members of the Longsford family had left for the Whalens' party and the household help had been dismissed for the remainder of the night.

Shelby sat in the kitchen eating a snack of cheese and crackers, listening to the wind that had begun to wail an hour before, promising the approach of a storm and welcome relief from the heat.

All evening her mind had been filled with thoughts of the murders and the possibility of alibis. In her heart, each time she contemplated who the murderer might be, her father's image always came to mind. It brought with it an ache of betrayal, a fury of contempt and the knowledge that he, more than anyone else, seemed a likely suspect. Fathers weren't supposed to be killers, she thought with a childlike hurt. Fathers were supposed to love and protect, be role models.

As she put away the food and cleaned up her dishes, she thought again of alibis. If even one of the murders took place while her father was on one of his frequent trips out of town, then he would no longer be a suspect.

With this thought in mind, Shelby decided to snoop around in her father's office. Located at the back of the house, the room had been off-limits to everyone for as long as Shelby could remember.

For a moment she lingered, her hand on the knob, aware that a childish taboo was about to be broken. Turning the knob, she walked into her father's private sanctuary.

It smelled like him, of strong cologne and expensive bourbon. She flipped the switch on the wall, a desk lamp coming to life and illuminating the room. The walls were adorned with pictures, photos of Big John with political allies and enemies, images chronicling the life of a power hoarder.

Shelby was surprised to discover one wall dedicated to his family. Professional portraits of them together as a group, and individual snapshots of each of the children in various poses. She walked from picture to picture, oddly touched by the display in a room where he spent so much of his time alone.

She smiled at the picture of herself seated at the piano, her face expressing utter distaste. She'd taken piano lessons for only a month, and had hated each and every one. Another photo showed her and Michael together, him playfully making rabbit ears behind her head.

"Michael." She breathed his name softly, remembering all the times he'd championed her against Olivia's tormenting ways, all the times he'd placed himself in the position to receive the punishment for something she had done.

She just couldn't find it in her heart to think he might have anything to do with the swamp serpent murders. Michael was a man of the cloth, had taken solemn vows, and there was no way she could imagine him using a knife rather than a rosary.

No, she couldn't believe Michael had anything to do with any of this. She didn't want to believe anyone she loved could have anything to do with any of this.

She turned her attention to the desk drawers, feeling like a thief as she began to search for records, daily planners, anything that might tell her where her father was on the nights of the most recent murders.

As she searched the desk, she was aware of the ominous rumbles of thunder and the brilliant lightning flashes that pierced the heavy draperies at the windows. Within minutes rain pelted the side of the house.

It took her nearly an hour to go through the contents of the desk, then she turned her attention to the massive file cabinets against one wall. "Bingo," she whispered as she spied a large folder containing internal revenue forms for the past twenty years.

Her father was nothing if not frugal and many of the trips he took were tax deductible. She knew if she dug around enough she'd find material supporting every claim he took, including dates of his travel.

It took her another hour to finally find what she was looking for, and eagerly she wrote out the dates, year by year for the past twelve. She had placed everything back where she had found it and had just turned off the light when she heard a noise. Different than a rumble of thunder, more intrusive than the gentle rain, it sent an ominous shiver walking up her spine.

She froze. Heart pounding frantically. Seconds passed as all kinds of scenarios rocketed through her head. What better way to silence her permanently than to sneak away from a neighbor's party and kill her?

The Whalens' house was less than a five-minute drive away. Easy for a guest to disappear for twenty or so minutes. How easy for the killer, to dispose of her, race back to the party, then be with the family when they discovered her dead body.

She took a step out of the office, wishing she'd thought to turn on a light in the downstairs hallway. A flash of lightning showed the hallway empty. Taking another step, she listened. Nothing. Maybe it had simply been her imagination.

She started for the stairs that led to her bedroom. The noise came again, louder this time. Stumbling, she fell to one knee, her heart nearly bursting out of her chest. The back door. The noise came from the back door. The jiggle of the doorknob, the brush of a large body against the wood. Somebody was trying to get in.

Another noise penetrated her consciousness. The rattle of paper. She looked down and realized the sheet of paper crackled as her hand trembled uncontrollably.

If she had any courage at all, she'd grab a knife from the kitchen drawer and confront whomever was outside. But Shelby wasn't a fool. She'd seen those horror movies, and always scoffed at the heroine's stupidity in confronting the horror head-on.

Shelby preferred crawling into a hole rather than direct confrontation with a killer. Unfortunately, a hole wasn't available. She jumped as someone banged on the door, all pretense of trying to be quiet gone.

"Shelby?" a familiar voice called.

The voice broke the inertia that had gripped her and she ran to the door. She unlocked it and flung it open to reveal Billy, his hair and clothing wet from the storm. "Billy, you scared me half to death," she exclaimed as he swept by her and into the kitchen. "What are you doing here?" She closed the door and turned to face him.

He grinned sheepishly. "I'm not sure. I got worried, started thinking all crazy thoughts."

Shelby smiled. "I know, the same thoughts crossed my mind."

"What time do you expect your family home?" he asked.

"I don't know, probably by midnight. Why?"

"Because I intend to stay here with you until they get home."

"Billy, that's not necessary. Besides, you're all wet. You need to get out of those clothes."

His wicked grin flooded her with heat. "That's exactly what I had in mind."

Chapter Seventeen

Billy. He was her first thought when she awakened the next morning. Her bed still held his scent, the pillow next to her still retained the imprint of his head. He'd sneaked out of her window the night before as her parents' car had pulled up the lane toward the house. And between the time he'd arrived and the time he had left, there had been magic.

She stirred languidly, knowing she needed to get up, but reluctant to leave the cocoon of Billy that surrounded her. For a couple of splendid hours there had been no swamp and town and there had been no killer. It had been just a man and a woman making love and whispering lover talk while a gentle rain pattered its rhythm on the roof.

She'd wanted it all to last forever, but knew that was the fanciful dream of a fool. Like the storm in the night, gone before dawn, there was no forever for her and Billy, no future at all. Always the faces of the swamp victims would be between them, and the knowledge that somebody in her family was responsible for the deaths.

Thinking of the swamp serpent, she remembered the piece of paper she'd written on the night before, a list of her father's travel dates for the past twelve years. Billy's unexpected appearance had made her forget about it, but now it preyed on her mind, making further sleep impossible.

Getting out of bed, she grabbed her robe and pulled it on then hurried over to the desk where the paper awaited her attention. She rummaged through her briefcase and pulled out the sheet of paper where Billy had written the dates of the murders. Laying the two pieces of paper side by side, she began to compare the dates.

It didn't take long to see that on the dates of all the murders Big John had been at the mansion, not out somewhere on the road. There was nothing in the dates to cast doubt on his guilt. She stared at the papers, her heart echoing the dull thud of dreadful certainty.

As much as she wanted to deny it, she knew there was more than a strong possibility that her father was the swamp serpent. She needed to talk to somebody, somebody other than Billy. She needed to talk to somebody who loved their father, someone who had grown up in the house. Michael. She wanted to talk to Michael.

It didn't take her long to shower and dress, and soon after she was on the road driving toward Michael's rectory. No remnant of the storm the night before remained. The sun was brilliant, the sky unmarred by clouds, making her feel as if she'd dreamed the thunder, the lightning... Billy.

Michael's church wasn't far from the mansion. Like the Longsford house, the church was bordered on the back by the swamp. It was a simple structure, complete with an old-fashioned bell tower. A short distance from the church was a well-kept little cottage, and it was here she assumed she would find her brother, probably preparing for the morning services.

She knocked on the door, then looked at her watch. It was just after eight. She knew the morning mass didn't start until ten, so hopefully Michael would have time to talk to her.

He opened the door and his face immediately lit with a warm smile. "Shelby, what a surprise. Come on in, I was just about to sit down for breakfast."

"I don't want to intrude," she said hesitantly.

"Intrude?" He took her by the arm and ushered her in. "You could never intrude. Have you had breakfast?" he asked as he led her into a small but cheerful kitchen.

"No, but I'm not hungry, although I wouldn't turn down a cup of coffee."

He grinned. "You'll probably turn down a second cup once you get a taste of my coffee. Sit down." He gestured her into a chair at the bright yellow enameled table. "So, to what do I owe this honor?" he asked as he poured them each a cup of coffee.

Shelby hesitated, unsure where to begin, what she wanted to say, what she needed to hear from him. She twisted the mug between her hands, wishing there was an easy way to tell him her suspicions.

"Shelby? What's wrong?" Michael's hand reached out and touched her arm, his eyes gazing at her warmly. "I can tell you're troubled. What can I do to help?"

She smiled, as always touched by his support, his concern. "There's nothing you can do to help, except listen. I need to tell somebody about some things I've been thinking. I need some objectivity."

Michael leaned back in his chair and took a sip of his coffee. "Objectivity about what?" he asked as he placed the cup back down.

"Big John."

Michael winced, a rueful smile curving his lips. "Ah, you don't make things easy, do you?"

"I also need to know that whatever I say will be kept in strictest confidence," she added.

"Shelby, I'm accustomed to hearing confessions. I keep confidences as part of my job."

She nodded, then took a moment to collect her thoughts, get them in order to tell Michael. It took her only minutes to tell him about Tyler and his connection to the swamp murders. She explained about the erased computer files, Big John's affair with Marguerite Boujoulais and finally the flowers she'd found in her bed and those that had been delivered to her. As she spoke, Michael's expression remained impassive, only his blue eyes flashing emotions too deep, too dark to release.

"I checked Big John's travel for the past twelve years and not one murder took place while he was out of town. Michael, I know it sounds crazy, but I think maybe he's the swamp serpent killer."

Michael sighed, leaned back in his chair and touched the collar around his neck as if for comfort. "God forgive me, but I've entertained the same thought."

"You have?" She looked at him in surprise. "But why?"

"I'm not sure, nothing specific, just a gut feeling that won't go away. Big John was always so vehement in his distaste of the swamp district. He fought long and hard to keep the community center from being built, a fight he lost." Michael smiled wryly. "Of course, now he embraces the center, aware that being associated with it can't hurt his political image. It struck me after the last murder that Big John has hatred as his motive, opportunity in that the mansion is close to the murder sites, and I've seen him walking in and out of the swamp in the evenings many times."

"Have you told any of this to Bob?"

Michael shook his head. "It's eaten at me for so long, but I haven't told Bob anything." Torment etched his features. "I keep telling myself I'm only speculating, that I really don't know anything for sure. But I'm so afraid there will be another murder and that blood will be on my hands."

Shelby pushed her coffee cup aside, unable to drink with the turmoil inside her. She hadn't realized it until this moment, but she had come here hoping Michael would tell her that her suspicions were ridiculous, that their father couldn't possibly be a killer. "I have to go to Bob," she finally said, a deep weariness tugging at her. "I couldn't live with myself if I didn't and somebody else ended up dead. I have to at least tell him Big John is a strong suspect."

Michael reached across the table and grabbed her hand. "It's a horrifying thought, isn't it? That the man who sired us and raised us could be a man who preys on the weak, pitiful people of the swamp."

"There's a part of me that finds it so hard to believe, and yet there's a part of me that finds it too easy to believe." She squeezed Michael's hand. "And I think that's the saddest part of all, that I can believe he's capable of such a thing."

"You know if it's true, Mama and Olivia will be destroyed by it."

Shelby nodded and withdrew her hand from his. "I know, but I can't keep silent and let more people die. Mama and Olivia will survive, and I can't allow the murders to continue."

"So this exonerates Billy," Michael said.

"Yes." She rubbed the center of her forehead, again feeling a weariness of spirit, an ache of pain that wasn't physical. "But Billy is so angry about the deaths in the swamp. The people who died were his people, his friends, his family. I'm afraid of his anger, afraid I might be defending him against another charge." As much as she loved Michael, as close as she felt toward him, she couldn't tell him that her greatest fear was the spillover of Billy's hatred destroying the memories of the passion they had shared.

"Ah, Billy will be all right. He's a survivor. Like us." Again his gaze was warm on her. "When are you going to tell Bob what you think?"

"Probably this afternoon. I can't put it off any longer. Even Tyler suspected Big John, and there is too much circumstantially to ignore."

"I'll go with you, if you want," he offered.

She shook her head. "That isn't necessary." She stood. "I'd better get out of here and let you prepare for your morning service."

"I'm glad you stopped by," he said as he walked her through the small living room and toward the front door.

"You've got a nice place here, Michael," she said as she looked around the cozy room.

"It's small, and the bathroom and kitchen need updating, but the church purse isn't exactly bulging, so I make do."

"It feels like a home," Shelby said. As she turned toward the front door her gaze fell on the cherry-wood secretary. The writing surface was cluttered with a variety of items—envelopes, bills, pens and paper clips. But it was the sight of one particular item that caused Shelby's blood to run cold. Pale blue stationery. It was the same kind of paper that had accompanied the flowers. Exactly the same.

"I'd better get home," she said, hanging on to her composure in desperation. She vaguely heard him say goodbye as she turned and walked toward her car.

Had Michael sent the bouquet? She fell into the car seat and started the engine, fighting a wave of nausea. Not Michael. Dear God, surely Michael wasn't involved in any of this. Please, don't let Michael be a part of the madness, she silently begged as she drove away from the church property. But the presence of the stationery refused to be silenced in her mind.

Along with the clamoring of the stationery came other memories. Michael, sitting at the dinner table, saying that he thought the killer was performing an act of mercy. Was it possible that the verbal abuse from Big John over the years had somehow made Michael snap? Was he now committing horrendous acts of murder and confusing them with acts of mercy?

It had been bad enough when she'd thought her father was responsible for the crimes, but to think Michael might be involved sent a dagger through her heart. Michael had been her sanity, her hero when they were growing up.

As always when she was upset, the first person she wanted to see was Billy. She stopped at the first pay phone she reached and called him, nearly sobbing in relief when he answered.

"I need to talk to you," she said.

"What's wrong?"

"I...I don't want to go into it over the phone." She needed his arms around her taking the chill from her body, she needed his strength buoying her to brave the face of her monster.

"I'll meet you in your backyard."

No questions, no need for explanations. She needed him and he was there. She drove home, her mind a chaotic mass of confusion. Thoughts of her father, of Michael and of Billy all swirled in her head.

Was it possible it had been Michael she'd seen on that night so long ago? Certainly the sight of her beloved brother stabbing a man to death would have been enough of a trauma to cause instant repression and horrible, haunting nightmares.

She parked her car and ran for the swamp without a backward glance at the house. Billy waited for her at the edge of the property, his arms open as if he knew her torment, recognized her need to be held.

For a long moment she remained in his arms, wondering what madness it was that drove her here to him and where the madness would eventually take her. Reluctantly she stirred from his embrace and stepped away. He took her hand and led her toward a fallen tree trunk, where together they sank down amid the jungle of greenery.

"What happened?" he asked.

"I went to see Michael. I wanted to talk to him about my father, my suspicions." She shuddered as she remembered that moment when she had spied the stationery. "I was getting ready to leave and saw that on his writing desk he had a stack of the same kind of stationery that came with the dead roses."

Billy nodded, appearing unsurprised. "You knew Michael was a possible suspect."

"Yes, but I never considered him seriously." Shelby dropped her head to her hands. "Michael was the one person in my family I thought I could always depend on. If he's capable of committing these kinds of crimes, then nothing is safe, nothing is sane in this whole world." Billy said nothing and she looked up to see him staring into the distance, his features as dark as the heart of the swamp. "Billy?"

He turned and looked at her, his eyes not radiating any light. "While I was looking over the autopsy reports, I discovered something interesting."

"What?" she asked, hoping it was something that would vindicate Michael.

"All of the victims were killed by knife wounds that thrust upward."

Shelby frowned. "You mean as if the murderer was shorter than the victims."

"Or on his knees."

Her frown deepened. "What would he be doing on his knees?"

Billy's gaze held hers. "Praying?"

NIGHT DESCENDED slowly, as if savoring the gulping of daylight. Shelby stood at her window, watching the dark shadows claim first the swamp, then the surrounding area.

Leaning her head against the pane of glass, she drew in a deep breath. She was exhausted, wearied beyond endurance. She'd spent the afternoon talking with Bob at the police station. It had been the most difficult conversation she'd ever had with anyone. Although she knew what she was doing was right, she felt like a traitor pointing an accusatory finger at the brother she loved.

Bob had agreed he had more than enough to bring Michael in for questioning. Not only did he have what Shelby had told him, he also had two witnesses who had seen Michael wandering in the swamp on the night of the last swamp murder.

Shelby had begged Bob to wait until the next day to pick up Michael. "It's Sunday," she'd protested. "Please, Bob, don't bring him in today. Wait and get him tomorrow."

But Bob had been adamant. He intended to leave to pick up Michael as soon as possible. Shelby had come home knowing that everything in her life, everything in her family, would change. Although her head told her Michael was the swamp serpent, her heart refused to completely accept the idea.

Something niggled at her, begging to be remembered but refusing to surface to her consciousness. She felt as if the puzzle was complete but she was left holding an extra piece.

Turning away from the window, she decided to call Billy and relay to him her conversation with Bob. As she went down the stairs to the living room, the house was silent around her. Her father, John junior, Olivia and Roger had all gone out to a fund-raiser dinner in Lake Charles and wouldn't be back until late that night. Shelby's mother had gone to her room right after dinner, stating she had a headache.

Before going to the telephone, Shelby wandered around the room where much of the family dynamics had played out over the years. It wasn't the same room from her memory. The decor had changed in the time she'd been gone. Even her memories now seemed to belong to somebody else. She had spent the years in Shreveport trying to reinvent her family. How sad that the one person she hadn't needed to reinvent was the most dysfunctional of all.

"Oh, Michael." She sighed as she sank down on the sofa. How could he be so warm, so loving to her, yet send her a hideous package to frighten her away? How could he preach the word of God on Sundays, then sneak through the swamp and commit murder in the night?

Picking up the phone receiver, she dialed Billy's number. He answered on the second ring, his deep voice a balm to her wounded soul. She told him about her conversation with Bob that afternoon, unable to hide the tremendous pain in her heart.

"You okay?" he asked.

"As well as can be expected. It just doesn't feel right. No matter how hard I try to put Michael's face on the figure I saw in the swamp with Layne Rocharee, it doesn't work." This time her sigh was one of frustration. "I don't know, maybe it doesn't feel right because I don't want it to be true. Bob was going to pick Michael up this afternoon. He said it would just be for questioning, but I have a feeling it will become a formal arrest. He indicated to me that Michael has been under suspicion for some time. He had several witness reports of Michael being in the swamp on the night of a couple of the murders. I haven't heard anything, but I assume Michael is now at the station." She swallowed against her tears. "If Michael has been arrested, I'm not surprised he hasn't called any of us. He wouldn't. He's always been very private." She wondered now if that privacy had instead been crafty secrecy.

"If that's the case and Michael really is guilty, then by this time tomorrow night the swamp serpent murders will be solved."

"Yes, and if Michael is the swamp serpent, then he probably killed Tyler and Fayrene, also." The words came with difficulty and she cleared her throat. "Tomorrow I'll ask Abe to drop all the charges filed against you. I'm sure he'd be quite agreeable. By tomorrow night you should be out from under the charges against you."

"And what will you be doing tomorrow night?" he asked.

"I don't know. Picking up the pieces of my family, I suppose."

"Your family has paid a high price for my freedom," he said.

Tears burned and she closed her eyes against them. "And the swamp has paid an enormous price because of my family."

For a moment silence fell between them, the gravity of the crimes creating a chasm Shelby didn't know how to bridge. She knew this was the beginning of the end of whatever had existed between Billy and her. Once Abe withdrew the charges against Billy, he wouldn't need her anymore.

"I'd better go," she finally said.

"I'll be in touch," Billy replied, then hung up.

Shelby slowly replaced the receiver into the cradle. Leaning her head back against the sofa cushions, she wondered how she had ever allowed herself to get involved with Billy. What madness had possessed her? She hadn't realized how much she'd come to depend on Billy's strong arms to hold her through rough times, hadn't recognized how deeply he was crawling into her heart until now when she was certain there would be nothing more between them.

Wearily she arose from the couch, deciding to go to bed. She was tired of thinking, tired of speculating. Everything was now out of her hands and there was nothing more she could do about the swamp serpent or Billy.

As she passed the gilt-framed mirror hanging on the wall of the stairs, she caught a glimpse of her reflection. She stopped and peered at the mirror image, for a moment surprised to see how much she looked like her mother. With her pale face and features taut with strain, it was a younger version of her mother peering back at her.

She continued to stare into the mirror, her reflection blurring as her vision turned inward. The events of that night so long ago unfolded in her mind just as they had every night since she'd returned to Black Bayou. She saw herself walking through the swamp, drawn off the path by the sound of voices. In her mind she watched as Layne Rocharee died, then saw herself running back home where her mother was on the front porch. Shelby stumbled onto the porch, half in shock, unable to comprehend what she'd seen. "Mama, in the swamp," she gasped, trying to catch her breath as the words tumbled over themselves in an effort to be heard. "Something bad, I saw something..."

"You saw nothing," Celia said, her breath sour with the scent of gin. "Running in the swamp like a savage," Celia said scornfully.

"But Mama...I saw something bad...but I don't remember...I can't think... I need to talk to Mama Royce."

Celia snorted indelicately. "Don't go running to that old woman. She's dead. She died this evening."

The visions dissipated, leaving Shelby to stare into the mirror images of her wide, frightened eyes. That's what had nagged her all along. That's what had been bothering her...the extra piece of the puzzle. How had her mother known about Mama Royce's death?

Shelby knew she wouldn't sleep without the answer, and the only person who could answer was her mother. Turning, she went back down the stairs and down the hallway that led to her parents' bedroom.

She knocked on the door and waited for an answer. There was none. She knocked again. Seconds passed. Minutes. Still no answer.

Drawing in a deep breath, Shelby turned the knob and eased open the door. The dim lamp on the bedside stand was on. The bed was empty and the French doors that led to the patio and the lawn beyond were open.

Shelby ran to the doors and stared outside. Her mother wasn't on the porch, nor was she visible in the spill of the full moon anywhere on the lawn.

Shelby's gaze moved toward the swamp, her heart pounding a frantic rhythm. She knew. She knew the swamp serpent was hunting again. She knew in her heart the swamp serpent was her mother.

Chapter Eighteen

Shelby paused only long enough to call Bob and tell him to get out to the swamp by her house. She spoke quickly, then hung up the phone and ran out the French doors.

The grass licked her ankles with dewy wetness as she raced across the lawn toward the tangled growth of the swamp. The moon hung low and full, just as it had all those years before, and the swamp beckoned like a familiar nightmare landscape.

Death and madness were in the heavy, humid air. She could smell them as clearly as she remembered the scent from her dreams...the scent of coppery blood mingling with pungent rotting vegetation and fragrant night-blooming flowers.

As she entered the thick greenery, memories exploded in her mind. Her mother, kneeling in front of Layne Rocharee, then rising up and at the same moment thrusting deep into his belly with a knife.

The moon had shone through the tops of the trees, fully illuminating her mother's face, a face Shelby didn't recognize, one filled with power, rage and madness.

Shoving the memory aside, she raced toward Billy's shanty, knowing if she was going to stop another serpent murder, she needed his help. The bridge to his place clattered beneath her feet and she didn't wait to knock, but rather threw open the door as she shouted his name.

She stopped short, surprised to see Gator, Angelique and Parker sitting at the table. "Where's Billy?" she asked without preamble.

"Your mother called and wanted to speak with him," Angelique said. "He went toward your place to meet with her."

Shelby's heart seemed to stop and yet she could hear the thunder of it beating in her ears. "My mother?"

Angelique's eyes narrowed. "What's wrong?"

"I...I have to find him. My mother...my mother is the swamp serpent." The words rode a sob as they escaped her. Without waiting for a response, she turned and ran out the door.

She didn't reflect on why her mother had lured Billy out into the swamp. It was impossible to speculate on the motive of madness. All she knew was that Billy was in danger. She ran through the swamp, half-crazed with fear, shouting his name over and over again. But there was no answer back. In fact, there seemed to be an unnatural hush pervading the swamp, as if it sensed evil and all the creatures silently waited for the danger to pass.

Shelby looked around, frantic. The full moon spilled down, ghostlike fingers of silver creating a dreamlike atmosphere and reflecting on the pools of water around her. Not a dream. A nightmare. Her nightmare. Her memory. And it was her memory that led her down an overgrown path toward the very place she had watched Layne Rocharee die.

She heard voices before she saw the figures. Two people in the clearing, silhouetted by the moonlight overhead. Her mother was stooped down, as if crying. As Billy took a step toward Celia, Shelby broke through the brush. "Billy, stop," she screamed. "Don't go any closer."

Billy paused, his face expressing surprise. "Shelby."

"Shelby, go home." Her mother stood, looking taller, more vital than Shelby had ever seen her before.

"No, Mama, I'm not going home." She stepped into the clearing where they stood.

"Shelby, you get on home. Billy and me are just having a little conversation. We were just saying that it's best if you leave Black Bayou and go back to Shreveport."

Shelby stared at her mother, new memories flooding back. "Trying to send me away, Mama. Like you did years ago?" She remembered now. Going to her aunt's in Shreveport had not been her idea. It had been a seed planted in her mind by her mother, nourished by the trauma of Mama Royce's death, the confusion over making love with Billy, and the unspeakable act she couldn't remember. "It's too late, Mama. I remember. I remember everything."

Even in the moonlight she saw the flash of rage flame from Celia's eyes. "Damn it Shelby, do as I say. Go home. We'll discuss all this later." Celia's lips twisted with cunning. "Go on, we'll fix this all later."

"Shelby?" Billy looked from her to Celia in confusion.

Shelby didn't answer him, but moved closer to where her mother stood. "Mama, it's over."

"No." Celia's voice echoed through the trees. "It's not over until I say it's over." The rage twisting her features fell away and she gazed at Shelby gently. "Shelby, we're Longsfords... family. Don't question my judgment. Now go on home and let me do what needs to be done."

"I can't do that, Mama." Shelby took another step toward her mother, close enough now to catch the scent of her familiar lilac perfume and the bite of the odor of gin. She was close enough to see the bloodlust in Celia's eyes, the flash of moonlight on a long, sharp knife. "I can't let you hurt Billy."

"Shelby, stay where you are." Where before Billy's voice had been quizzical, this time it was deep with the knowledge of danger, the recognition of being in the presence of unstable evil.

"Mama, give me the knife." Shelby ignored Billy's warning, knowing if she didn't get the knife away from her mother, Celia would try to harm Billy. She couldn't let that happen. In an instant she realized if the knife pierced Billy, she would feel the pain. She'd rather feel the sting of the knife herself than to have him hurt.

"Shelby." The cry came from a distance.

"You hear that, Mama. Bob is on his way. I told you, it's over." Shelby inched closer and Celia raised the knife to ward her away. "Billy, stay back," she exclaimed as he tensed and started forward.

"Mrs. Longsford."

All three turned at the sound of Angelique's voice. Angelique stepped into the clearing, her face a mask of ancient sorrow. "You killed my sister," she said, her gaze not wavering from Celia.

"Don't be ridiculous," Celia scoffed.

"And my Remy." A deep keening burst from Angelique. A haunting sound of deep pain that echoed eerily through the trees.

As the noise died, Angelique lunged for Celia. The sudden movement broke the inertia that had held Shelby and Billy and they rushed forward, as well.

Angelique cried in pain and at the same time Bob, Michael and several deputies rushed into the clearing. In moments Celia and Angelique were separated, Angelique's shoulder bleeding copiously as Billy held on to the knife.

"What in the hell is going on?" Bob asked.

"She killed my sister...my husband," Angelique said, leaning weakly against the trunk of a tree.

"That's ridiculous." Celia tried to struggle out of Bob's grip. "That woman attacked me and I want her arrested."

"We need to get Angelique to a doctor," Billy said, pressing a handkerchief over Angelique's shoulder to staunch the flow of blood.

Bob frowned in obvious frustration. "I don't know what the hell is going on, but let's get out of this swamp to sort it out."

Bob held on to Celia as Billy supported Angelique. Michael and Shelby silently followed as they moved out of the swamp and to the Longsford mansion. Shelby knew she was in shock. Her mind was curiously numb, her skin unnaturally cold as she wrapped her arms around herself and walked toward the house.

Her mother was the swamp serpent, responsible for seventeen deaths. She knew it was true, felt the knowledge settle with her memories. The extra piece of puzzle fit. But nothing could dispel the horror. Nothing could take away the utter abhorrence that inundated her as she tried to understand why.

Big John, John junior, Olivia and Roger were seated in the living room as they all walked in. Apparently they had just arrived home from their fund-raiser, as they were still dressed in their formal attire. "What's this?" Big John stood as they entered the room. "What's going on here?"

Billy went directly to the phone and placed a call to Doc Cashwell. Angelique leaned against the doorframe, looking proud and noble despite the paleness of her skin and the blood that still seeped from her wound.

"Will somebody please tell me what the hell is going on?" Big John boomed.

"I'm hoping we'll figure this all out right now," Bob said, his expression still one of confusion.

Shelby sank onto the sofa, her gaze directed at her mother, who once again looked small, almost pitiful in her cotton nightgown. "Mama?" Celia refused to meet Shelby's gaze.

Billy hung up the phone and moved to stand next to Angelique. "Mrs. Longsford stabbed Angelique," he said.

Big John turned and stared at his wife in amazement. "Why would you do a damn fool thing like that?"

"She is the swamp serpent," Shelby said softly.

Big John's gaze focused on Shelby, even more amazed than before. There was a moment of heavy silence, then Big John threw back his head and roared with laughter.

The change in Celia was immediate, as if her husband's laughter caused something to snap inside her. She raised her head, eyes flashing malevolence. "What's the matter, John? Don't believe I'm capable?" She jerked out of Bob's grip and advanced toward her husband. "You were going to leave us for that swamp tramp. I had to do something, had to take care of the problem, protect our family."

"No." Olivia stumbled backward, her face drained of all color. "It can't be you. I . . . thought it was Daddy. Tyler thought it was Big John. Tyler was going to tell." She clamped her mouth shut, her eyes darting wildly as if seeking a means of escape.

"Good God, Olivia, what have you done?" Roger asked.

Tears began to stream down her face and she looked at Big John pleadingly. "I did it for you. I thought…I needed to protect you. I love you, Daddy." A deputy moved next to her, ready to grab her should she attempt to run.

The laughter that had been on Big John's features transformed into revulsion. As Shelby watched, her father grew old. Confusion tugged his features downward and his eyes became haunted. Michael gripped the crucifix around his neck and prayed beneath his breath.

"He's not man enough to do what I've done," Celia boasted, and now the madness was full in her eyes, a shining wildness that sent a shiver up Shelby's spine. "That woman was evil, she had to be disposed of before she stole all that belonged to me."

"You killed Marguerite?" Big John asked.

"And all the rest of them," Celia replied, pride ringing in her voice.

"Mrs. Longsford, perhaps you'd better contact your lawyer before you say anything more," Bob said.

"I don't want a lawyer. I know what I did and I want everyone to know." Her eyes gleamed and she tossed her head like a coquettish young woman. "They tell stories about me, bedtime tales about the swamp serpent who eats people for dinner."

Shelby felt as if it was all a dream. She listened numbly as her mother spoke candidly of the murders, explaining that Layne Rocharee had been the first, a test to make certain she was capable of stabbing a person to death. He'd been a practice run for Marguerite. "Every time you moaned her name in your sleep, I killed another piece of swamp scum," she told her husband. "And it didn't take long for me to realize I liked the feeling it gave me." She gestured around. "Here I've always been nothing, a shadow of you. But in the swamp I was something. I was powerful.''

"But Mama, why tonight? Why Billy?" Shelby asked.

Celia looked at her, eyes cold and distant. "I overheard you talking to Billy, knew they were picking up Michael tonight. I couldn't let Michael go to jail, so I knew there had to be another swamp serpent murder tonight."

"But why Billy?" This time it was Michael who asked the question.

Celia smiled, the cunning smile of insanity. "If Billy died I knew Shelby would leave." She looked at Shelby. "You couldn't leave it alone. You kept picking and prodding to find the killer. I made you forget once. I figured I could make you forget again."

Minutes later Olivia and Celia, handcuffed, were placed in two patrol cars. Doc Cashwell arrived and took off with Angelique, insisting the wound required more treatment than he could give on the spot. As the cars drove off, Shelby turned to her brother and stumbled into his embrace.

The tears she'd stifled from the moment her full memory returned now fell. She cried for the child she had been, betrayed by a mother obsessed and crazed. She sobbed for the victims, innocent people who had fallen to her mother's madness.

"I'm sorry, Michael." She finally stepped away from him. "I . . . I was afraid it was you. I told Bob I thought it was you."

"Shh, that doesn't matter now. Thank God I had solid alibis for several of the murders." Michael touched her cheek. "Are you okay?"

"I'm not sure. I think it will be a very long time before I'm really okay." She leaned against him. "Oh, Michael, I can't understand any of this."

"Everyone said it was a crime of passion. And it was, the passionate hatred of one woman, and the passionate distorted love of another."

Shelby turned, seeking Billy. She caught sight of him running across the lawn, and in an instant he disappeared into the darkness of the swamp. Her mother had killed his friends and neighbors. Her sister had murdered his best friend and wife. No wonder he had run. The Longsfords had destroyed too much of what had been important to him. Surely he hated them . . . hated them all. Not for the first time in her life, Shelby was sorry she'd been born a Longsford. She knew Billy was out of her life for good. Now all she had to figure out was how to pick up the shattered pieces of her life.

"ANGELIQUE?" Shelby pushed open the hospital room door and peered in.

"Come in." Angelique gestured her inside, looking as regal, as proud as a queen even though she lay in the hospital bed, her side and shoulder bandaged.

"I . . . I brought you some flowers." Shelby set the arrangement on the table, then remained awkwardly standing. "I don't know what to say, how to tell you how sorry I am. I know they're nothing but words, and there's no way they can ease your pain."

Angelique pointed her to the chair next to the bed. Her eyes, so dark and mysterious, stared intently into Shelby's. "You owe me no apologies."

"Yes, but my mother—"

"Exactly." Angelique cut her off. "Your mother. Not you."

Shelby sank into the chair, grateful for her words of absolution, yet discomforted by the woman's probing gaze. "How are you? They told me your lung was punctured."

"Bah, I'm a fast healer. I'll be out of here in a day or two. And you . . . are you a fast healer?"

Shelby smiled. "I'm not sure. Time will tell."

Angelique raised herself against the pillows, wincing slightly, then refocused her gaze on Shelby. "I sent the dead flowers to you."

"Why?"

Her gaze shifted to the window. "Since Remy's death, my life has been empty. Billy's friendship filled a space for me, and for a while I thought that friendship might become something more." She sighed. "You frightened me. Whenever Billy spoke your name, I heard something in his voice that I'd never heard before." She turned and looked back at Shelby. "I sent them to scare you, to make you go away and leave Billy alone. But it didn't work, did it? You love him."

"No." Shelby felt the blood rush to her face. "I . . . it doesn't matter what I feel for Billy. There can never be anything between us."

Angelique smiled. "Ah, you sound like a woman who thinks she can control such things. What you feel for Billy is far stronger than anything you can control. You don't throw away emotions so great."

"Perhaps not, but if you leave them alone long enough, eventually they go away," Shelby replied softly.

Again Angelique smiled. "Ah, were it all that easy."

As Shelby drove home minutes later, she thought of Angelique's words. She knew it would not be easy, knew that forgetting Billy would be one of the most difficult things she'd ever faced. She cursed herself now for her weakness, for allowing herself to get involved with him in any way other than a strictly professional one. She'd been a fool, and now she would pay a fool's price, extracted through sensual dreams, hollow yearning and heartbreak.

She hadn't seen Billy since two nights before, when Bob had taken her mother and her sister away and she had seen him fleeing back into the swamp.

She'd spent the morning with Abe, who had agreed to drop the charges against Billy. Shelby knew she needed to see Billy one last time, to tie up loose ends concerning his case.

As she pulled up to the mansion, she saw her father sitting on the rocker on the front porch. In the past two days she'd watched her father grapple with all that had happened. The events had humbled him, caused him to retreat into the shell of an old man. Gone was his bluster, his zest for life, as if the tragedy had sucked it all out of him.

She got out of the car and walked to the chair next to him. Easing down, she fought the impulse to take his hand, knowing he had always loathed signs of weakness in himself or in others.

"I loved her, Shelby." His chair rocked to and fro in a slow rhythm.

"I know."

"She took me by surprise. My life was settled, then she appeared, full of life and laughter."

It was at that moment Shelby realized her father wasn't talking about Celia, but rather Marguerite Boujoulais. She didn't answer, slightly uncomfortable but knowing he felt the need to talk, to somehow explain.

"I have to admit, your mother was right. I wanted to leave her and marry Marguerite, but I couldn't. I was afraid." He frowned and stopped the rocking motion. "I was a fool. I cared too much what people would say, a Longsford taking up with a swamp girl. I knew I should break it off with Marguerite, but I couldn't do that, either. And so I snuck around like some lovesick schoolboy."

"Dad, nothing you did justifies what Mama and Olivia did," Shelby said.

"I know that, but I've never been one to shirk my responsibility and I have to accept partial blame for this mess."

This time Shelby didn't fight her impulse. She reached over and took her father's hand in hers, fully expecting him to pull away, but needing to make the gesture nevertheless. To her surprise, he didn't pull away but rather folded his fingers to tighten their grip around her hand. "I've never been much of a father to you, Shelby. But you've thrived despite my mistakes. That speaks well of you, your strength."

The crimes of her mother and sister had left holes in Shelby's heart, but as she sat there holding her father's hand, she realized they stood on the threshold of a new, different relationship. One that would be healthy and good for them both.

They sat there for a long time, not speaking, having no need for words. Finally it was her father who broke the silence. "So, what are your plans? You heading back to Shreveport?"

Shelby shook her head. "No. I'm going to close my law office there and move it here. I figure there are lots of people in the swamp who can't afford adequate counsel for charges leveled against them. It's time they had an advocate besides Billy." Besides, she refused to let her mother win, to once again leave her home because of the actions of others.

Big John nodded and eyed her knowingly. "Don't make the same mistake I did, Shelby. Don't be afraid to follow your heart. If it takes you into the swamp, then so be it."

"But sometimes in following your heart there are just too many obstacles to get around to reach the end of the journey," she replied.

His hand squeezed hers once again and they went back to watching the sun set over the swamp.

SHELBY WALKED through the woods, the morning sun her companion as she made her way toward Billy's shanty. She'd put off this final visit as long as possible, but knew she needed to see him once more. This time there would be closure so she could move on with her life.

The swamp was different this morning, filled with the sound of life. Birds sang in the trees and creatures scurried amid the brush and foliage. Fish jumped and slapped the surface of the ponds as if joyously celebrating the end of the reign of the serpent.

As she walked, visions of those nights in Billy's arms haunted her, just as she knew the faces of the victims would haunt her, as well. It would take her a long time to be able to forget those faces and she hadn't even personally known them. For Billy, she was certain it would take an eternity for him to forget.

Walking across the bridge, she heard the sound of laughter emanating from the shanty. She wasn't sure who was there, but Billy's laughter was as familiar to her as her own heartbeat. Low and seductive, it beckoned her closer, yet made her want to run.

It was at that moment she realized Angelique had been right. She was hopelessly, helplessly in love with Billy Royce. The knowledge filled her with incredible joy and

blistering rage. Damn him for making her love him. It was
not supposed to have happened. She had been so confident that she could work as his legal counsel, verbally spar
with his wit, make love to him and still not fall beneath the
seductive spell he'd wrapped around her years before.

She'd been wrong. Billy was in her blood, seared into her
heart, and she knew time would heal the wounds, but the
scars would be there forever.

Billy answered her knock, the smile on his face instantly
fading as he saw her. "Shelby," he said in surprise. "Come
in."

She stepped inside to see Gator seated at the table, a can
of grape soda in his hand. Parker sat on the floor nearby,
a hand-held video game absorbing his total concentration.

"Ah, just the person I wanted to talk to," Gator said as
he waved for her to sit down in the chair next to him.

"Me?" Shelby asked in surprise.

Gator nodded. "I want to know if you'll represent me if
I get arrested for letting one of my dogs bite one of those
infernal tax men."

Shelby bit the side of her cheek to stifle a smile. "Why
don't you come see me in the next day or two and we'll see
if we can't find somebody to handle your tax problem before you have to let your dog bite anyone."

Gator grunted, obviously satisfied by her answer. He
swigged the last of his soda, then crushed the can with his
good hand. He looked from Shelby to Billy, then stood.
"Come on, Parker, let's you and me go for a little walk, let
your daddy and the lawyer lady talk private-like."

All too soon Shelby found herself alone with Billy, his
expression as always inscrutable. "I came to tell you I've
spoken with Abe and all the charges against you have been
dropped."

"From what you said to Gator, it sounds like you intend to stay here in Black Bayou," he observed.

"I've told you all along I'm here to stay. This is my home." She paused a moment, the silence heavy between them. "I heard that you spoke to Jonathon and Laura LaJune about Sissy."

He nodded. "I figured if Jonathon fought Sissy for custody of the baby, I'd finance a lawyer for her."

"From what I've heard that won't be necessary. Laura has taken Sissy under her wing, and I imagine when the time comes Jonathon will be handing out cigars." Again the silence grew. "It was Angelique who sent me the flowers. She took the stationery from Michael's place. She was hoping I'd be scared out of Black Bayou. We spoke and I think we will be friends." She frowned and sighed. "If only things were as easily fixed with Olivia."

"She loved your father very much," Billy said.

"Too much. She lived her life trying to get something from him he couldn't give her. She married Roger to make him happy, worked in politics to gain his respect. And finally she committed the ultimate crime to protect him, and he didn't even need protection." Shelby shook her head softly. "I imagine she'll have a lot of time to think about what she's done."

She stood and moved toward the door. There was nothing left to say, no unfinished business left between them. It was time to leave and put Billy firmly in her past.

She held out her hand, intending to end things on a professional note. "Then I guess that's it."

Billy took her hand in his, the sexy, seductive smile on his face making her wish she hadn't initiated the simple tactile pleasure she found in his handshake.

She started to pull her hand away, but he held it fast and instead drew her closer, into the heat of his body, against the hard strength of his chest. With one hand he stroked the side of her cheek. That simple touch was her undoing.

"Damn it, Billy, don't touch me." She started to step away from him but he held her fast.

"Why not?" he asked, his breath warm on her neck. "I like touching you. I like kissing you, and I think if you're honest you'll admit that you like it, too."

"I do like it," she agreed, tears suddenly burning her eyes as she managed to break away from him. "That's the whole problem. I like it too much. And it isn't just your touch that I like." Like a crumbling dam, once the emotions began to seep, they swelled to flooding stage. "I like the way your lips curve when you smile. I admire how you care for Parker and your passion for the swamp. I love how I feel when I'm with you, strong yet protected, safe yet adventurous—" She broke off with a sob of frustration. "Damn you, Billy, I hate you. I really hate you."

He smiled, the sexy, seductive smile that twisted her heart. "How you do sweet-talk a man, Shelby." The smile faded and his dark eyes seemed to absorb her, so intent was his gaze. "If I didn't know better, that would sound like you love me."

She closed her eyes, not wanting to admit it, remembering she had sworn to herself long ago she would never feel that way about him again. She looked at him once more. "I said those words to you once a long time ago, and you threw them back in my face. I won't say them again. Besides, it really doesn't matter what I feel." She closed her eyes once again. "I know you can never forgive my mother and sister. How you must hate all of us."

"Oh, Shelby, if only it was that easy." He placed his hands on her shoulders and she couldn't help but look at him. "I think I fell in love with you years ago when I found you crying in the middle of the swamp and without saying a word you placed your hand in mine." He smiled at the memory. "Of course, we were just kids then. Then on the night of Mama Royce's death, when you told me you loved me, I was afraid to believe you. To me you were still little more than a kid. What in the hell could you know about love?" His thumbs moved in caressing circles on her shoulders.

"But Billy, my mother—"

"Shh." He stilled her protest with his lips against hers, kissing her with a tender passion that whispered of love. "As far as I'm concerned, you're as much a part of the swamp as I am. And the mother who raised you and made you the woman I love was Mama Royce. You were born a Longsford, but I'm hoping you'll live the rest of your life as a Royce."

Shelby held her breath, wondering if her ears deceived her, if what she saw shining in his eyes was a joke. "Is this a marriage proposal?"

He nodded solemnly. "I love you, Shelby, but I'm warning you. It won't be easy. We're bucking tradition here, swamp marrying town."

She stared up at him. In his eyes were the dark mysteries of the swamp, but in his heart was the goodness of Mama Royce. She could almost hear Mama Royce's sigh of contentment riding in the air. Town and swamp. What difference did it make? Shelby belonged here. She knew it with a clarity she'd never felt before. She belonged here amid the buzzing mosquitoes and the sweet memories and Billy.

She smiled, unafraid of what they might face as long as they faced it together. "It's time somebody bucked tradition. I suppose it might as well be us." She leaned against his chest, her smile wickedly playful. "I guess I'll have to marry you, Billy Royce. I believe it's my civic duty."

He grinned. "Ah, Shelby, how you do sweet-talk a man," he said just before his lips descended to claim hers in a kiss that spoke of forever.

HARLEQUIN®

I N T R I G U E ®

COMING NEXT MONTH

#381 RULE BREAKER by Cassie Miles
Lawman
Aviator Joe Rivers was hell-bent on discovering the real cause for
his wife's fiery death in a plane crash. But he didn't expect to find
himself falling in love again—and with a prime suspect. After all, it
was sexy Bailey Fielding who helped pilot the craft in which Joe's
wife was killed....

#382 SEE ME IN YOUR DREAMS by Patricia Rosemoor
The McKenna Legacy
Keelin McKenna dreamed through other people's eyes...victims'
eyes. And when Keelin came to America in the hope of reuniting the
McKenna clan, the dreams intensified. This time she couldn't ignore
them—because somewhere out there was a father whose teenage
daughter was missing. Tyler Leighton would come to rely on Keelin
much more than she ever dreamed possible.

#383 EDEN'S BABY by Adrianne Lee
In the past, a woman had killed for Dr. David Coulter's love. Now
the lovely Eden Prescott has pledged her love to David. But when
she discovers her pregnancy, should Eden turn to the father of her
baby...or will that make them all—her, David and the coming
child—mere pawns in the game of a jealous stalker?

#384 MAN OF THE MIDNIGHT SUN by Jean Barrett
Mail Order Brides
Married to a stranger.... They're mail-order mates, and neither one is
who they claim to be. Cold Alaskan nights roused a man's lust for a
warm woman—and Cathryn matched Ben's every desire. He would
enjoy sweet-talking her into divulging her deepest secrets...for she
had slipped right into the ready-made role he had planned for her.
And right into the trap he'd set....

AVAILABLE THIS MONTH:

Look for us on-line at: http://www.romance.net

HARLEQUIN®

I N T R I G U E®

WANTED

12 SEXY LAWMEN

They're rugged, they're strong and they're WANTED!
Whether sheriff, undercover cop or officer of the court,
these men are trained to keep the peace, to uphold the
law...but what happens when they meet the one woman
who gets to know the real man behind the badge?

Twelve LAWMEN are on the loose—and only
Harlequin Intrigue has them! Meet one every month.
Your next adventure begins with—**Joe Rivers**

in
#381 RULE BREAKER
by Cassie Miles
August 1996

LAWMAN:

There's nothing sexier than
the strong arms of the law!

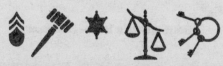

LAWMAN2

BRIDE'S BAY RESORT

UNLOCK THE DOOR TO GREAT ROMANCE AT BRIDE'S BAY RESORT

Join Harlequin's new across-the-lines series, set in an exclusive hotel on an island off the coast of South Carolina.

Seven of your favorite authors will bring you exciting stories about fascinating heroes and heroines discovering love at Bride's Bay Resort.

Look for these fabulous stories coming to a store near you beginning in January 1996.

Harlequin American Romance #613 in January
Matchmaking Baby by Cathy Gillen Thacker

Harlequin Presents #1794 in February
Indiscretions by Robyn Donald

Harlequin Intrigue #362 in March
Love and Lies by Dawn Stewardson

Harlequin Romance #3404 in April
Make Believe Engagement by Day Leclaire

Harlequin Temptation #588 in May
Stranger in the Night by Roseanne Williams

Harlequin Superromance #695 in June
Married to a Stranger by Connie Bennett

Harlequin Historicals #324 in July
Dulcie's Gift by Ruth Langan

Visit Bride's Bay Resort each month wherever Harlequin books are sold.

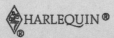

HARLEQUIN®

BBAYG

You are cordially invited to a

HOMETOWN REUNION

September 1996—August 1997

Where can you find romance and adventure,
bad boys, cowboys, feuding families, and babies,
arson, mistaken identity, a mom on the run...?
Tyler, Wisconsin, that's where!

So join us in this not-so-sleepy little town and
experience the love, the laughter and the
tears of those who call it home.

WELCOME TO A
HOMETOWN REUNION

Twelve unforgettable stories, written for you by
some of Harlequin's finest authors. This fall,
begin a yearlong affair with America's favorite
hometown as **Marisa Carroll** brings you
Unexpected Son.

Available at your favorite retail store.

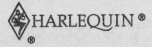

Sabrina   It Happened One Night
Working Girl   Pretty Woman
While You Were Sleeping

If you adore romantic comedies then have
we got the books for you!

Beginning in **August 1996** head to your
favorite retail outlet for
LOVE & LAUGHTER™,
a brand-new series with two books every
month capturing the lighter side of love.

You'll enjoy humorous love stories by favorite
authors and brand-new writers, including
JoAnn Ross, Lori Copeland, Jennifer Crusie,
Kasey Michaels, and many more!

As an added bonus—with the retail purchase,
of two new Love & Laughter books you can
receive a **free** copy of our fabulous
Love and Laughter collector's edition.

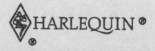